Raquel

To Grandma—who always insisted that I play for her,
to Dad—who continues to play,
and to Asher and Beau—whose song has just begun.

Lincoln Middle School,
May your lives be filled with light, fellow warriors of the King!

D. B. K. Miller
(aka Ms. Miller :)
Eph. 6:10-18
DKMillerAuthor.com

Her mom asked her if she was losing weight. Raquel was overjoyed that she'd noticed, but her mom looked worried rather than pleased. She would point out that she could see her collarbone, and to Raquel this was like music to her ears. But she soon tired of her mom's constant nagging and succumbed to wearing sweatshirts around the house to get her mom off her back. She actually didn't mind too much since she was noticing that she was starting to feel cold more easily than she used to. But once out of her mom's sight, it was back to tank tops and tight jeans (which, incidentally, weren't nearly as tight as they used to be).

She smiled at her reflection in the mirror; she was looking more and more like the models in the magazines!

The belt of truth kept showing up in her reflection, as well, but she was learning to see around it.

Table of Contents

Christmas Eve Dinner

Christmas.

The word was supposed spark feelings of joy, peace, comfort, and happiness. Images were supposed to spring to mind of sleigh bells, horses, and children playing in the snow.

But there was no snow. Not in Texas. Not in her thirteen-year lifetime. Just one more thing that had gone wrong.

Raquel absently reached behind her back to fiddle with her waist-long blond hair. Her hand felt nothing but air. Enraged, she pounded the windowsill and continued to stare vacantly out her second-story bedroom window. Why had she decided to cut her hair off? *Stupid.* That's what she was. Just *stupid.*

Of course, she knew the events surrounding her decision. Or *event*. The *night*. How could she forget that? But had it really been her *decision?* Had she really been thinking at all that night, or merely reacting? If she'd been thinking, she knew, she never would have done it. But that's what months—or really *years*—of hearing her parents yell at each other had done to her: made it hard for her to think.

Maybe it was for the best, she decided. Maybe it was best that her dad had come into her room with suitcase in hand, given her a quick good-bye, and left. Maybe he should have done that a long time ago. At least then maybe she would still remember how to think. But that night something had snapped inside of her and all rational thought flew out the window. She'd sat down in front of the mirror, grabbed up the pair of scissors on her dresser, and in less than a minute her long, blond hair lay in a heap at her feet. It took that long to destroy the beauty that she had; it would take months before she could get it back.

Stupid.

But she only thought the word for a second before she let it go. Thinking hurt too much. It was less painful not to care. She didn't care about her relatives sitting in there eating Christmas Eve dinner without her. She didn't care that her dad wasn't one of them.

She resumed her blank stare out the window and allowed her mind to become as barren as the snow-less front yard.

Her bedroom door opened abruptly. Raquel heard it, but she didn't turn. Not even after several seconds of silence, which was unusual.

"Get out here, Raquel!"

Her mom sounded mad. She didn't care.

She heard the door squeak to a close. She didn't turn to see if her mom was inside the room or out.

"Get out here!" her mom whispered abrasively. She was inside the room.

"No," Raquel said absently.

"You're *not* going to ruin Christmas for the entire family, young lady! You get out here and stop worrying about your precious hair!"

Raquel smirked. Her mom thought she didn't want to eat Christmas Eve dinner with the relatives because of her *hair*. Funny.

"I can see you smiling in your reflection!" her mom said, speaking in a loud whisper. "You think this is funny? You think it's funny that I'm left to explain to everybody why your father left the week before Christmas?"

"Not my problem."

"Well, it's *gonna* be your problem if you don't get your tail out here! It's bad enough that your father's gone; I'll be blasted if I'm gonna let you spend Christmas Eve in your room."

This time, Raquel couldn't help but chuckle. "As if you're disappointed he's gone," she said, turning to look at her mom. "You and I both know it's the best thing that's ever happened to us."

In several rapid strides, her mom crossed the room and slapped Raquel soundly across the face. She wasn't surprised; it wasn't the first time she'd been slapped by her mother. She looked up at her mom—a tall, beautiful woman—and smiled. Her mom always hated it when she smiled at her after being slapped.

"Now you listen to me, young lady," she said, sticking a long, painted fingernail in her face. "You don't disrespect your father, you hear me? I won't allow that kind of talk!"

"You can't control what I say," Raquel responded coldly.

"The heck I can't! Your father may have made a mistake, but he's a good man."

"Oh, yeah, mom—a *good man*. Whatever. A *good man* cheats on his wife."

"I told you, don't you disrespect your father! Everybody makes mistakes."

Raquel smirked, shaking her head. "Whatever, Mom."

"Now you *will* get out here and be pleasant in front of our guests."

"And put on a 'happy face,' just like you, right, Mom?"

Her mother stared while Raquel smiled triumphantly up at her. Then she spun on her heels and marched out of the room, slamming the door behind her.

Satisfied, Raquel turned back to the window. She always won fights with her mom. Her mom knew how to hit, but Raquel knew how to use words as effective blows to the gut.

I wonder what Sara is doing tonight, she thought.

Raquel's heart immediately sank. Sara: the one friend she'd had a little over a year ago while living in southern Texas... until Sara had left. People were always leaving.

What did it matter, though? Raquel had left, too—moving back to this same crummy town she'd lived in before. How many times had she moved? Six? At *least* six. Nearly *half* of her lifetime had been spent moving! At least this house was the best out of all of them. Even though she'd been forced to move in the middle of the school year back to this friendless town in north-eastern Texas a couple weeks ago, at least she had a mansion to live in this time with a bedroom as big as a bowling alley.

At first, Raquel had hoped to run into Sara; hadn't Sara said her home was in north-eastern Texas? Raquel had soon dismissed the possibility. Who was she kidding? Texas was a big state; there were *lots* of towns in north-eastern Texas. Sara was probably nowhere near here.

Raquel sighed and turned away from the window. She heard her stomach growl. When her mom had opened the door, the aroma of the Christmas Eve dinner feast had wafted in. She sighed again. She didn't want to face her relatives, but she didn't want to starve, either. Besides, they couldn't make her talk. She could eat without talking to anyone.

Her stomach rumbled again and she headed out the door.

She reached the bottom of the staircase and entered the dining room, taking a seat at the enormous dining room table surrounded on every side by aunts, uncles, and cousins. A few of them tried to talk to her, but she kept her mouth shut. She scooped a heaping portion of mashed potatoes onto her plate, grabbed a dinner roll, and stabbed at a good-sized slice of ham. Christmas Eve dinner was always a big to-do; Raquel was suddenly glad she'd decided not to turn it down.

She reached for the brown gravy.

"Better leave off the gravy," her uncle chortled. "Looks like you've been eating a tad too much gravy lately." He laughed a guttural laugh and went back to his meal.

Raquel felt all the blood rush to her face. She let her fork fall to her plate. She looked down at her stomach; what did he mean? Was she fat? She didn't think so.

Nobody came to her defense. Nobody chided him or told him he was being rude. Everybody went right on eating as though the comment had never been made—consummately unaware that this side comment would soon turn Raquel's entire world upside down.

Chapter 2

Christmas Morning

Raquel wasn't interested in dessert. She darted for her room as soon as she'd stayed long enough to ensure that her mom wouldn't follow her.

She sat down in front of the large mirror on her dresser. Her whole head was hot; she felt like crying, but she refused. She swallowed. *Do I look fat?* The words kept ringing in her head.

For a moment she wondered why she even cared. She thought she'd made up her mind not to care about anything. But somehow the thought of being fat terrified her. She looked down at her dresser: All of the models on the covers of the fashion magazines were thin. Raquel had always prided herself in keeping up with the latest fashions. Since it was December, most of the models were wearing clothing that covered them from head to foot, but anyone could still tell how thin they were.

Raquel sighed and slouched in her chair. As usual, she reached behind her back for her hair before remembering that it was gone. At that moment, something exploded inside of her and she went crazy—shoving all of the magazines on her dresser onto the floor into one gigantic heap.

Except for one.

Underneath the recent issues was a summer issue of the magazine. The woman on the cover had long, blond hair... just like she used to have. The woman was beautiful.

Raquel's eyes roamed from the woman's hair and face to her body. The woman was thin. Amazingly thin. *Unbelievably* thin. Because it was a summer issue, the woman was wearing clothing that revealed her midsection. Raquel studied the woman's stomach; it was practically concave. She had seen pictures of women's stomachs before, of course, but tonight she studied it. It was beautiful. *She* was beautiful. And for the first time, Raquel decided that it was not because of her hair or even her face that the model was so beautiful; it was because of her stomach.

Raquel stood and studied her own stomach in the mirror. Raquel had always been tall and thin—or so she'd thought up until about ten minutes ago. She looked down again at the woman on the magazine. The woman was thinner. She was prettier. Raquel had to admit that she looked nothing like this woman.

But she could change that. She could go on a diet. She could start exercising. How hard could it be? Weren't they always advertising new dieting products on TV? Weren't there all kinds of exercise programs? Why hadn't Raquel realized it before? Dieting and exercising were the keys to beauty. She'd been so clueless... up till now. She could be beautiful. With a little time and effort, she could look *just* like the woman on the cover of that magazine. And in that moment Raquel decided that she *would* look just like the woman on the cover of that magazine.

She smiled at the thought and bent down and began to pick up the magazines from the floor—placing them back on her dresser. As each cover model passed by her vision, her smile got a little wider. *Soon I will look like them,* she thought excitedly.

Raquel slept better that night than she'd slept in a long time. She felt alive... like she had something to live for. Raquel couldn't remember the last time she'd felt like that.

When she awoke, she was surprised to find that it was still dark. She tried going back to sleep, but she didn't feel the least bit tired. She rolled over to find a new position but this didn't help.

Frustrated, she finally kicked the covers off and sat up on the edge of the bed. It was dark, and yet there seemed to be a strange glow coming from outside. Curious, Raquel stood and walked over to the window. What she saw made her mouth drop open: Covering the lawn was a layer of freshly-fallen snow, with huge flakes continuing to fall!

Raquel became like a little kid and ran from her bedroom, down the stairs, through the darkened living room, and to the front entryway where she flung open the front door. She froze. Not because of the icy chill that was in the air. And not because of the beauty of the winter wonderland that had become her front yard. But because of what was standing *in* her front yard.

At the bottom of the porch steps, a giant white horse shook its massive head violently, sending snowflakes flying. Then it looked at her. Raquel gasped: The horse had glowing red eyes!

Raquel was both terrified and enthralled at the same time. This was the most beautiful creature she had ever seen. Even against the snowy backdrop of the front lawn, the horse seemed to stand out—so white that the snow hardly looked white in comparison! And a soft glow of light surrounded the horse as though a light were shining on it. Or being emitted from it.

She found that she couldn't stop looking at its eyes. She felt herself being drawn to the creature. Raquel took a step forward. At that moment, she noticed two things at once: Even though she was now standing barefoot on her front porch wearing only a nightgown and housecoat, she didn't feel cold. She also noticed for the first time that the horse had two gigantic white wings resting on its back! How could she have missed it before? Raquel jumped as the horse unfurled its wings and flapped them several times—creating a gust of wind—before nestling them gently back onto its back.

Raquel grinned. Now *this* was beauty!

She took another step forward, then halted—amazed at her own boldness. What was she thinking? Why was she walking *toward* this creature when she should have been running *away* from it? The fire in its eyes still terrified her.

She took another step forward and stopped again. This was *crazy;* the horse was *enormous!* And who knew whether or not it was safe? But the longer she looked into the horse's eyes, the stronger the desire became to get closer to it. She tried to look away but found that she couldn't. Before she'd realized what she was doing, Raquel found herself running toward the horse, jumping from the porch onto its back.

The horse was incredibly soft, yet powerful. She settled in between its two massive wings and grabbed handfuls of the silky mane. A feeling overtook her that this was the most natural place she could be—that this was where she should have been all along.

Raquel was a bit startled when the wings suddenly unfurled and the horse took off running. Rather than feeling afraid, Raquel found that she felt elated as they raced through the snowy night. The intense beating of the horse's wings soon caused them to become airborne and Raquel found herself sailing through the night sky—rising higher and higher over the town. She looked down and discovered that she didn't feel afraid in the least—even at this altitude. Only a few lighted windows could be seen down below as they sped quickly by.

Deciding that this was the sweetest dream she'd ever had, Raquel sighed contentedly and loosened her grip on the horse's mane, laying her head against its neck. The neck remained stabilized as the horse flew. She closed her eyes—her cheek resting against its downy mane. The rhythmic beating of the horse's wings soon lulled her to sleep.

Chapter 3

Relámpago

Raquel awoke to the sound of running water. In the back of her mind she wondered where it was coming from, but the dream she'd just had was so beautiful that she hesitated waking up fully. Besides, her bed was so incredibly soft...

Her bed? She felt of her pillow; it didn't feel like a pillow. It felt like soft and silky angel's hair—like the horse's mane in her dream.

Raquel opened her eyes. Everything was still dark. Was it still night time? Surely not; it had to have been close to morning when the horse showed up.

The horse. But it had all just been a dream. Right?

She felt around in the darkness: in front of her was the horse's silky mane; to her left and right were velvety wings.

Surely this couldn't be happening...

She lost her balance and tumbled headlong off the side of the horse and landed with a splash in a pool of water. Raquel panicked and flailed around for something she could grab a hold of, but she couldn't find anything. The water only came up to her waist so she was able to get her feet up under her, but she was quickly knocked off her feet again from the rapidly-moving water. Raquel felt herself being carried downstream at an alarming rate. And to add to her fright, everything was still pitch-black!

Then something large blocked her path and she clung to it with all her might. The object was solid and immovable. And soft. She blinked her eyes and noticed that objects were slowly coming into focus—blurry at first, then clearer the more she blinked. She saw a large white object looming above her. It was the white horse, knee-deep in the water. She saw its long neck curved down toward her. Where was its head? Its head was what she was clinging to!

At this moment of realization, the head jerked up from the water—taking Raquel along with it, a steel grip on its mane. Raquel swung there momentarily as from a rope, then quickly climbed the soft but sturdy mane to the horse's neck. (This didn't seem to hurt the horse in the slightest!) Upon reaching its neck, she clung to it like a cat clinging to a large tree branch and began shinnying her way to the horse's back. It was here that Raquel finally heaved a sigh of relief.

Sitting upright, she noticed that even though she had nearly drowned just moments ago, she wasn't even wet. She also noticed that she could now see perfectly—more clearly, in fact, than she had ever been able to see before.

And this is what she saw:

She sat atop an enormous waterfall that towered over a land more beautiful than anything in her wildest dreams. Far below were forest glades of various shades of green that Raquel had never seen, and to her right was a magnificent mountain chain made up of such a variety of colors that the individual mountains seemed to take on a life of their own. Beyond the forest were patches of white (Raquel couldn't tell if they were snow or clouds), and several gorgeous mansions randomly dispersed throughout dotted the landscape like jewels in a crown.

The roar from the waterfall caused her to look down. Raquel marveled that the horse was able to stand so stationary in such turbulent water. She noticed for the first time just how close she was to the waterfall's edge. The horse had saved her from going over just in time.

Raquel studied the horse. She couldn't see its eyes because it was facing forward. She wasn't sure she even *wanted* to see its eyes; she hadn't forgotten how much they terrified her. But at the same time, she felt that she would die of despair if she never got to see them again.

The horse curved its neck and looked at her. Raquel caught her breath. What did she see in those eyes? Love? Not just love, but a powerful kind of love that Raquel was unfamiliar with. An all-consuming, unconditional love. A love that accepted her for who she was and despite what she did. She didn't understand this kind of love at all.

The horse faced forward and the spell was broken; Raquel found that she could think again.

Love? From a *horse?* It wasn't possible. But then again, neither was a *flying* horse.

As if to prove her wrong, the giant wings to her left and right unfurled. Raquel grabbed fistfuls of mane and braced herself for the takeoff. Her stomach was left behind as the horse lifted into the air. But Raquel was glad to find that the horse chose not to fly too quickly; it flew at a slow enough pace that Raquel could take in the scenery below and around her. She saw fields of flowers far below with every color of the rainbow—their sweet aroma drifting up to her as they flew past. There was a winding street made of gold with a river running through it, with fruit trees on either side. There were children playing a game down below in one of the patches of white she'd noticed earlier. It looked like fun. She wondered how many other people lived here.

Far too soon, the great horse quickened the beat of its wings to prepare for a landing. It landed in a grove of cherry blossom trees with a long, rectangular table nearby. On the table was an assortment of delicious-looking food that put even Christmas Eve dinner to shame. The aroma was nearly overwhelming; it was all Raquel could do to keep from jumping off the horse and begin devouring the feast.

"Why don't you?"

Who had spoken? Raquel looked at the horse, then she looked back at the table. A Native American man with dark hair past his shoulders sat dressed in ordinary, every-day clothes, but there was something about him that seemed unordinary. Maybe it was the fact that he was so *big*—both in height and muscular build. He sat there eating, not paying her a bit of attention.

Was it he who had spoken? No one else was around...

"Why don't you eat?"

Raquel looked at the man, startled. He had put his food down and was staring at her. She had never seen eyes like this before; they were dark brown, but they seemed to possess a light. She sat there open-mouthed for several seconds before the man finally went back to his eating.

As soon as he looked away, Raquel found that she could think again. The spell had been broken—just like with the horse. She immediately became conscious of the fact that she was wearing her nightgown. She was glad that she'd thought to grab her housecoat.

Raquel looked around; there was nothing else to look at other than the table... and the man. They were seemingly alone inside a forest, although it wasn't dark the way most forests are. The white cherry blossoms were so bright, in fact, that she found herself continually blinking her eyes.

Again, the scent of food caught her attention and she looked back at the table. The man was eating ravenously as though he hadn't eaten in months. Raquel felt her stomach growl. It *did* look delicious. Maybe she should take the man up on his offer and eat something.

Then she remembered: She was on a diet. Just the night before, she'd decided to try and lose weight by going on a diet. *Remember, Raquel?*

"You're not fat."

Raquel felt her blood begin to boil. "Excuse me?"

"You're not fat," the man repeated, not looking up from his food.

"Who said I was?"

"You did," he said matter-of-factly, pointing a finger at her with one hand while holding onto his food with the other.

Enraged, Raquel slid off the side of the horse and marched over to the man sitting at the table, then stopped dead in her tracks. He was not as easily intimidated as she had hoped; in fact, *she* felt intimated just standing here next to him... and he wasn't even looking at her—he was still eating. Even in a sitting position, the man was taller than she was—and for the first time, she noticed that the man had wings! Giant, snowy-white wings... just like the horse!

The Native American continued eating; he sure was enjoying himself. Like most Native Americans, the man had sharp features and dark, bronzed skin. He had high cheek-bones... and *enormous* arm muscles! Raquel made a mental note to never try and intimidate him again.

"Sit," the man said between mouthfuls, not looking at her.

Without taking her eyes off him, Raquel sat down at the table.

The man swallowed his mouthful. "Eat," he said.

This guy certainly didn't have the gift of conversation. Raquel looked at the food in front of her. It made her mouth begin to water. She quickly looked away.

"Eat," the man said again, keeping his eyes on his food.

This guy's choices of words were short and to the point, but Raquel could be short and to the point, too. "No," she responded curtly.

He paused and looked at her. Raquel caught her breath. His dark brown eyes were somehow bright and hard to look at. "Why don't you eat?" he said again.

Raquel swallowed. "Be-because I don't want to," she stammered.

"Why?"

Get ahold of yourself, Raquel! she told herself. *Nobody can make you do anything, remember?* "I just don't feel like it," she responded. She was trying to sound tough, but it was hard to feel tough sitting next to this guy.

The winged man held the food he was eating out to her—right under her nose. Raquel looked at it briefly then closed her eyes and turned her head. "I don't want it," she said resolutely.

"You lie."

Raquel opened her eyes and attempted to stare the man down—sitting up as straight as she could. "No, I *don't* lie!" she said defensively. "And is it possible for you to say more than two words at a time?"

The man had gone back to eating, and upon hearing this he chuckled. The laugh was deep and rich, just like his voice.

"What's so funny, you... you winged freak!" It was all Raquel could think of to say.

One of the man's wings hit her so hard that Raquel found herself face-first in a bowl of pudding. The man snorted. "Sorry," he said, looking at her with a huge grin. "I forget my own strength sometimes. You want it *now?*"

Raquel had gotten some of the pudding in her mouth and was hesitating lifting her head from the bowl. Then she remembered her diet and suddenly jerked her head up from the bowl—shoving it away. "No!"

The man started laughing—a loud, thunderous sound.

"*Now* what's so funny?" Raquel demanded.

He held the bowl up in front of her face.

"I *told* you, I don't—" But Raquel stopped. The bowl was so shiny, it served as a mirror. She had the pudding all over her nose and chin. Embarrassed, Raquel looked for a napkin, but she didn't see any.

The man's arm appeared in front of her—covered in a white garment. His ordinary clothes had somehow been replaced by a long white robe. He looked more regal now, and his smile more welcoming than mocking. "Use my sleeve," he said, a wide grin covering his face. "It automatically rejects all stains."

Raquel hesitated, then took the man's long, draping sleeve in her hands and quickly wiped her face with it. True to the man's words, the stain immediately faded and the sleeve became perfectly white again.

Raquel suddenly felt different after having wiped her face with the man's robe. She felt more relaxed and less angry.

The man appeared more relaxed, too. He propped his elbow on the table and rested his head on his hand, still donning a huge grin. "I am Relámpago," he said in a booming voice. "You are Raquel, yes?"

Chapter 4

Dante

Raquel couldn't deny answering the question in the affirmative. "Yes," she said.

"You are wondering why I have wings, yes?" asked the Native American.

That was just one of the many things Raquel was wondering. "Yes," she answered again.

"I am a criado, little warrior!" the man responded, as though that should clear everything up. "Welcome to Paraíso!"

Apparently excited, the man began to flap his wings. Raquel quickly scooted away from him.

Relámpago burst out laughing. "I promise I will not hit you again," he said with a grin, and held up a hand as though he were taking an oath.

"How do I know you can be trusted?" Raquel challenged.

"In Paraíso, only the truth is told."

"Well, not where I'm from," she said. Raquel attempted to drive home her point by looking away, but when she looked away she saw the table full of food, so she quickly looked back at the criado.

"Why don't you eat?" the Native American criado asked.

"We've been through this!" said Raquel angrily. "I already told you... I'm not hungry!"

"You didn't say that before," the criado pointed out. "You said, 'I don't want to.'"

"Yeah, well, that's the same thing," Raquel said, turning around and crossing her arms, her back to the table.

"Not the same thing at all," Relámpago said, shaking his head. "It is quite possible to be hungry and not want to eat, just as it is possible to want to eat and not be hungry."

"It's also possible to not want to eat *and* not be hungry," Raquel stated emphatically, not looking at him.

"You want to eat *and* you are hungry," the criado informed her.

"Says who?" Raquel demanded, turning to face him. "How do *you* know what I want? Maybe I'm on a diet, okay? Ever heard of a 'diet' here in—wherever we are?"

"Paraíso."

"Yeah, Paraíso!"

"Yes, I have heard of it, but not in Paraíso."

"Why? Is everyone here so perfectly thin that they don't need to diet?"

"You are not fat."

Raquel pounded the table with her fist so hard that plates and bowls rattled. "I didn't say I was!" she shouted. "I'd greatly appreciate it if you wouldn't put words in my mouth!"

Relámpago turned back to his plate. "If you are neither hungry nor want to eat," he replied calmly, "why do you sit at the table of food?"

"I have no earthly idea!" Raquel exclaimed, jumping to her feet and marching away from the table.

"The food is good for eating, little warrior," the criado called to her between bites.

"I'm sure it is," she called back. "Enjoy stuffing your face. And quit calling me that!"

She heard a sudden commotion behind her, but she didn't turn to look. Suddenly, the criado landed directly in front of her. It startled her momentarily, but then she remembered that the man had wings in this strange dream of hers. She attempted to walk around him but he extended a wing—blocking her way.

"You said you wouldn't hit me again!" she said angrily, attempting to glare at him but not really making eye contact. The guy must have been at least seven feet tall! Plus his eyes still freaked her out.

"And you can trust me to keep my word," he said with a nod, his arms crossed.

"Can I trust you to go away and leave me alone?"

"Decidedly no," the criado said, shaking his head.

Exasperated, Raquel attempted to go around him the other way, but his other wing snapped out in front of her.

"What do you *want?*" Raquel screamed up at him.

"I want you to eat," he said, looking down at her.

"What's it to you?" Raquel demanded. "Why should you care whether I eat or not?"

"I want you to live."

"Um, in case you hadn't noticed, I *am* living—unless I've died and this is the afterlife... a horrible afterlife where people force you to eat!"

Relámpago chuckled.

"And I would *very* much like to *go on* living just like I was before I came to this annoying place!" Raquel spun around and started walking away.

"You don't like the way you are living."

Raquel halted in her tracks. Slowly, she turned to face him. "What do *you* know about my life?"

The criado uncrossed his arms and folded his wings, appearing less menacing, and began walking slowly toward her. "I know that you are unhappy with your life," he said, a note of sadness in his voice. "You are angry at your father for what he did to your mother, and for leaving you."

Raquel blinked.

"You are angry at your mother," he said, continuing toward her, "for mistreating you. You are even angry at yourself, Raquel."

Relámpago was now standing directly in front of her. She looked up at him and heard herself ask, "For what?"

The criado smiled warmly and reached down to her, gently tracing her face with his large hand. "For not being good enough," he said tenderly. "But you are, Raquel. You are *beautiful*."

For a moment, Raquel believed him, and it did something to her. Looking into his eyes, she suddenly felt like a princess—like a priceless jewel that the whole world looked upon in wonder. She felt the same unconditional love that she'd felt when she'd looked into the horse's eyes. She began to smile.

Then she caught herself. She would *not* be a sucker for anymore lies! She turned and walked away.

"It's not a lie, Raquel," Relámpago called after her.

"And why should I believe you, huh?" Raquel demanded, turning on her heels to face him. "Why shouldn't you be a liar just like everyone else I've ever met? Why should *you* be any different?"

The criado looked pained enough to cry. In fact, Raquel wasn't completely sure she didn't see a tear on his cheek. Raquel was shocked. She'd seen plenty of people cry *because* of her, but she'd never seen anyone cry *for* her.

Some movement came from within the trees. Raquel turned to see a stocky eleven- or twelve-year-old Asian boy run out to embrace the white horse. "Espíritu!" he cried. The horse flapped its wings in greeting as the boy held tightly to the horse's head.

Raquel looked back; Relámpago was gone.

The boy paused to look at her. Raquel looked back. It became a kind of staring contest. Finally, the boy spoke up. "Who are *you?*" he asked, rather rudely, Raquel thought.

"Who are *you?*" Raquel fired back.

The Asian boy looked back at the horse and said something in another language. Raquel distinctly heard her name mentioned. The horse nodded its head.

"What are you saying about me?" she demanded. "And how do you know my name?"

The boy gave her a skeptical look—scanning her from head to toe.

"What's your problem?" Raquel spat. "What are you looking at?"

The boy's expression didn't change as he responded, "You're in your nightgown."

"*And* housecoat!" Raquel countered, tying the loose ends of her housecoat tightly around her waist. "And would you mind answering at least *one* of my questions? Who *are* you?"

The boy sighed and shook his head, turning back to the horse. He said something else in another language, and again the horse nodded its head.

"Would you cut that out!" Raquel demanded. "I already know you can speak English!"

The heavy-set boy glanced her way, then began to meander his way over to her. As he approached, Raquel began to feel intimidated—just as she had with Relámpago. The boy was younger than she was but he carried himself with such an air of confidence that it made Raquel feel uncomfortable. He had short black hair and long shaggy bangs that covered his forehead, and there was something about his eyes that bothered her—just like the horse's and the man's. "Fine," the boy said, now reaching her. "You want English? You got it."

Raquel felt at a loss for what to say, but only momentarily. "What language were you speaking to the horse?" she asked.

"To Espíritu?" said the boy. "Korean. I speak both Korean and English, but I use Korean when speaking with Espíritu."

"Is Espíritu the horse?"

The boy looked over his shoulder at the horse and then back at her again. "Y-y-yes," he said slowly, mockingly.

"Well, I didn't know," Raquel said, annoyed. "And for the third time, who *are* you?"

The boy sighed again and extended his hand. "Ayudante," he said. "Some call me 'Ayu,' but most call me 'Dante.'"

"And this place is called Paraíso?" she asked, not shaking his hand.

The boy let his arm fall to his side. "Yep," he said with a smile, seemingly unaffected by her lack of geniality. "You're learning!"

"Yeah, well, I haven't exactly gotten much help since I've been here."

The boy spread his arms wide. "That's why I'm here," he announced with a grin, sticking his hands in his pockets and rocking back and forth on the balls of his feet.

"So I get a chubby Chinese kid to help me?"

The boy's grin never faded. "Korean," he corrected her.

He seemed to have missed the "chubby" part, so Raquel decided to repeat herself. "My mistake," she said. "A chubby *Korean* kid."

"That's me!" he exclaimed, seemingly unfazed.

"Are you going to just stand there and let me call you 'fat'?"

"Why not?" he shrugged. "It's the truth, isn't it? Why should I be ashamed of the truth?"

"You could go on a diet."

"Why should I?"

"Don't you even *care* what others think about you, or are you crazy?"

"Don't know about the latter," Dante said with a smile, "but I can tell you for sure that I don't care what others think about me. Nobody but the King, that is."

"You care about your king's opinion of you, but no one else's?"

"Yep."

"Why?"

"Because I live to serve the King and nobody else."

"Not even yourself?"

"*Especially* not myself."

"You *are* crazy!"

Dante just shrugged again. "If serving the King makes me crazy, then I guess that makes me crazy. Better crazy than dead."

"So your king kills people who don't serve him? Sounds like a nice guy."

Dante quit rocking, his expression turning serious. "I didn't say that! The King is Love; you won't find a deeper love than His. People end up dead not because of the King but because of themselves. The King loves us so much that He sent His Son to die in our place. But people choose to die when they reject the King's gift and decide to serve themselves instead."

"What are you talking about? Who's choosing to die?"

"Anyone who doesn't accept the King's free gift."

"And his 'free gift' is his own son's death?"

"You got it!" Dante exclaimed.

"So, wait a minute, let me get this straight," Raquel said. "Everybody was gonna die, so your king stepped in and said, 'Hold everything, let my son die instead'?"

"That's right," Dante nodded, his eyes shining.

"Why?"

"Because that's what love *does*. He loves me, and He loves you, too."

"Why? Why would your king love *me?* He doesn't even *know* me."

"Sure He does!" Dante exclaimed. "You may not know Him, but He sure knows you!"

"If that's true," Raquel said, "then now I know for *sure* that He doesn't love me! I haven't done anything to earn His love."

"That's the great thing about the King," Dante smiled. "You don't *have* to earn His love! In fact, you *can't* earn His love! It wouldn't be love anyway if you could earn it."

Raquel decided she'd need some time to think that one through. "So... you don't care what others think about you because you know your king loves you?"

Dante's grin got wider as he began to rock again. "That's right!"

"Do others make fun of you?"

"No one in Paraíso cares what you look like," he told her. "Every type of body—fat, thin, tall, short—is considered beautiful. But really, everyone thinks about the inside of the person so much that they really don't have time to consider the outside."

Raquel felt her face crack a smile. "I need to move here," she decided.

Dante laughed. "That's easy to do!" he exclaimed. "Just tell the King you love Him and that you want to serve Him and that you want His Son's death to take your place... and that's it! Your name will be found in Paraíso's registry—also known as the Book of Life."

"The Book of Life?"

"I'll show you!" he said excitedly, grabbing a hold of her hand and pulling her over to Espíritu. Raquel was amazed at how easily he flung himself onto the horse, and at how easily he was able to help pull her up.

Chapter 5

The Song

It was a short flight to their destination. Sitting behind Dante on Espíritu, Raquel could see that they were approaching what looked to be a *very* tall golden staircase extending upward into the sky. It was so tall that Raquel couldn't see the bottom of it. As they circled around it, Raquel noticed that criados—the men with wings—of all different nationalities stood guard along the staircase dispersed at intervals in groups of two. Like Relámpago, the criados all had huge muscles and enormous white wings, but unlike Relámpago every single criado had fastened around his waist a golden belt with a golden sheath attached to it. Inside each sheath was a sword, and the criados' left hands were resting on the hilts of their swords—causing them to appear even more intimidating than Relámpago had appeared. The expression on every one of their faces was incredibly solemn; Raquel couldn't imagine what creature on earth would dare mess with them. She also couldn't imagine what awaited at the top of the staircase that warranted being guarded by so many criados.

Espíritu continued circling the staircase until the top finally came into view. It was a large platform on which a criado stood guard at each of the four corners. In the center of the platform was a tall golden podium surrounded by four more winged criados—these with their swords already drawn. On top of the podium sat a massive book.

"Is that the Book of Life?" Raquel wondered.

"Yep," Dante replied over his shoulder to her.

"Are we going to land next to it?"

"If the criados can make room."

The criados themselves seemed to be wondering if they could make room. After spotting Espíritu, they all bowed in reverence to him then abandoned their military stance—all of them moving to one side of the platform to make room for the giant horse. One of the criados got too close to the edge of the platform and nearly fell off before another criado grabbed a hold of his hand and steadied him—both of them laughing. *He has wings,* Raquel thought to herself. *It's not like it would even be that big a deal if he fell.*

Now that space was available, Espíritu swooped in and landed next to the giant book—and the crowded criados. The book, of course, was now completely unguarded, but the criados didn't seem to mind. In fact, with the arrival of Espíritu, they seemed to have forgotten all about the book—smiling and sheathing their swords. They even began to talk amongst themselves, appearing more like children than armed guards.

"Don't they care about guarding the book anymore?" Raquel wondered.

"Not with Espíritu here," Dante answered, sliding down off the horse onto the platform. He reached for her hand. Raquel slid down without his help.

Once Raquel slid down, the criados stopped their chatter and turned to stare at her. Raquel found herself stepping behind Dante. "Can't they go away?" Raquel asked angrily. She wasn't intimidated by their size so much as their eyes.

She felt certain they wouldn't harm her, but the brightness of their eyes scared her (though she didn't even know why).

Dante must have understood because he took a step toward them—seemingly feeling no fear, Raquel noted—and began to speak to them in Korean. The criados looked at him for a moment then turned their attention to Espíritu. The great horse nodded his head. The jubilant criados began again to talk amongst themselves in some foreign language, then one by one took off from the platform with a beating of wings—creating a giant wind that blew Raquel back against the horse. Espíritu seemed unaffected by the turbulence. After what seemed like a lot longer than it really was, the criados were all gone—leaving Dante and Raquel alone on the platform with Espíritu.

"Quite a wind, huh?" laughed Dante. "You should see what it's like when there's a thousand of 'em!"

Raquel was still trying to catch her breath, and hearing this didn't help.

Dante smiled gently and took her by the hand. Raquel jerked her hand away. "Follow me," Dante smiled, unflustered.

She followed him over to the giant podium. At the base of the podium, Raquel looked up. The closed leather-bound book was extremely large with words from another language written on the cover. The podium on which it sat was obviously made for someone closer to a criado's height than her own.

"The Book of Life," Dante said reverently.

Raquel looked at him, then up at the book. She reached as high as she could to try and open it.

An ear-piercing scream caused her to quickly recoil and drop to a squatting position with her hands over her ears. She looked up to see Espíritu reared up over her head—his giant hooves hanging precariously over her, then she held her breath as his forelegs came down nearly crushing her, missing her by inches. He looked down at her—his nostrils flaring, his red eyes aflame.

"Don't touch the Book," Dante said calmly but resolutely, helping her to her feet.

"Uh, yeah, I kinda figured that out," Raquel said, backing slowly away from the Horse.

"Don't worry," Dante told her. "If Espíritu had wanted to harm you, He would have."

"Is there any chance of that happening again?" Raquel asked fearfully, not taking her eyes off the Horse.

"What, of Espíritu commanding both fear and awe? I'd say there's a really good chance of that."

Raquel just wanted out of here; she would try and get this over with as quickly as possible. "So tell me about the book," she said, daring to take her eyes off the giant Horse. "What makes it so important?"

Dante smiled gently. "The Book of Life," he told her, "has everyone's name in there who will end up living in Paraíso. It was written at the foundation of the world. The King knew ahead of time who would reject and who would accept the gift of His Son."

"And those who accept him are written in the book?"

"That's right," Dante said with a nod.

"And if your name's in there," Raquel continued, "it means that you get to live in Paraíso?"

"That's right," Dante said again.

"What about those who choose to reject him? What happens to them?"

Dante sighed. "They are forced to live in the Land of Lamento—a terrible place where you're always on fire but can't ever die. Everything's dark so you can't even see your loved ones if they happen to be there with you. In fact, there's no love at all in that place. It's basically the opposite of here."

"The king makes all that happen just for rejecting him? Isn't that a little harsh?"

"Isn't it a little harsh to reject the King's sacrifice of His only Son?" Dante countered.

"Maybe," admitted Raquel, "but not to that extent. I don't think *anybody* deserves that kind of punishment, no matter *what* they've done."

"Do you think anybody deserves to live here in Paraíso?"

Raquel thought about it and chuckled. "Maybe Mother Teresa," she said with a laugh, "but not me."

Dante grinned. "Even Mother Teresa's not perfect," he said. "*Everybody* messes up once in a while. By the way, that's the first time I've heard you laugh."

Raquel smiled and looked down, embarrassed. "Yeah," she said sheepishly. "I guess there's something about this place that brings out the best in me. I honestly can't remember the last time I laughed. I don't have much reason to laugh back home."

"Accepting the King won't make all your problems go away," Dante informed her, "but you'll at least have peace knowing Espíritu—and knowing that Paraíso is waiting for you some day."

Raquel shifted her weight from one foot to the other. "When you say, 'accept the king,'" she said hesitantly, "what does that mean, exactly?"

"I already told you," Dante said. "It means that you tell the King you love Him, you want to serve Him, and you want His Son's death to take your place."

"The king's son died in my place?"

"Y-y-yes."

"Why?"

"So that you could live in Paraíso for eternity and not in the Land of Lamento."

"I'm not a bad enough person to live in the Land of Lamento for all eternity."

"Have you ever done anything bad?"

"Well, yes..."

"Then you're a 'bad enough person.' You have to be *perfect* to live in Paraíso."

"That's ridiculous!" Raquel exclaimed. *"Nobody's* perfect! You said yourself that even Mother Teresa's not perfect!"

"Exactly," Dante nodded. "That's why the King sent His Son to die—so that in the King's eyes we could be *made* perfect. Even after people accept the King's gift of His Son, they'll still make mistakes, of course. But in the King's eyes, they're absolutely perfect. Pretty good deal, huh?"

"The king is powerful enough to forgive us like that," Raquel marveled, "and yet he's not powerful enough to find a better way for us to be forgiven? Allowing his son to die was the only option he could think of?"

"Yes," Dante said gravely. "To us, the bad things we do are just kinda bad, but to the King they're repulsive. Remember, unlike us, the King *is* perfect. Evil cannot be allowed to live in His Kingdom. That's why His Son, the Prince's, death was required. Like the King, the Prince is perfect, so He made a perfect sacrifice for us. That's how much the Prince loves us—enough to be willing to die for us."

"You talk about the Prince as though he's still alive," Raquel observed.

"He is!" Dante said excitedly.

"But you said—"

"I said He died," Dante interrupted, "but I didn't say He *stayed* dead. After He died, He came back to life again! That's how powerful the Prince is!"

Suddenly, Espíritu reared up and let out another ear-piercing scream—violently beating His wings. Apparently knowing this was coming, Dante quickly grabbed a hold of Raquel's hand and with the other grabbed a tight hold of Espíritu's mane—long enough to reach Dante without Dante's feet ever leaving the platform. The smile never left Dante's face, and his eyes never left Raquel. As Espíritu came crashing back down onto the platform (and the windstorm was over), Dante calmly released the Horse's mane as though nothing had even happened. "I knew that was coming," he laughed. "Espíritu does that when He gets excited."

Raquel stood there, open-mouthed. "You really *are* crazy," she laughed, partly out of fear and partly out of joy. "You would grab onto Espíritu when he's acting like that?"

"Acting like what?" Dante asked, stroking the now-calm Horse. "That's normal behavior for Espíritu. He gets excited when you start talking about the Prince. Just like the King and the Prince, Espíritu experiences all ranges of emotions, and He's not shy about sharing them with the rest of us. In fact, you get to know Espíritu and you'll find that you're getting to know the King and the Prince, as well."

Raquel looked at the Great Horse and found herself smiling. "I might like that," she said humbly.

"It's easy to get to know them," Dante told her. "They're waiting to talk with you. You can talk to the King right now, if you want."

"Right now? But he's not even here."

"Sure He is! You can't see Him, but He's always nearby—especially in Paraíso!" Dante laughed.

Raquel looked over at Espíritu. He was looking at her. The love in his eyes was still powerful, but it didn't frighten her as much as it had before. She decided that she *did* want to get to know him better... and the King, too.

She could talk to the King right now? How?

Raquel didn't know who to look at, so she closed her eyes. "King," she began, "I'd like to get to know you. If you're anything like Espíritu, then I know you love me. And I... I love you, too. Teach me how to serve you. You gave your Son's life for me—thank you for doing that. Thank you for being willing to die, Prince; that was... really nice of you," she said awkwardly. "Thank you for dying in my place," she said, feeling tears spring into her eyes, "and for making me perfect in your eyes. Thank you for forgiving me." She couldn't say another word.

At that moment, a commotion caused Raquel to open her eyes. Espíritu had left the platform and was zooming around over their heads—laughter in His eyes—doing all kinds of flips and turns with the ease of a tiny sparrow. He shown brightly as though lit up from the inside—the light causing His whole body to appear as though it were on fire. He let out a scream, but Raquel could tell that it was a scream of joy.

Then, from out of nowhere, criados flew in from all directions—joining Espíritu in His jubilant celebration. The air over their heads became filled with wings and singing and laughter and light. The song they sang was so powerful that Raquel dropped to her knees on the platform. She knew she would never forget this moment for as long as she lived.

Dante got down on his knees beside her.

"What are they singing about?" Raquel asked him in awe, her eyes still on the sky.

Dante's voice revealed that he was equally in awe. "They're singing about *you*, Raquel," he said.

Chapter 6

First Day Back

A song played on the alarm clock. Six-thirty Monday morning. *Snooze*.

Sara rolled over—grateful for even nine more minutes of extra sleep. She would stay in bed all day if she could.

"Sara, get up," she heard her dad call from the hallway.

With a moan, she covered up her head. Maybe he'd go away.

No such luck. "Sara, I know you hear me," she heard his voice say. "C'mon, you don't want to be late for your first day back."

Her moan turned into a groan as she kicked her covers off. *First day back*. Why couldn't Christmas break last a little longer? It *never* seemed long enough.

It *was* a nice break, though. She lay there a little longer reminiscing. Christmas had always been her favorite time of year. The songs. The presents! The *food!* The good old-fashioned warm feeling of being with those you love... not to mention celebrating the Prince being sent to earth. Yes, it had been a good Christmas.

But now it was back to reality. She'd made it half-way through seventh grade, but she wasn't sure she could make it the rest of the way. At least she'd been able to start the school year at her own school. The year before, she'd been forced to start sixth grade at her cousin Jaime's school because her dad's health issues had kept them from returning home in time for school to start. His health had improved, thank goodness, but his doctor had warned him to watch what he ate. Her dad wasn't that old, but eating unhealthy foods all his life was finally catching up with him.

Sara smiled. She and her dad were becoming closer. Their relationship was still not where she'd like it to be, but at least they were talking. Ever since her mom died when Sara was very young, her dad had clammed up and just stopped talking—at least to Sara. Then she'd had an encounter with Espíritu and all that changed.

Her smile widened into a grin. *Espíritu*. What she wouldn't give for another ride on that magnificent Horse. How she *wished* she could live in Paraíso instead of being forced to toil through seventh grade. Paraíso: that amazingly beautiful City beyond the clouds...

At least she knew her mom was there—happy and free from the burdens of this life. And some day she would join her!

Back to reality, Sara, she told herself. *School, remember?* Paraíso was very real, but it would have to wait.

Throwing her legs over the side of the bed, Sara stumbled to her feet and shuffled into the bathroom. She looked at herself in the mirror. *Whew!* She had a lot of work to do.

"Where is my hairbrush?" she asked, searching the countertop. Finding it, she started brushing her long, dark hair. Being Mexican-American wasn't so bad. She still hated being short, but she admired the light that she saw from her own eyes. She knew that it was because Espíritu lived inside her—although, admittedly, she still didn't understand how that was possible. She wasn't the prettiest girl in school—not by a long shot—but she was pretty, nonetheless.

She sighed heavily, slamming the hairbrush down on the countertop. If she was pretty, then why was she *still* not getting any attention from the boys at her school? She didn't used to care about dating and thought girls were silly who chased endlessly after boys... crying over them when they broke up... feeling hopelessly dejected until they were reunited. She thought all of the drama was a waste of time.

Until this school year. Now pursuing a guy didn't seem like such a far-fetched idea. Especially a guy like Gabe.

Sara leaned dreamily against the bathroom door. *Gabe.* He was *so cute!* Her heart began to race just thinking about him. She'd tried dropping him hints that she was interested—smiling at him in the hallway, talking to him every chance she got. So why did he continue to ignore her?

She turned to the side and looked at herself in the mirror. *Oh, that's why.* While most other girls at her school were starting to develop, Sara still had the body of ten-year-old. What a difference two years can make... for some girls, that is. Some of the girls at her junior high whom she'd grown up with were, like her, not even teenagers yet but you'd never know it to look at them. And they didn't mind flaunting the fact, either. Clothes for preteens were getting more and more provocative every year, it seemed, and the well-developed girls were taking full advantage of the fact. Naturally, the guys were noticing. They also noticed when things were lacking.

Things were definitely lacking on Sara. She wouldn't be a preteen much longer; in just four months she'd be a teenager. There would need to be some *serious* growth take place in the next four months.

She knew she should be content with how she looked. After all, she was a child of the King; there was no greater honor than that. The King fashioned her exactly the way He wanted her to look. Still, when all your friends are changing and you feel left behind, it's just plain tough.

She sighed again, taking in her profile. Her eyes stopped on her stomach. What was this? From the side, her stomach seemed to bulge out. Was it just her imagination? She sucked in and couldn't believe the difference! She looked so much thinner—and *prettier!* She let her breath out and watched as the bulge returned. Maybe she needed to go on a diet...

"Sara, are you getting ready?"

She immediately grabbed up her toothbrush and squeezed on the toothpaste. "Yes," she called, the toothbrush in her mouth. She'd have to think more about the diet later. The bus would be here to pick her up at 7:30 and she couldn't be late.

After getting dressed in her room, Sara sat down on her bed, the Book of Light in her lap. She'd made it a daily routine to be sure and read from the Book of Light before leaving for school in the morning. This had taken some getting used to, but now she found herself looking forward to this time. It was time spent with the King. It was the King's Book, and the King always seemed to "speak to her" through its pages. Since she no longer had the Power of Paraíso—enabling her to see things from Paraíso's perspective—she couldn't see the light coming out of the Book but she knew it was there. Not only was she in the habit of reading from it before school, but she'd been taking it with her to school, as well. A warrior can never be too careful. It had been a little over a year since her last encounter with a sombra, but the encounter was enough to convince her that she needed to be armed and ready for battle. She knew that the big, black shadows could attack at any time, and she needed to be prepared even if she couldn't see them. It was certainly fine with her if she couldn't see them. She kind of missed seeing Fuego, though.

Sara smiled and looked to her left. Even though she couldn't see him, she knew that her red-bearded, dry-humored guardian criado was keeping watch nearby. Fuego wouldn't let any harm come to her.

She looked down at the Book of Light again.

Don't say, "I will get even for this wrong." Wait for the King to handle the matter. The King detests double standards; he is not pleased by dishonest scales. The King directs our steps, so why try to understand everything along the way?

Proverbs. She *loved* the proverbs in the Book. And the cool thing was that they were so *practical*. Who knew that such an old Book could be so useful for a preteen in the 21st century?

Don't say, "I will get even for this wrong." Wait for the King to handle the matter.

Yep, she'd learned the truth of that one. She used to think it was acceptable to take revenge on her enemies—and even that it was acceptable to ask *the King* to take revenge on her enemies—but she'd been wrong on both accounts. As she'd just gotten through reading, the King *will* handle the matter, but it wasn't right for warriors to *ask* Him to. Warriors of the King must love their enemies, even when it's hard.

Sara chuckled to herself. It sure had been hard to love Raquel! They'd become close friends, but initially Sara didn't think she would like Raquel at all. The fact that Raquel had slapped her in the face the first day they met probably had something to do with it.

But Sara had forgiven her, and look what had come from it: a close friendship. Forgiveness must *always* be the path of a warrior.

A close friendship. Well, at least they *used* to be close. It had been a year since they'd seen each other. *I wonder whatever happened to her?* Sara thought. Although Raquel had been quiet and withdrawn—or maybe *because* of this—Sara could tell that Raquel wasn't happy with her life. Sara had never been able to find out why. They'd pretty much stuck to surface-level conversations. She never did find out why

Raquel had such a low self-esteem. She'd openly admitted to Sara that she didn't feel pretty. Sara had thought she was insane. She had to have been the most beautiful girl in the whole school! Tall, thin, waist-long golden hair. Sara would give anything to look like that.

Raquel had said that she'd moved from somewhere in north-eastern Texas, which was where Sara lived. Too bad Texas was such a big state; they might have lived close to one another without even realizing it. But Sara realized that the chance of this was slim. Besides, Raquel was in southern Texas now; there was no reason to think she was anywhere near here. It *would* be nice to run into her again, though.

"Sara, your bus is here!" she heard her dad call.

"Coming!" she called back. Sara snapped the Book of Light shut, cutting off its light (even though she couldn't see it), and stuffed it into her backpack.

Her dad was waiting for her at the base of the stairs. He was impatient, but at least he cared. In the past, her dad would have been sitting in his easy chair—not even bothering to give her eye contact as she left for school. He looked mad, but at least he was looking at her. That was an improvement.

She hurried down the stairs—giving her dad a quick hug as she passed by. "Love you, Dad," she said quickly. He didn't say anything in response, but she hadn't expected him to. It wasn't all that easy for him to say, "I love you." She'd have to be patient and give him some more time.

Sara flew out the front door and jumped onto the bus. As usual, she took a seat near the back. There weren't as many kids back here and she liked the solitude. She would be around other kids all day long; at least here she could be alone for five minutes on the ride to school.

Soon after taking her seat, Sara noticed something: She'd ridden this same bus all school year and she knew where everybody sat. But here was a back-of-the-head she didn't recognize. Sitting alone in a seat a little farther up was a tall girl with blond hair. For a fleeting moment, Sara imagined that it was Raquel. *It's just 'cause Raquel is on your mind,* she told herself. The girl turned her head to face the window. Sara saw that the girl's hair was cut above her shoulders. *Nope, not Raquel,* she decided.

When they'd reached the school and the school bus screeched to a stop, she tried to catch a glimpse of the girl's face but the other kids were blocking her view—and besides, the girl was one of the first ones off the bus.

Chapter 7

Gabe

As Raquel hurried off the bus, the only thought going through her mind was, "Here we go again." She'd had to start mid-year at a school before, and it was about as much fun as getting your gum scraped at the dentist. To make matters worse, she was starting mid-year as an eighth grader! In this particular school district, seventh and eighth grades made up the junior high, so she was supposedly at the "top"—although she didn't feel at the top.

She'd felt at the top in Paraíso, and she'd been quite literally at the top when Espíritu and the criados had sung their magnificent song over her at the top of the golden staircase. Soon after, she'd gotten back on Espíritu and once again fell asleep during the ride. She had awakened to find herself in her own bed.

That had been a little over a week ago, and she'd had plenty of time to consider this crazy dream of hers. Maybe all the moving she'd done in her life was finally getting to her. Maybe she was going crazy. There must *really* be something wrong with her.

But then again, if it had all been a dream, why did she wake up to find that she was wearing her housecoat over her nightgown? She *never* wore her housecoat to bed...

Not important, she'd decided. She'd been upset that night; she'd had an argument with her mom. She'd been known to do irrational things when upset.

She had soon after remembered the other reason she was upset that night: her uncle's comment. Her uncle thought she was fat, and upon close examination in the mirror, she'd decided he was right. She would go on a diet so that she could look like the supermodels on her magazine covers. She had to do *something* to fit in at this school; after all, she was an eighth grader—she had to establish herself as someone at the "top."

The hallways in this school were *huge*—more like a high school than a junior high, she thought. And everybody seemed to know everybody. Of course they did; they'd been together in school half a year already. Raquel was already beginning to feel like an outcast.

Raquel scanned the lockers for her number, and when she found it she quickly began applying the combination to the lock—careful to keep her head down and her eyes straight ahead of her. There were lockers, of course, to the left and to the right of her, but she tried to be invisible as she quickly completed the lock's combination and opened the locker. Her hands were so shaky that when she tried to unzip her backpack and take out her books, she dropped a book on the floor. She heard some kids laugh but she didn't look at them; she bent down quickly to pick it up.

"Here ya go," a boy said, grabbing the book before she could and holding it out to her.

Raquel snatched it out of the boy's hand, then quickly regretted her decision. She looked up at him: He was *drop-dead gorgeous!* He had black hair that swept over his forehead and dark brown eyes. And he was smiling at her!

Say something, Raquel!

"Uh, thanks," she said quickly. Was that *really* all she could think of to say?

The boy was still smiling. He laughed. "Do you want your book back or not?" he asked.

"Oh, yeah," she said, taking it from him. "Thanks."

"No prob," he said with a laugh, standing to his full height. As the boy stood, so did Raquel. He was *tall!* And just *look* at those muscles...

"I don't think we've met," he said, extending a hand. "I'm Gabe."

Gabe. What a *sexy* name!

"Hi," said Raquel, choking on the word. She cleared her throat. "I'm Raquel."

"Are you gonna shake my hand, or what?" he laughed.

"Oh, yeah," she said, attempting to shake his hand but realizing she was still holding the book. She quickly put the book in her locker. "Sorry," she said, smiling nervously and shaking his hand.

"That's okay," he laughed again. "Raquel... that's a pretty name."

I'm gonna melt, she thought.

"Did you just move here, or something? The locker next to mine hasn't been used all year."

"Yeah," Raquel said, again clearing her throat. She stood gazing into his eyes.

"You don't talk much, do ya?"

Raquel felt her face go red.

"That's okay, though," Gabe said quickly, scanning her body. "Your looks make up for it."

Now Raquel blushed for a different reason. She looked down at what she had on. Was he commenting on her clothes or on her body? Or both? Despite the fact that there was still snow on the ground from last week, she had on a yellow low-cut spaghetti-strap top and some low-riding blue jeans that were too tight on her (but not after her diet). She'd spent half the morning searching her closet for the sexiest clothes she owned—clothes that hopefully accentuated her full bosom. She must have succeeded.

Gabe laughed again when he saw Raquel looking at herself. Raquel looked up quickly, embarrassed.

"You wanna get together some time?" he asked.

Is that a trick question? "Yeah, sure," Raquel managed to say.

"Are you free today after school?"

I'm free the rest of my life! "Yes," she answered.

"How 'bout we meet here at our lockers right after last period?" Gabe suggested. "Then we'll figure out something to do."

Raquel couldn't believe this! Her heart was pounding a million miles an hour. She heard herself say, "Sounds good."

Gabe gave her a wink and Raquel felt her knees go weak. "Since our lockers are right together," he said with a dreamy smile, "we'll probably be seeing a lot of each other."

Raquel could stand here looking at him all day. *Did I answer him? I can't remember…*

Gabe chuckled and threw his backpack over his shoulder, displaying a muscular bicep. "See ya after school," he said, and gave her another wink before tossing his head (and his hair) and turning to walk away.

Even after he was gone, Raquel continued to stand there as though in a trance. What had just happened? Had the cutest guy in the whole school *really* just asked her out? Even though he was the *only* guy in the whole school she'd even met, he *had* to be the cutest! *And* the most popular! And he wanted to go out with *her!* Maybe things would be okay at this new school after all. If she was going out with the most popular guy in school, then soon *she* would be popular, too!

In the midst of all these pleasant thoughts, an unpleasant thought suddenly entered her mind: She'd been in this situation before—wanting to be popular. She'd befriended Cassie, the most popular girl in school, hoping that would make her popular, too—only to find out that Cassie wasn't who she had appeared to be. When the friendship ended, things were worse than they'd been at the beginning; Cassie had turned the whole school against her. She would have been better off avoiding her completely.

But this situation was nothing like that, she told herself. This was no girl—this was a *guy!* And a *nice* guy, at that... not to mention *cute!*

Things would be different this time. And besides, she'd never been asked out by a guy before. She would be *crazy* to turn this one down!

She heard an alarm beep three times. She looked around; kids were slamming their lockers closed and rushing to class. That must have been the warning bell. Raquel quickly figured out which book she needed for first period, grabbed it and her binder, and stuffed the rest in her locker along with her backpack. Then she slammed her locker door closed and hurriedly looked at her schedule to figure out what room number first hour was.

After finding the room and taking a seat at a desk, Raquel began to relax. And she found that thinking about Gabe all through first hour made her relax even more.

Chapter 8

The Meeting

Last hour couldn't come fast enough. Raquel kept looking at the clock throughout the day, but that only seemed to make time go by slower. When last period finally arrived, the hour dragged by so slowly that Raquel thought she was going to go crazy with anticipation. After an eternity of boring lecturing by the teacher, the final bell rang and Raquel was the first one out the door.

Her last hour class was a mile away from her locker, and everyone in the congested hallway seemed to be moving at a snail's pace. Raquel tried to push by people, but there simply wasn't enough room. She'd never seen so many people in one place.

She finally reached her locker. Gabe wasn't there. Hadn't he said to meet here after school? Raquel began to panic. Had he said to meet somewhere else? She'd been so fixated on his eyes that maybe she hadn't paid close enough attention to what he said. *Did he say to meet somewhere else?* she thought frantically, looking around. *Maybe his last hour class is even farther away than mine*, she decided.

Raquel forced herself to relax. She took a deep breath and determined to be patient. *C'mon, Gabe, don't keep me waiting here forever.*

The hallway was slowly clearing out. Raquel found that she needed to use the restroom, but she couldn't leave her post for fear that she'd miss him. When she couldn't wait a moment longer, she hurried to the nearest restroom. By the time she came out, the hallway was nearly empty. She took off running. "You need to walk!" she heard a teacher yell. She ignored her.

She arrived at her locker out of breath. Gabe wasn't there, and neither was anybody else. Everyone had gone to the buses. She'd missed the bus, but that was the least of her concerns. She'd missed Gabe.

Raquel felt her eyes sting with tears. *Get ahold of yourself, Raquel,* she reprimanded herself. *His locker's right next to yours; do you honestly think you won't see him again? You'll see him again tomorrow, for goodness sake, so pull yourself together!* Knowing she'd see him again tomorrow didn't help; she wanted to see him *now!* How could he have stood her up like this? Was it *her* fault? Had he come while she was gone to the restroom? If only she'd gone to the restroom *before* last period instead of waiting till after! *Stupid!*

It was all Raquel could do to keep from bursting into tears. She somehow managed to gather up the books she needed for homework, put them in her backpack, and drag herself to the office to wait for her mom to come pick her up. Her mom would not be happy about having to leave work early, but Raquel didn't care.

As suspected, her mom was irate when she arrived at the school, and she lectured her all the way home about responsibility and this being the very first day of school and she being old enough to know what to do and how she'd better not ruin this new job for her. Raquel wasn't listening; she was staring forlornly out the window. Never once did her mom ask her how *her* day was or *why* she missed the bus. Of course she didn't; her mom never bothered to make conversation with her. Yelling and screaming was more her style.

It was pouring down rain all the way home, which fit Raquel's mood just fine. When she got home, she went straight to her room and stayed there, content to never come out again. Throwing herself onto the bed, she began to sob.

Raquel awoke to find that she had cried herself to sleep. She could still hear the rain pounding outside. She looked out her window; night had fallen. She considered changing into her nightgown, but decided she didn't care. She didn't care about *anything* anymore. She tried going back to sleep, but after several seconds of finding this impossible and discovering that being awake meant thinking about Gabe, she decided she needed a distraction. She got up and went downstairs to the living room.

She turned on the computer. The light hurt her eyes as the sudden light lit up the room. It was a big room, though, and certain parts of the room were still hidden in darkness. As she glanced around the room, waiting for the computer to "warm up," Raquel found that she felt nervous, though she didn't know why. She felt like someone was watching her. *It's probably just because it's a brand new house,* she told herself. *I haven't totally gotten used to it yet.* She turned her attention back to the computer, but she couldn't shake the feeling that she was being watched.

Her attention was drawn to a statue standing over in the corner to her left. It was not unusual to have statues in the house; her parents had bought all kinds of unique (and expensive) artifacts over the years. Raquel didn't remember this one, though. Had her mom just recently bought it? She must have bought it as recently as that evening, because Raquel made a habit of using the computer every day and she didn't remember seeing the statue earlier.

A sudden flash of lightning lit up the room followed by a crash of thunder. Raquel jumped. She'd gotten a better look at the statue, and it seemed strangely familiar to her. The figure was dressed in a long white robe with a gold belt around its waist and a golden sash vertically across its massive chest. A long sheath was attached to the belt, and the statue held in its right hand an enormous sword—blade pointing toward the ceiling. She looked up at its face: It was a Native American.

Raquel's heart began to pound. But Paraíso had all been a dream. Right?

The figure took a step toward her. Raquel gasped and fell over backwards in her chair—hitting the floor with a crash. Before she could get up, she saw the huge Native American with wings coming toward her—now illuminated with his own light. This was no statue: this was Relámpago!

Raquel scrambled to her feet. "Get back!" she shouted.

The criado stopped and held up his hand—palm facing her.

"Get away from me!"

"You will wake your mother," Relámpago told her. His voice was deep and strong, just like Raquel remembered it.

"I don't care!" Raquel screamed at the top of her lungs. "Get out of my house! *Now!"*

"You are under my protection."

"I said *GET OUT!"*

The stone-faced criado took a step toward Raquel, and Raquel froze. He stopped, then glanced around the room. Spotting the overhead light, he reached up with his left hand and snapped his fingers. The light came on.

Raquel caught her breath. "How did you do that?" she managed to say.

The criado motioned toward the couch with his massive sword. "Sit," he said.

Raquel backed away from him. "No, thank you," she said, hoping she didn't sound as scared as she felt.

"Why are you afraid?"

"Uh, maybe because there's a huge man with wings and a sword standing in the middle of my living room in the middle of the night."

Relámpago smiled. "If you were *very* afraid," he said, "you would not have told me that."

"I'd just assume you leave."

Relámpago chuckled.

"Am I really so amusing that you want to hang around me?"

"Amusing or not," he said, sheathing his sword, "the King has placed you under my care, so you will be seeing quite a bit of me from now on."

"I don't need a babysitter," Raquel informed him. "I'm quite capable of taking care of myself, thank you very much. Your services are no longer required, so good-bye."

"This is just the beginning, little warrior."

"Quit calling me that!" Raquel shouted up at him. "Why on earth do you keep calling me that—it doesn't make any sense! Do I look like a warrior to you?"

"Admittedly no... not yet, that is."

"Then why—"

"But you will," he interrupted.

"Will what?"

"You will begin to look like a warrior. And more importantly, you will begin to *act* like a warrior."

Raquel put her hands on her hips defiantly. "Don't *tell* me how to act! I'll act..."

But Raquel didn't finish her sentence. The giant criado's eyes flashed as he reached for his sword and pulled it half-way from its sheath before he froze. He stared at Raquel with fire in his eyes, then a second later shoved the sword back into its sheath with the sound of scraping metal.

Raquel stood staring up at him with wide eyes. Her defiance had suddenly been replaced by fear. "Were... were you about to hurt me?" she dared to ask.

"I will not hurt you," Relámpago stated firmly, his expression still of one ready for war, his hand still on his sword.

Raquel was keeping a close eye on his sword to make sure it didn't move again. "But, it looked like you were about to—"

"I will not hurt you," the criado repeated emphatically. "I was sent by the King to protect you, not to harm you. What you witnessed is my automatic reaction to sin."

"To sin?"

"I am in the habit of cutting down sin where it stands."

Raquel's throat felt dry. She swallowed.

The fire began to leave Relámpago's eyes, and he released his sword. Raquel visibly relaxed. The criado walked over to the nearby couch and slowly sat down. "Come and sit," he said.

Raquel decided she'd better obey. It was a long couch, and Raquel sat down at the opposite end of where Relámpago had sat. She let out a cry as the criado suddenly took to the air and landed himself directly beside her. "You really *aren't* going to leave me alone, are you?" she said.

Relámpago smiled. "You will be glad of that fact in the days to come."

Raquel looked down. He was holding an open book. Where had the book come from?

"This is the Book of Light," Relámpago informed her. "It is the King's Book. He will teach you how to be a warrior through this Book." He held it out to her.

Raquel hesitated. The book had a beam of light shooting out from its pages. She took the book from him, then screamed as soon as she looked down at it. She dropped the book; Relámpago caught it. "You didn't tell me it would make me blind!" she said angrily, rubbing her eyes.

"On the contrary," the criado said warmly. "It will make you see. Seeing will come in time."

"How am I supposed to read a book I can't even look at?"

"Your eyes will adjust," he assured her. "In the meantime, I will teach you what it says."

The book had closed when she dropped it. Without taking his eyes off Raquel, Relámpago opened it again to the center of the book—a powerful beacon of light shooting out. "This chapter is the longest chapter in the entire Book," he told her. Then he added, "It is one of my favorites."

Then he began to quote it—not read from it, but actually quote it; his eyes never left her. She listened as the criado spoke—his voice as strong and powerful as the light itself. Now that the book was in the criado's hands and she was no longer directly in its light, Raquel found that she could lean over and follow along in the book without the light getting in her eyes. She was amazed to find that Relámpago was quoting it word-for-word—not missing a single word or phrase! Even though his eyes were on her (and at times even closed), he seemed to know exactly what the book said:

"Joyful are people of integrity, who follow the instructions of the King. Joyful are those who obey his laws and search for him with all their hearts. They do not compromise with evil, and they walk only in his paths. You have charged us to keep your commandments carefully. Oh, that my actions would consistently reflect your decrees! Then I will not be ashamed when I compare my life with your commands. As I learn your righteous regulations, I will thank you by living as I should! I will obey your decrees. Please don't give up on me! How can a young person stay pure? By obeying your word. I have tried hard to find you—don't let me wander from your commands. I have hidden your word in my heart, that I might not sin against you. I praise you, O King—"

"You're not going to quote the entire chapter, are you?" Raquel asked worriedly. "We'll be here all night."

Relámpago opened his eyes—reluctantly, it seemed—and smiled. "However long it takes for you to learn it," he replied soberly.

Chapter 9

The Confrontation

"What does this mean to you?"

Raquel was confused. "What does *what* mean to me?"

"This chapter," said Relámpago.

"Ummmm. . . ." Raquel said with a laugh. "I didn't know I was going to be quizzed on it afterward."

"It is not a difficult question."

"Maybe not for *you,*" Raquel said, trying to make eye contact with the criado but finding that his eyes were too powerful to look at for very long. "You understand this stuff because it's obvious you've read it before."

"Many times," Relámpago said with a nod, "along with the rest of the Book."

"So naturally you understand it."

"What do you not understand?"

"It's not that I don't understand it," Raquel replied defensively. "It's just that... oh, never mind."

"So what does this mean to you?"

"Would you *please* stop repeating yourself all the time!" Raquel said, careful to look anywhere but at his eyes. "It's *really* annoying."

"Then answer my question," Relámpago stated calmly but firmly.

Raquel sighed. "If I answer your question—"

"I *won't* leave you alone," Relámpago finished for her with a smile.

Raquel managed a smile. Relámpago was learning to speak her language; what a refreshing change around here. "I was afraid of that," she said with feigned disgust. "You won't jump all over me if I get the answer wrong, will you?"

"I won't 'jump all over' you," Relámpago said with a chuckle. "I'm asking what something means *to you*. It is impossible to answer incorrectly."

"Okay," Raquel said hesitantly. She looked over at the Book of Light that Relámpago was still holding and skimmed the passage again. "I guess it means," she said, "that we should follow the King's rules?"

"Is that a statement or a question?"

It sounded like Relámpago was issuing her a challenge. "It's a question," she fired back.

"Do you question whether or not you should follow the King's rules?"

"I thought you said it was impossible to answer wrong," Raquel objected.

"You have not answered at all; you have answered my question with another question."

"My mom does that to me all the time."

"And how does it make you feel?"

"Frustrated."

"So..."

Raquel smiled. "So you're feeling frustrated right now?"

"Not yet," Relámpago said, returning the smile.

"Well, I've seen what happens when you get frustrated..."

Relámpago gave her a wink.

Raquel laughed. "...so I guess I'd better answer you. Um, yeah, I guess we should follow the King's rules."

"Why? Why should we follow them?"

"These are hard questions, Relámpago." It occurred to Raquel that this was the first time she'd referred to the criado by name.

"The reason is given right there in the chapter, Raquel," he insisted.

Raquel looked over at the passage again and began to read it aloud. "'*Joyful are people of integrity, who follow the instructions of the King. Joyful are those who obey his laws and search for him with all their hearts.*' I guess we're supposed to obey his laws so that we'll be joyful," Raquel concluded.

"That is correct," Relámpago nodded, "but there is more. You overlooked some key verses. Look at this one." He pointed to the correct verse without so much as glancing at the Book. "*'They do not compromise with evil, and they walk only in his paths,'*" he quoted. He moved his finger down the page—again, without looking at the Book. "*'Oh, that my actions would consistently reflect your decrees! Then I will not be ashamed when I compare my life with your commands,'*" he quoted again. His hand continued moving as he quoted the Book. "*'As I learn your righteous regulations, I will thank you by living as I should!... How can a young person stay pure? By obeying your word... I have hidden your word in my heart, that I might not sin against you.'*" He finally paused. Relámpago removed his hand from the book. "What reason do these verses give for following the King's commands, Raquel?"

"I—I'm not sure," Raquel answered honestly.

"*'They do not compromise with evil,' 'they walk only in his paths,' 'living as I should,' 'stay pure,' 'that I might not sin against you'...*"

"They help us act the right way?" Raquel offered.

"Raquel," said Relámpago proudly, "I could not have given a more suitable answer."

Raquel smiled.

"They help us act the right way. This is no small thing, Raquel. It is not easy for humans to act the right way."

Raquel snorted. "Tell me about it," she said.

"But by following the King's commands," he told her, "you will be acting the right way."

"I don't really like the idea of someone telling me how to act."

"So I gathered from the statement you made earlier," Relámpago replied, smiling weakly, "but consider this, Raquel: What results from bad behavior?"

"In school, you get a detention for it... unless, of course, you don't get caught!" she added with a grin.

Relámpago shook his head. "In life," he said, "there are *always* repercussions for bad behavior—whether you 'get caught' or not. You may never see the repercussions, but they are there."

"When we do something bad," Raquel clarified, "something bad always happens... whether we know about it or not?"

"That's right," the criado nodded. "So which is wiser, Raquel: to accept direction and be told the right way to act, or to go your own path and inevitably have bad things happen?"

"To accept direction, I guess," Raquel admitted, "but let me be honest with you, Relámpago: I *hate* people telling me what to do. People are *always* telling me what to do, and I'm *sick* of it!"

"I can see that," Relámpago replied softly.

"So if the King is going to be putting even *more* demands on me—"

"It is not the King's nature to be demanding," Relámpago said, shaking his head. "The King is patient with us, Raquel. He asks things of us; He does not demand. The King does not push us from behind but rather leads us from ahead. Whether or not we choose to follow Him is our choice."

"And if we follow him," Raquel concluded, "bad stuff won't happen to us?"

"No, that is the wrong conclusion to make," Relámpago stated emphatically. "Bad things *can* still happen even after an appropriate behavior is chosen; but bad things *will* happen if a *wrong* behavior is chosen."

"So, basically, you're saying that bad stuff is gonna happen to us no matter what, but *less* bad stuff will happen to us if we do what's right."

"Again, I could not have stated it better myself," the criado smiled.

Raquel sighed. "Well, yeah, then I guess it would be smart to do what's right, huh?"

"Again, well spoken."

"But it's really hard sometimes to know what's right..."

With a knowing smile, Relámpago lifted the Book of Light. "The Book of Light is the King's guide on how to live," Relámpago explained. "The King loves His warriors greatly; He does not leave them to figure out life on their own. He wrote this Book to guide them along the right pathway for their life. By following His decrees, humans are automatically given the best life possible."

"Not a *perfect* life," Raquel reminded him, "just the best life *possible*."

Relámpago chuckled. "That's right," he said, smiling down at her.

"Guess I'd better start reading right away then," she said, taking the book from Relámpago's hands, careful to keep its light pointed away from her eyes. "I don't want to miss out on *one second* of my best life possible with Gabe!"

The criado's face fell. "With Gabe?" he asked dubiously.

"Yeah," said Raquel, excitedly flipping through the pages of the Book of Light. "If the King wants me to have the best life possible," she said, scanning the pages for Gabe's name, "there's gotta be *something* in here about me ending up with Gabe! You should *see* him—"

"I've seen him," Relámpago said grimly, "and your best life possible does *not* include Gabe."

Raquel's hand froze on the page she was about to turn. "Excuse me?" she said.

"I have seen this boy you speak of," Relámpago told her, "and it would be wise for you to avoid him."

"*Excuse* me?" Raquel said, raising her voice. "Says who?" She held up the Book of Light. "Does the book say, 'Raquel, stay away from Gabe'?"

"Not in so many words, no."

"Well, then—"

"But it says to avoid people *like* him."

"What, people who are drop-dead gorgeous?"

"There is more to people than what is on the *outside*, Raquel."

"And how do *you* know what he's like?" Raquel demanded, getting angrier by the moment. "You can read his thoughts, I suppose?"

"No, but I can read his eyes."

"Read his *eyes?* What in the world is *that* supposed to mean?"

"Raquel," Relámpago said calmly, "please hear me out. I know that you have feelings for Gabe, but Gabe is not what he seems. I have seen far too many like him. Trust me, you're better off without him."

"*Trust* you?!" Now Raquel was shouting. "Why on earth should I trust *you?* I don't even *know* you!"

"You don't know Gabe, either," Relámpago reminded her.

"Shut up!" Raquel shouted, slamming the book shut, cutting off its light. "First you're going to try and tell me who to date, and now you're going to start telling me what I *know?"* Raquel jumped off the couch and threw the book in his face.

Relámpago didn't even flinch; he just looked sad. "I don't need you or anybody else to tell me how to live my life!" Raquel announced. "If the King really loves me like you say he does, he'll let me date Gabe! End of story!"

"He'll let you," Relámpago said softly, "but it's not the path He would choose for you."

"I said *end of story!*" she yelled. "I'm choosing my own path, got it? I don't need the King to tell me what to do, and I *sure* don't need any help from *you!*"

Raquel spun around and marched out of the room—flipping the living room light off as she left.

Chapter 10

The Lunch Date

When Raquel walked into the living room the following morning dressed for school with her backpack on her shoulder, the only reminder she had of the previous night's conversation with Relámpago was the computer being on... and even this wasn't proof that the conversation had taken place. Besides, the chair wasn't overturned like it should have been. (Of course, her mother could have picked it up when she came in, but Raquel chose to overlook this fact.) No, the conversation had *definitely* been a dream.

But wait... what was this? There was an open book lying over on the couch. And light was shooting up out of it.

The Book of Light!

Raquel approached it cautiously as though she were approaching a snake rather than a book. The book's light reached all the way to the vaulted ceiling. But how was this possible? Unless...

As she neared the book, Raquel looked over at its pages. It was turned to the same chapter that Relámpago had been quoting from the night before.

But hadn't she started flipping through it? And closed it? And threw it in his face...

"Good morning."

Her mother's voice coming from behind startled her. "Mom, don't sneak up on me like that," Raquel said, quickly reaching over and slamming the book closed. Had her mom seen the book?

"Well, *sorry,*" said her mom sarcastically, continuing on past her into the kitchen. "You sure are jumpy this morning. Have a bad dream?"

Raquel was relieved; she hadn't seen the book—or its light. *"No,"* she said, scooping up the book from the couch and stuffing it into her backpack.

"Well, *something* must have scared you last night," her mother continued, talking to Raquel over her shoulder, "because the computer chair was lying on the floor when I came in this morning. Oh, and you left the computer on."

"Can we just change the subject, please?" Raquel asked, following her mother into the kitchen.

"Alright," said her mom, getting an apple from the refrigerator and starting to cut it. "But remember the rule, Raquel: No unsupervised use of the computer."

"I'm not a *baby,* Mom," Raquel said, taking a seat on a bar stool. "I don't need to be *supervised."*

"Just remember the rule, or the computer's history," her mom said without looking up from the apple.

"Whatever."

"Excuse me?" said her mom, glaring up at her.

"You use the computer just as much as I do," Raquel informed her. "You're not gonna get rid of it."

"Don't tell me what I will or will not do," her mom ordered. "And when I say it's history, I mean for *you,* young lady, not for me."

Raquel shrugged. "As long as it's in the house, I'm gonna use it," she said.

"Not without supervision, you're not."

Raquel shrugged again. "Try and stop me," she said.

Her mom's face got as red as the apple in front of her. Satisfied, Raquel jumped off the bar stool, walked behind her mother, got an apple out of the fridge, and walked out the door—slamming it behind her. She would be a full thirty minutes early waiting for the bus, but she didn't care. She couldn't stand being in there with her mom for one more second.

The morning was cool and crisp—and a little on the chilly side. It was January; of course it was going to be chilly. But Raquel cared more about fashion than she did about freezing. Like the day before, she'd found a sexy top and some tight jeans to wear. She liked the fact that they were tight—although maybe they *were* just a little too tight; sometimes she felt like she could hardly walk in them. Well, her new diet would change all that. After all, she needed to look good for Gabe.

Feeling invigorated at the thought of Gabe, Raquel took a huge bite from her apple. What would she say to him? She wouldn't act mad at him; that would just make her look like a jerk. And she wasn't mad at him, anyway; she was mad at herself.

So what should she say to him? *Hey, what's up?* No, that was too casual. *Sorry I missed you yesterday, I completely forgot.* That was a stupid lie. Why would she want him to think she'd forgotten? How about, *Sorry I missed you yesterday, my last hour teacher kept us late*. Raquel decided that would have to do.

She took another bite of her apple. Should she ask him to lunch with her? Was that too forward? She wasn't even sure if they ate lunch at the same time. There were three separate lunch periods: one for seventh grade only, one for eighth grade only, and one for seventh and eighth grades combined. Raquel didn't know if Gabe went to the eighth grade lunch or the combined lunch. She knew for sure that Gabe was an eighth grader; for one thing, he was *really* tall! For another thing, his locker was right next to hers, and the school was split into a seventh grade wing and an eighth grade wing.

Should she invite him to lunch? Well, it didn't hurt to ask, did it?

Relámpago's words from last night echoed in her mind: *"It would be wise for you to avoid him... Gabe is not what he seems. I have seen far too many like him... you're better off without him."* She angrily took a huge bite out of her apple. *What does* he *know?* she thought. *Gabe is a nice guy, that's obvious. He helped me with my book, didn't he?* Relámpago was probably just trying to keep her from having fun—just like her mom.

And Gabe had told her she looked good!

Raquel leaned against the nearby streetlamp with a dreamy smile. *Gabe said I look good,* she thought. Maybe her uncle was wrong; maybe she *wasn't* fat. After all, if she could get the attention of the cutest guy in school, then obviously she didn't need to go on a diet, right? He wouldn't have told her she looked good if she were fat.

The school bus rounded the corner, jolting Raquel from her daydream. She smiled. Soon her daydream would become a reality. Soon she and Gabe would be a couple! They would be seen all over school together...

Once at school, Raquel couldn't reach her locker fast enough. Gabe was already there—head and shoulders above everybody else. He was leaning against his locker with his arms crossed and a serious expression on his face. *How sexy!* He appeared to be waiting for someone. Was he waiting for *her?*

Upon seeing her, Gabe smiled. Raquel noticed that it wasn't a particularly big smile, but she didn't care; a little smile looked sexier, anyway.

"Hey, girl," he said, looking her over and eventually arriving at her eyes. "Glad to see you're not letting the cold dictate your clothes."

All of the lines Raquel had rehearsed flew out the window. She searched her memory frantically for something to say, but her mind was blank.

Gabe laughed. "I also see you're still shy, but that's okay in my book."

Come on, say something, Raquel! Raquel cleared her throat. "Sorry I was late yesterday," she said, her voice sounding more like a chipmunk than anything else. "My teacher—"

"Not important," Gabe interrupted, waving off her comment. "I was busy after school yesterday anyway."

This news hit Raquel like a ton of bricks. He was busy after school yesterday? He'd remembered their date but had chosen not to show up?

Her disappointment must have been obvious, because Gabe quickly came back with, "But I'm free today at lunch."

Suddenly, all was forgiven. "Great!" Raquel exclaimed.

"I'll find you," Gabe said off-handedly, opening his locker and rummaging through his stuff. He continued talking to her without looking at her. "I know where you sit," he said. "I saw you yesterday at group C Lunch. My lunch is group A, but I'll skip study hall today to come and sit with you."

He would do that for her?

"See you then," he said, glancing at her quickly with only the slightest hint of a smile before slamming his locker shut and turning to walk away.

Raquel wished he'd stayed longer to talk, but who cares, she decided: *She would be eating lunch with Gabe!* They'd have *plenty* of time to talk then!

Raquel excitedly put her stuff away and then somehow managed to make it the first half of the day without going crazy with anticipation. At lunchtime, she didn't know where she should sit, but Gabe had said that he knew where she sat yesterday, so she sat down in the same exact spot so he wouldn't miss her.

Raquel looked down at her tray. It was a disgusting conglomeration of mac and cheese, brown beans, mixed fruit, and a dinner roll.

"Not exactly delectable, is it?"

Raquel looked up quickly, startled. *It was Gabe!* Unlike this morning, he had a huge grin on his face. Maybe he was *really* hungry. He certainly seemed eager to sit down next to her.

"I hate this school's lunches," he said, taking a seat beside her, "but at least I have someone beautiful to sit with today."

Beautiful? Had he really just called her *beautiful?*

Raquel couldn't stop staring at his eyes. They were the most beautiful brown eyes she had ever seen, and a *lot* less scary than Relámpago's.

"So where ya from?" Gabe asked, cutting off a piece of his Salisbury steak and sticking it in his mouth.

It took Raquel several seconds to respond. Gabe seemed to have been prepared for the delay, although he didn't seem all that much more patient for it. "My family moved here from southern Texas," Raquel finally managed to say.

"Oh, yeah?" said Gabe, chewing with his mouth open. "And ya just moved here?"

"Yeah," replied Raquel. "Right before Christmas."

"Mmmm," Gabe said with a nod. Raquel couldn't tell if he was responding to her or enjoying his food. Raquel noticed that his eyes kept wandering down below her face. She found herself surprised that this bothered her. She should have been enjoying the attention she was getting, but for some reason it made her squirm instead.

She quickly thought of something to say. "You have lots of friends here?"

Raquel immediately regretted the question. Gabe started to laugh—a little at first and then louder and louder until he was drawing the attention of the whole lunchroom. "Raquel," he said, "you are *so* funny!"

Raquel felt her face go red.

"I'm sorry," he said, though not very sincerely, considering the fact that he was still laughing. "It's just—you're so funny!" He reached over and put a hand on her leg—giving it a squeeze.

Raquel froze. She felt her heart begin to race. He quickly removed his hand and went back to eating his steak, but the effect of what he'd done lingered. Even though she was wearing jeans and hadn't been able to feel his hand on her skin, she'd still felt as though a bolt of electricity had shot through her. It didn't take Raquel long to decide that she liked the feeling.

Gabe looked up at her, chewing his steak with a satisfied smile on his face. For someone who "hated" the food, he sure seemed to be enjoying it.

Raquel stared back at Gabe so long that it became awkward. She quickly reached for her dinner roll and took a big bite.

"Whoa, slow down!" Gabe laughed. "You don't wanna go ruining that pretty figure of yours with carbs, now do ya?"

The dinner roll felt out of her hand and onto her tray. First her uncle, and now Gabe? She *was* fat!

"Look," said Gabe quickly, gathering up his tray and standing to his feet. "I gotta go. I'll see ya later, Raquel." Raquel watched as he dropped his uneaten lunch into a nearby garbage can before exiting the lunchroom.

Raquel sat there in a daze. She'd never before felt such a wide range of emotions within such a short period of time. She wasn't sure what she felt; all she knew for sure was that she'd liked it when Gabe had touched her. He'd embarrassed her, sure—but for just a moment Raquel had felt special... *important*...the moment he touched her. The embarrassment he'd caused seemed microscopic in comparison.

She wanted to be touched by him again. She *needed* to be...

"Raquel?"

Raquel jumped at the sound of the familiar voice. She couldn't believe who was standing there. No, it couldn't be.

"Sara?"

Chapter 11

The Warning

ll thoughts of Gabe were forgotten—at least for the moment. "Sara?" Raquel couldn't believe her eyes.

"Raquel! Oh, my gosh!" Sara exclaimed, immediately putting down her lunch tray, plopping down next to Raquel and smothering her in an embrace. "What in the world are you doing here?"

Raquel didn't return the hug. Raquel had never been happier to see anyone, but she wouldn't show it. She wished she knew how to open up to people—especially Sara—but she didn't. Knowing how to open your heart is something that is taught by example, and Raquel had no example to go by. "What are *you* doing here?" she asked with a small smile.

Sara loved Raquel, but she knew Raquel had trouble with showing love. She chose not to be offended by Raquel's lack of enthusiasm. "I *live* here!" she laughed, her spirits not dampened in the least. "Remember how I told you I was from north-eastern Texas?"

"Y-y-yeah."

Sara spread her arms wide. "This is it!" she said with a laugh. "Did you just move here, or something?"

Raquel wasn't sure why, but the excitement of seeing Sara was quickly wearing off. There was something about her that made her feel uncomfortable. Something about her eyes; they were brighter than they used to be. "Yeah," Raquel responded, looking down. "I used to live here when I was in the fifth grade. Then we moved."

"So that's how we missed each other!" Sara exclaimed. "I'm one grade below you, and in this town fourth and fifth grades are in separate schools!"

Raquel started to mess with her food with her fork. "Yeah," she said detachedly.

Sara could tell something was wrong. She didn't expect Raquel to act very happy; she never did. But she was acting moodier than usual. "What's wrong?" she asked sincerely.

Raquel looked up at her. "What do you mean?" she asked, her eyes shifting.

"You're acting funny," Sara said plainly.

Raquel looked down at her tray. "I just have a lot on my mind, that's all."

"Do you want to talk about it?"

"*No.*"

Sara situated herself on the bench next to Raquel and began to open her chocolate milk.

"What are you doing?" Raquel demanded.

Sara took a bite of her salad and looked at Raquel with a half-smile. "Eating my lunch," she said, taking another bite.

Raquel felt annoyed. Sure, she was glad to see her, but did she tell her she could sit next to her? *No*. She didn't want to be rude to her friend, but she also wanted to get rid of her. "This seat is taken," she said.

"Oh, yeah?" Sara responded happily, unaffected by Raquel's rudeness. "By who?"

Raquel hesitated. She didn't want to open up to Sara, but it may be the only way to get her to leave. "Gabe," she said simply.

Sara dropped her fork onto her tray. "Gabe?" she exclaimed.

Raquel couldn't hide her smile. "Yeah, Gabe," she said.

"You're already eating lunch with Gabe the Babe?"

Raquel snorted. "Is that what people call him?"

"Don't *you* think he's a babe?"

Raquel rearranged her mac and cheese on her tray and shrugged, her smile giving her away. "I guess," she said.

"You *guess?*" Sara laughed. "He's the cutest guy in the *whole* school! *Probably* the whole *town!*"

Raquel was grinning now.

"Did he ask you out?"

Raquel shrugged, unable to stop smiling. "Sort of," she said.

"Wow," Sara said, shaking her head. "Some girls have all the luck! You just moved here and already Gabe's asking you out! How did you run into him?"

"His locker's right next to mine."

"Really? Any chance you could put in a good word for me?"

Raquel laughed before she could stop herself.

"You laughed," Sara said kiddingly. "You actually laughed."

"Yeah, well..." Raquel chuckled, then couldn't think of anything else to say.

Sara studied her. "You look different, Raquel."

Raquel's face fell. "My hair," she said dryly.

"That's it! Why'd you cut it?"

Raquel decided her mac and cheese needed some more attention.

Sara decided not to force the issue. "That's okay, you don't have to tell me," she said respectfully. "You're pretty anyway."

Raquel had forgotten how kind Sara was. She looked up at her and searched her eyes. They looked sincere. *And bright.* "Thanks," she smiled.

"Your eyes look different, too," Sara observed.

Raquel looked at her, confused.

"Your eyes look...I don't know, brighter. Almost like you've been reading the Book of Light, or something."

Raquel couldn't hide her surprise.

"*Have* you been reading it?" Sara asked excitedly.

Unable to restrain her amazement, Raquel reached over and unzipped her backpack, pulling out the Book of Light and setting it on the lunch table.

"Oh, my gosh!" Sara exclaimed, opening it.

The instant the book was opened, a beacon of light shot out to the very top of the lunchroom. Raquel reached over and slammed it shut. "Don't do that," she scolded.

"Can you see its light?" Sara wanted to know.

Raquel was taken aback. "Can *you?*"

Sara was beside herself with excitement. "Oh, my gosh, you *can* see it!" she laughed. "You've been to Paraíso! Did you get to go for a ride on Espíritu?"

"I thought I'd dreamed the whole thing up," Raquel admitted.

"Nope," Sara laughed, shaking her head. "Although that's what I thought at first, too. What else can you see?"

"What do you mean?"

"Can you see your armor?"

Raquel was confused. "My armor?"

"I guess that answers my question," Sara said, taking another bite of her salad. "Don't worry, though, it'll show up."

Something was bugging Raquel. "Can you see..."

"What?" Sara asked, her mouth full of salad.

"...big guys with wings?"

"Criados!" Sara said excitedly. She motioned up and to the left with her fork. "Fuego's probably standing over there somewhere." She turned her head. "What's up, dude?"

Raquel looked in that direction. "Um, Sara?" she said, amused. "There's no one there."

"Oh, he's there alright," Sara said, going back to her salad. "Laughing at me right now, no doubt. Just 'cause I don't have the Power of Paraíso anymore doesn't mean Fuego doesn't still hang around."

"The name of your criado is Fuego?"

"Yeah, what's yours?"

Raquel hesitated. How much should she tell Sara? It sounded as if she already knew everything anyway. "Relámpago," she said.

"Cool name," Sara nodded, taking another bite of food. Raquel was amazed; Sara was talking about criados and light coming out of books as casually as if she were talking about the weather. "What's he like?"

"Who, Relámpago?"

"Yeah."

"Annoying."

Sara laughed. "Yeah, Fuego was annoying at first, too." She looked over her left shoulder. "*Really* annoying," she added.

Raquel laughed. She decided that her friend had gone crazy. But then again, if she was crazy, then that would make her crazy, too. Maybe all of this was for real after all. "You *used* to be able to see him," Raquel clarified, "but now you can't?"

"Yeah," Sara admitted, stabbing some more salad onto her fork. "I gave up the Power of Paraíso because..." She paused and set down her fork, looking directly at Raquel. There was concern in her eyes.

"Because why?" Raquel wondered.

"Have you seen any sombras yet?" Her tone of voice had changed. She no longer sounded excited.

"What's a sombra?"

"Oh, trust me, you'd know if you'd seen one."

Raquel shrugged. "I guess I haven't seen one then."

"You will," Sara said, boring holes into her with her eyes. "You're a warrior now, right? You've decided to follow the King?"

Raquel nodded, unsure whether or not she was glad about it.

Sara smiled, but it was a pensive smile. "That's great, Raquel. That's the best decision you could have ever made. But you should know something about sombras: They go after warriors. You'll have the King's armor and Relámpago to protect you, but make no mistake about it: it's a war you're about to face. You'll need to use this as your sword." She held up the Book of Light.

Raquel snatched it away from her. "Don't open it again," she warned.

"No one but you can see its light," Sara said calmly. "You *need* to be opening that Book, Raquel."

Raquel didn't like the direction this conversation was going. Sara was starting to sound way too much like her mother... *and* Relámpago. "I'm at school," Raquel reminded her. "I think I'm safe here, Sara."

Sara snorted. "If only that were the case," she said, more to herself than to Raquel.

Raquel ignored the comment. "You don't sound too scared," she said, more of a challenge than an observation. "These *sombras*—or whatever they're called—must not be too bad."

Sara gave Raquel her full attention. "They're dangerous, Raquel," she said. "Remember Cassie?"

Raquel felt her stomach tie in knots. She nodded.

"Cassie's secret club was run by sombras."

Raquel laughed nervously.

"I'm serious, Raquel," Sara said, looking her friend directly in the eyes. "Remember how you were so easily persuaded by Cassie to be her friend, just like I was? Cassie was being influenced by sombras. Sombras are sneaky; you don't usually know they're influencing somebody until it's too late."

Raquel squirmed on the bench.

"Sombras are good fighters," Sara continued. "They know a warrior's weaknesses and go after them."

Raquel wanted to turn this conversation around as quickly as possible. "What are *your* weaknesses?" she challenged.

Sara managed a smile. "Same as yours," she said simply.

"You don't seem scared of them, as 'dangerous' as they are."

"That's 'cause I know how to fight 'em," said Sara matter-of-factly. "And if you're smart, Raquel, you'll learn, too."

"From the Book of Light, I suppose."

Sara nodded. "Exactly."

Raquel went back to moving her food around on her tray with her fork. "I haven't exactly found it to be all that interesting to read," she said coolly.

"Raquel," Sara said seriously, "listen to me." Raquel looked up at her, annoyed. "I didn't, either," Sara said with conviction. "...at first. But then I wised up. Trust me..." She picked up the Book of Light. "You *need* to be reading this Book."

Raquel snatched the book out of Sara's hands and stuffed it into her backpack. She didn't need one more person in her life telling her what to do. "I'll read it when I'm good and ready," she said quickly, picking up her tray and getting up from the lunch table.

"It might be too late by then," Sara said softly.

Raquel heard her friend, but she ignored her.

Chapter 12

The Website

Raquel looked over her shoulder at her mother, annoyed. Why couldn't she just go away? Even though she was sitting over on the couch watching TV without paying any attention to her, it bugged Raquel that she felt she had to be in the same room with her. Why didn't her mom trust her to be on the computer without a babysitter? What was she afraid of?

"Feel free to leave."

Her mother completely ignored her, her eyes glued to the television.

Raquel turned back to the computer screen, fuming. She knew it was no use; she'd argued this out with her mother before and it never did any good. Raquel had asked for her own computer that she could keep in her room; it's not like they couldn't afford one. Her mom had said no, that she wanted her within plain sight. It made Raquel feel like she was two years old. Her mom didn't care about any other aspect of her life, it seemed. Why did she care so much about this?

She tried to calm down enough to continue surfing the internet. Usually this relaxed her; it was the one time of the day she felt in control. She could go to the websites *she* wanted to go to; no one could dictate to her where to go or what to do. She could call the shots without anyone—teachers, parents—breathing down her neck. There was freedom here... not *complete* freedom, of course, as long as her mom was in the room, but freedom nonetheless.

Rather than reading up on the latest celebrity gossip or the latest fashions, Raquel had a different preoccupation today: the latest diets. After having lunch with Gabe (and feeling the effect his touch had had on her), she was more determined than ever to look good for him. She couldn't lose him. She just *couldn't*. He was the best thing that had ever happened to her.

Raquel was amazed at the number of different dieting plans that were available. She had thought that going on a diet would be a simple thing, but she was finding out that everyone seemed to have a different idea on how to do it. Which plan was best?

She found a website that seemed helpful. "Want to lose weight fast?" it said. "Start by counting those calories!"

In order to lose one pound, it said, you have to lose 3,500 calories. *Good grief,* Raquel thought. *This is going to be impossible!* Then it made it sound more plausible by saying that if you want to lose one pound per week, that comes down to cutting back on 500 calories a day. Raquel thought that still sounded like a lot.

She read on. The article went on to offer ideas on exactly how to accomplish this feat. Rather than eating a bagel for breakfast, for example, eat an English muffin and cut back on 220 calories. Eat only half a cup of cereal instead of a full cup to cut back on 200 calories. Use skim milk rather than whole milk and cut back on another 70 calories. Instead of eating pork sausage, eat turkey sausage and cut back on 125 calories. Suddenly, dieting didn't sound so hard, after all. The suggested changes sounded feasible, and just these four changes alone would equal a cutback of *more* than 500 calories.

But the article didn't stop at breakfast foods; it had suggestions for lunch and supper, as well. For lunch, it said, use mustard instead of mayo and a roll instead of sliced bread on a sandwich and this would cut 200 calories out of your diet. Raquel grimaced; she didn't even *like* mustard. But maybe she could learn to develop a taste for it. Eat a salad instead of fries and you could save yourself from a whopping 300 calories! *That's 500 calories right there,* Raquel thought, her excitement building.

For supper, it suggested using smaller plates; going from a 12-inch plate to a 9-inch plate would save her from 500 unneeded calories! And eating slower helped, too. Women who chewed their food at least 20 times before swallowing ended up eating 70 calories less than those who ate fast. The reason? Because it takes the body 20-30 minutes to feel full. *That makes sense,* Raquel thought. *If you eat slower, you'll feel full faster.* It said not to eat more than 400-500 calories per meal, and the "absolute maximum amount" of saturated fat that anyone should eat per day, it said, was 20 grams.

The article didn't stop at suggestions for eating. Exercise, it said, was equally important. A brisk 15-minute walk would burn about 100 calories. *That's easy!* Raquel thought excitedly. *I can walk 15 minutes every day after school! And forget 15 minutes; I can walk 30 minutes and burn twice as many calories!* Raquel's heart raced with anticipation. She could do all of this stuff and end up losing even *more* than 500 calories a day! She could lose 500 calories *every meal!* That way, she'd lose more than just one pound per week. One pound a week didn't sound like much, anyway. How about one pound a *day!* Now *that* was more like it!

"What's that?"

Raquel spun around in her chair; her mom was looking over her shoulder. *"Mom!"* Raquel yelled, quickly clicking the website off the screen. "Go away!"

"What were you looking at, Raquel?"

"None of your business!"

"Are you trying to lose weight?"

"I said none of your business!"

"Tell me what you're up to or the computer's history."

"Whatever, Mom." Why did her mom bother with empty threats? Raquel turned her attention back to the computer and opened a different website. "Go away," she said, still looking at the screen. She felt her mom's eyes still on her. She spun around in her chair. "I said *go away!"* she demanded.

"Don't you raise your voice with me, young lady!"

"Then go away!"

Her mom cast one more skeptical glance at the screen before walking back to the couch.

Finally! Raquel thought. *Never a moment's peace when she's around!* She decided she would have to do her dieting research at night, even if it meant breaking the rule; it was the only way to escape her mom's watchful eye. She couldn't tell her mom about her plan to lose weight; she wouldn't understand. She would probably just tell her that she didn't need to lose weight, and Raquel knew that she did. Besides, it was none of her business; it was *her* body.

She waited till her mom fell asleep on the couch to finally turn the computer off. Raquel knew that when her mom woke up and saw the computer off, she'd think that Raquel had gone to bed and so she'd go to bed, too. Then, with her mom gone, she could come back and get on the computer without having to worry about being watched.

Raquel waited in her room till she heard her mom's bedroom door close. Then she quietly slipped back downstairs and turned the computer back on. Raquel sat back in her chair and waited as the computer made noises in an attempt to start up. She couldn't help but remember the last time she'd used the computer at night. It had turned out that she wasn't alone like she'd thought. Relámpago had shown up unexpected and unwanted. Would he show up again?

Just the thought of being watched gave Raquel the creeps. She looked to her left. Was Relámpago standing there? Sara had talked to her own criado as though he were really there, even though she couldn't see him. What if Relámpago was there, too, only invisible?

Raquel shook her head. *I'm getting to be just as crazy as Sara,* she thought. Still, she decided that sitting here in the dark was more than she could handle. For extra measure, she got up and went to turn on the living room light. Before she could flip the switch, the light came on by itself.

She spun around, heart racing. Relámpago was sitting in the computer chair—sword in its sheath. He looked relaxed, but there were daggers in his eyes as he stared her down.

"What are you doing here?" Raquel demanded, trying to keep her voice down. She didn't want to wake up her mother—mainly because she didn't want to get caught down here with the computer on.

"Helping you out," said the Native American criado flatly in his resonant voice.

"I could've done that."

Relámpago chuckled and his eyes softened. As he stood casually to his feet, Raquel was reminded just how big he was—*and* how muscular! He made Gabe look like a toothpick; the criado could break him without even trying. "I was not referring to the overhead light, little warrior," he said, a gentleness returning to his voice.

"If you *really* want to help me," Raquel said, trying to sound braver than she felt, "you can just leave."

The computer made a sound, indicating that it was now fully on and ready to go. Both Raquel and the criado glanced in its direction. Then Relámpago looked back at her. "Why are you accessing the computer at night?" he wanted to know, his eyes indicating that he already knew.

Raquel considered saying, "None of your business," but she dared not talk back. Talking back to Relámpago was nothing like talking back to her mother; she'd nearly gotten "cut down" the last time she tried it. "I... I was just going to check my email," she lied, her voice trembling.

Relámpago didn't appear fooled. He crossed his arms and flicked his enormous wings—resulting in a breeze that startled her. "Why did you not check it when you were on the computer earlier?" he asked.

So he *was* following her around!

Raquel's throat felt dry. "I forgot," she said hoarsely.

"I don't take well to lies, Raquel," he said, his tone of voice indicating that he meant business.

Raquel felt the color drain from her face.

"Where is your backpack?" he inquired, his voice deep and resolute.

Raquel decided to tell the truth this time. "In my room."

"Go and get it."

Raquel obeyed. When she came back down, carrying her backpack, the criado was gone.

She looked around tentatively. Was he *really* gone? Or was he still there but she just couldn't see him? And why did he want her to go and get her backpack?

Raquel searched the room—and even the kitchen—before finally deciding that Relámpago was in fact gone. She cautiously made her way back to the computer and sat down—clutching her backpack to her chest. Did she dare turn her attention to the computer? What if Relámpago showed up again? Would he ask her questions about why she was reading about dieting? She didn't want to have to answer any more questions.

With Relámpago out of sight, Raquel felt her courage returning. She decided that she didn't care what Relámpago thought. After all, where did he get off telling her what to do? She dropped her backpack on the floor and swiveled around to face the computer.

She quickly did a search for the website she'd been looking at earlier and found it. She learned that using two egg whites and one egg for an omelet rather than three eggs saved her 125 calories, and that a cup of granola cereal had 600 calories whereas a cup of high-fiber cereal only had 120.

Something to her right caught her attention; she turned to look. She gasped: Her backpack lay on the floor unzipped—a bright light shooting out of it.

She sat staring, mouth agape. How did the backpack get unzipped? Did Relámpago unzip it? Was he trying to get her to read the Book of Light—even after she'd thrown it in his face?

With trembling hands, Raquel reached over and picked up her backpack, reaching inside for the Book of Light. She laid it in her lap—careful to keep the beam of light from hitting her face. She looked down at the page:

The King blesses those who patiently endure testing and temptation. Afterward they will receive the crown of life that the King has promised to those who love him. And remember, when you are being tempted, do not say, 'The King is tempting me.' The King is never tempted to do wrong, and he never tempts anyone else. Temptation comes from our own desires, which entice us and drag us away. These desires give birth to sinful actions. And when sin is allowed to grow, it gives birth to death.

Raquel sat very still, contemplating the words she'd read. *Temptation comes from our own desires, which entice us and drag us away. These desires give birth to sinful actions. And when sin is allowed to grow, it gives birth to death.*

Did Relámpago want her to read this? Did *the King* want her to read this? Why? What "temptation" was she falling prey to? *Entice us and drag us away.* She didn't like the sound of that; it made her think of a mouse being eaten by a cat. *Sinful actions*. What had Relámpago said about sinful actions? He'd said that there were always negative consequences for bad behavior—whether or not you got caught. *And when sin is allowed to grow, it gives birth to death*. Not only negative, but *deadly* consequences! According to the Book of Light, temptation leads to sinful actions, and sinful actions lead to death.

But what did this have to do with her?

Raquel slowly closed the Book of Light and put it back in her backpack, not bothering to zip it. Reading the words from the Book of Light gave her a strange feeling—like she was in danger, or something. But what was she in danger of?

She turned her attention back to the computer, trying to forget what she'd read. But the words from the Book of Light kept echoing in her mind. Finally giving up, she turned off the computer and went to bed.

Chapter 13

The Encounter

"Raquel, aren't you going to have breakfast?"

Raquel had found some orange juice in the fridge and was pouring herself a glass. "I am, Mom," she said, putting the orange juice back in the fridge and closing the door. She didn't know how many calories orange juice had, but since it was made from fruit, she figured it probably didn't have too many. If she hadn't been so distracted by the Book of Light last night, she would have researched it.

"That's not breakfast."

Raquel sighed, taking a seat at the breakfast bar.

"You need to *eat* something," her mom insisted.

"You sound like Relámpago."

"Who?"

"Never mind."

"Raquel, I'm not going to let you go to school on an empty stomach. It's not healthy."

"Since when do you care so much about me eating breakfast?"

"Since I noticed you're not doing it," she said, stirring her coffee.

"I don't see *you* eating breakfast," Raquel pointed out.

"I had a bagel before you came down," her mom told her. "You want a bagel?"

Raquel considered it. She remembered the website saying that English muffins had fewer calories than bagels. "Do we have any English muffins?" she inquired.

Her mom looked up from her coffee. "English muffins? You've never asked for an English muffin in your life."

"Well, I'm asking for one now, aren't I?"

"Why do you want an English muffin?"

"Don't give me the fifth degree, Mom, it's a simple question. Do we have any English muffins or not?"

"Of course we don't," her mom replied, clearly curious about her daughter's request. "We've *never* had English muffins in the house because you've never even told me you *like* English muffins."

"Well, I'm telling you now."

"What's this all about? Does this have anything to do with that website I saw you on last night?"

"Good grief, Mom!" Raquel exclaimed, jumping off her bar stool, her backpack slung over her shoulder, and marching over to the sink—pouring out the remainder of her juice. "I can't even ask a simple question without you jumping all over me!" She walked out the door before her mom could say another word.

At school, Raquel was dismayed to find that her mom was right; she should have eaten *something* for breakfast. Her stomach kept growling all through first hour and into second. She couldn't even concentrate on what her teachers were saying but kept looking at the clock and counting down the minutes till lunchtime. It didn't help that Group C Lunch was the very last lunch period of the day. She decided that she would definitely eat breakfast tomorrow; it was no good starving herself.

Sara was waiting for her in the cafeteria at the same place they'd sat the day before. Raquel considered finding somewhere else to sit, but Sara had already spotted her so she knew she couldn't ignore her. She just hoped that Sara wouldn't give her a hard time about her food the way her mom did.

"Hey, Raquel!" Sara said with a smile.

Raquel grimaced. Why was it that Sara was happy all the time?

"I saved a seat for ya!"

Raquel sat down next to her without making eye contact. "Thanks," she said quickly, turning her attention to her carton of skim milk.

"So…?"

Raquel snorted and looked at Sara out of the corner of her eye. "So… what?" she asked.

"Any news?"

"About what?" Raquel asked, taking a sip of her milk. *Yuck!* She'd definitely have to get used to skim milk.

"Gabe the Babe, of course!" Sara laughed.

Raquel had almost forgotten about Gabe. *Almost*. "Not really," she shrugged. "I haven't seen him today."

"I thought you said his locker was right next to yours."

"It is," Raquel said defensively, looking up at her sharply. "But I still haven't seen him today, okay?"

Sara looked hurt. "Okay," she said softly, turning to her lunch tray.

Raquel felt bad. She shouldn't have jumped down her friend's throat; Sara was just trying to make conversation. "I'm sorry," she said before she realized what she was saying.

Had she really just apologized? Wow, she couldn't remember the last time she apologized to anybody about *anything*. When did *this* start? Did it have anything to do with the fact that she was a warrior now?

Sara was surprised by Raquel's apology, too. "That's okay," she said with a smile, her eyes shining. "Thanks for apologizing, Raquel."

Embarrassed, Raquel looked down at her lunch. She'd gotten food that looked healthy, but she found herself wondering how many calories everything had. There was a salad without dressing, a ham and cheese sandwich, and a couple of orange slices. Why had she gotten orange slices? She'd had orange juice for breakfast; orange slices didn't appeal to her in the least. She took a bite of the dressing-less salad. It was like eating air. She sighed and picked up the mustard packet and began to apply it to her sandwich. She already knew it would be gross, but it was better than nothing and mustard had fewer calories than mayo.

"I'm really glad that you're a warrior now, Raquel," Sara said reflectively. "After my dad and I came back here, I thought about you a lot. I asked the King to make you a warrior."

Raquel looked up from her mustard sandwich. "You did?"

Sara nodded. "Yeah," she said, smiling.

"Why?"

Sara's smile broadened, her eyes shining even brighter. "Because I want you in Paraíso with me some day," she said.

Raquel looked away. Why were Sara's eyes so hard to look at? In a strange way, they reminded her of Relámpago's, though not nearly as bright as his.

"The King listens to His warriors, Raquel," Sara went on. "In the Book of Light, the Prince said, '*I tell you the truth, my Father will give you whatever you ask in my Name. Until now you have not asked for anything in my Name. Ask and you will receive, and your joy will be complete.*' We don't have because we don't ask. The verses don't mean that the King is like a genie in a bottle—granting our every request. But rest assured that if what we want is the same as what the King wants, the King will give it to us." She paused, then added with an extra sparkle in her eye, "Being a warrior has its perks, you know!"

"You take this 'warrior' stuff pretty seriously, don't you?"

"You will, too," Sara told her, turning to her lunch, "once you find out what you're up against."

"So far," Raquel said smugly, "I don't see why being a warrior is such a big deal."

"It's a *huge* deal, Raquel," Sara exclaimed, food still in her mouth. "When you decide to follow the King, *everything* changes! Your attitude changes, your dreams change... even some of your old habits start to change. You begin to view life with hope. The King made us to enjoy life, and He helps us do just that!"

Raquel held her sandwich without eating it. "I haven't found that to be the case," she said dejectedly, determined not to look at Sara anymore.

"You will, Raquel," Sara said tenderly, touching Raquel's arm. Raquel scooted away. "The King never gives up on us," Sara continued. *"Never.* He *loves* us, Raquel."

Raquel squirmed.

"He won't leave you alone. He'll stay after you until He has your whole heart."

"Relámpago said the King wasn't demanding," Raquel said, concentrating on her sandwich.

"He's not, Raquel, but He *is* relentless. Somewhere near the beginning of the Book of Light, the King actually describes Himself as 'jealous.' In other words, He wants our full attention and devotion."

"So he *is* demanding, then."

Sara shook her head. "I know it sounds weird to refer to the King as 'jealous,' but that just means He wants our love and our undivided attention. He *deserves* our love and undivided attention."

Raquel took a small bite of her mustard sandwich and grimaced at the taste. "He sounds like a dictator to me," she said, quickly taking a swig of her milk. "Anybody who tries to make people love him..."

"You can't *make* somebody love you," Sara reminded her. "Love isn't love at all if it's forced."

Raquel rolled her eyes. Dante had told her nearly the exact same thing. "You sure seem to know a lot about the King," Raquel observed, glancing at her. She meant it presumptuously, but unfortunately for her, Raquel didn't take it that way.

"I've been studying," she smiled proudly.

"Don't you have enough homework without adding another book to the list?"

"The Book of Light isn't just 'another book,' Raquel," she stated emphatically. "I used to think the same thing—back when I first became a warrior—but that Book really is a lifesaver for warriors. If you don't take the time to read it, you're sunk."

"Maybe I never should have become a warrior in the first place," Raquel said, looking at Sara to catch her reaction. "Then I wouldn't have all this to worry about."

"I used to think that, too," Sara said seriously, looking her directly in the eyes. "But listen, Raquel: Those who aren't warriors go through life blind. They can't find their purpose in life because the only purpose to be found is in loving the King. It's why we're here: to have a relationship with the One who made us. Be glad you're a warrior and have access to the Book of Light. People who aren't warriors may not have the extra studying to do, but they're drowning, Raquel; they're sinking and they don't even know it."

Raquel had had enough mustard sandwich for one day. "This is all very interesting," she said, grabbing her backpack and standing to her feet, "but if you'll excuse me, I have *math* to study for."

Raquel headed straight for the nearest restroom, dropped her backpack on the floor, and stood bracing herself on the countertop. She felt like she might get sick. She felt queasy—and not just from having eaten a dry salad and mustard sandwich for lunch. All this talk about the King and the Book of Light was making her head spin. *"The King never gives up on us.* Never. *He* loves *us, Raquel."* Sara's words kept replaying in her mind.

Love. What a joke!

She looked up at herself in the mirror. What was there to love? No one had ever taken the time to show her love; why should the King be any different? If the King loved her so much, then why hadn't he kept her family together? Why did he let her dad be stupid and cheat on her mom?

Raquel cut off the flow of thoughts. Asking 'why' never did any good anyway.

Something shiny caught her eye. She stared curiously at her reflection. Around her waist was a bright, silver belt.

Confused, she stepped back from the counter. She looked down at her clothes; the belt wasn't there. In the mirror, she appeared to be wearing a thick metal belt several inches wide. A long, silver sheath without a sword inside was attached to the belt's left side. She looked down again and even put her hands on her hips; the belt wasn't there. What was going on?

She looked up again at her reflection. By moving and catching the light at just the right angle, she noticed a letter in the center of the belt's buckle: the letter "T."

Then something else caught her attention. Her hands were still resting on her hips—now touching cold metal. But Raquel didn't notice. Her focus was on the huge black shadow standing in the middle of the room.

Chapter 14

The Rescue

Raquel stood frozen in fear. No more than a few feet from her—standing between her and the door—was a large figure the size and shape of Relámpago. It looked like a criado's shadow—complete with outstretched wings—but it was like looking at a dark cutout of where a criado *should* be. She couldn't see the figure's face: only darkness. She could see the outline of the figure's muscles, though, and they were just as big if not bigger than Relámpago's. One marked difference between Relámpago and this creature was that it didn't carry a sword; its arms were down by its sides—long, curved claws on the ends of its fingers.

Raquel did what any rational person would do; she screamed at the top of her lungs.

The scream didn't seem to have any effect on the shadow. It continued standing there stock still. Raquel couldn't see the creature's eyes, but she knew it was looking at her; she could feel its icy stare.

Raquel screamed again as loud as she could. *Could no one hear her?*

Just when she thought she was about to pass out from fear, she heard the restroom door slam open and bang into the opposite wall. Even this didn't deter the shadow; it continued to face Raquel and even took a step toward her. Raquel gasped.

"Raquel, what's wrong?"

Raquel couldn't see past the giant shadow, but she immediately recognized the voice: *It was Sara!*

The creature's reaction to Sara's voice was instantaneous: The giant shadow suddenly lost its composure and dropped to the floor—cowering like a frightened rat. It looked toward Sara with bared fangs; Raquel was horrified to see a forked tongue come out of its mouth! In the next instant, it unfurled its wings and took off through the ceiling.

Raquel shrieked and dropped to the floor, covering her face. The next thing she knew, Sara was kneeling by her side. "What's wrong, Raquel?" Sara was asking, her arm draped over her protectively. Raquel was trembling violently and breathing heavily—her heart beating so fast she thought it would explode.

"*Say* something, Raquel!" Sara insisted. "You're scaring me."

"You... didn't see it?" Raquel struggled to say.

Sara's eyes lit up with understanding. "You saw a sombra," she said methodically.

Raquel nodded.

Sara didn't react the way Raquel had expected she would. Rather than acting afraid or at least unnerved, a look of frustration and anger darkened Sara's face. "C'mon," she said, helping her friend to her feet. "Try standing up."

Knees still shaking, Raquel almost fell but Sara caught her. "Here, put an arm over my shoulder." Raquel obeyed. "Can you stand, or do you need to sit down again?"

Raquel was slowly getting her breath back. "No," she said between breaths. "I'll be okay."

"Do you need a drink of water?"

Raquel tried to laugh. "I think I need something stronger," she said.

Sara laughed. "Raquel!" she chided her, shaking her head.

"Thanks, I'm okay now," she said, removing her arm from around Sara's shoulder and bracing herself on the counter instead. She was still breathing heavily.

Sara stood there silently, unsure of how to help her friend. "Pretty scary, aren't they?" she finally said.

Raquel laughed again. "That's the understatement of the year," she said.

"I remember the first time I saw one," Sara said compassionately. "I was scared out of my wits, too."

Raquel couldn't remember ever being this scared—not even as a child when her mother had slapped her for the first time. She'd always denied being afraid, but there was no denying it this time.

"Don't worry," Sara said consolingly, gently rubbing her arm, "it's gone now."

Raquel's heart was still racing, but she refused to be treated like a child. "I'm fine," she said angrily, stepping away from Sara's gentle touch.

Sara looked hurt, but only for a moment. She stuck her hands in her pockets. "So will you be ready for the *next* sombra that comes along?" she asked with a knowing smile.

What kind of a question was that? "I just want this *whole business* to stop!" Raquel said furiously. "I wish I'd never set foot in Paraíso!"

"Going to Paraíso didn't make sombras show up," Sara reminded her, "it just made them visible."

"Well, I'd much rather they stay *in*visible!"

Sara could sympathize. "I see your point," she nodded, taking Raquel's hand, "but at least this way you'll know when you're under attack."

Raquel jerked her hand away. "I was *fine* before I ever decided to follow the King!"

Sara looked her in the eyes. "No one is *ever* fine before deciding to follow the King, Raquel."

Raquel turned and faced the opposite wall. She felt her anger subsiding. "I need answers, Sara," she said meekly.

It was a moment before Sara responded. "You know where to find them, Raquel," she heard her say.

Raquel hesitated. "In the Book of Light," she said softly.

"In the Book of Light," Sara agreed.

After a moment, Raquel slowly reached down and picked up her backpack from the floor—setting it on the countertop. With trembling fingers, she meticulously unzipped it and pulled out the Book of Light. She laid it down gently next to the sink. Then she looked at Sara. Sara looked down at the Book and then back up at her. Raquel expected her to say or do something, and it frustrated her when she didn't. "Well?"

Sara laughed. "Well, what?" she said.

"Aren't you going to get excited to see it or something?"

She laughed loudly. "I see mine every day!" she exclaimed with a smile. "I've got a copy of it in my backpack right now!"

"But it's a *'lifesaver for warriors,'*" she said, mocking her.

Sara laughed so hard Raquel thought she was going to fall over. "Glad to see you were listening," she said, grinning from ear to ear.

"So this is all just a big joke to you?" Raquel asked agitatedly.

Sara's face became grave. "No, Raquel," she said solemnly. "It's not a joke at all. I'm sorry for laughing. I take the Book *very* seriously."

"So what does it say about fighting sombras?" Raquel challenged.

Sara sighed and, with a smile, picked up the Book. She looked knowingly at Raquel. "I'm about to open it," she warned. "Is that okay with you?"

Raquel rolled her eyes. "Whatever," she said.

Sara opened the Book. The sudden light caught Raquel off-guard and she let out a gasp. Sara laughed. "You'll get used to it," she said, the Book's light shining up in her face, making her eyes sparkle even more than usual.

Raquel swallowed. "So what does it say?" she asked humbly.

She watched in amazement as Sara effortlessly turned the Book's pages—despite the powerful light shooting up at her. She found the spot she was looking for and began to read aloud:

Finally, be strong in the King and in his mighty power. Put on the full armor of the King so that you can take your stand against the enemy's schemes. For our struggle is not against flesh and blood, but against the rulers, against the authorities, against the powers of this dark world and against the spiritual forces of evil in the heavenly realms. Therefore put on the full armor of the King, so that when the day of evil comes, you may be able to stand your ground, and after you have done everything, to stand.

"Wait a second, hold on," Raquel interrupted. *"'Forces of evil'?"*

Sara nodded. "That's just another name for 'sombras,'" she explained.

"How can you stand there and read about 'forces of evil' like it's no big deal?" asked Raquel incredulously.

Sara's lips curved into a smile. "They can't touch me," she said shrewdly.

Raquel was shocked by her answer. And the way Sara was smiling at her, she believed it. Sombras really *couldn't* touch her! That's why the monster had flown away like a frightened sparrow the second it knew Sara had entered the room. "Sombras are *scared* of you?" Raquel asked in amazement.

Surprisingly, Sara shook her head. "Not of me," she said, "but they're scared of the Prince, and the Prince lives inside me. Whenever somebody chooses to become a warrior, the

Prince actually comes to live inside them! I know it doesn't make sense, but it's really true! That's how I knew *you* were a warrior, Raquel: I could see the light of the Prince in your eyes." Raquel blushed. "Sombras can see it, too, and it scares 'em. They're afraid of the Prince's power. And... just think! We now have this power living inside of *us!*"

"It didn't seem scared of *me,*" Raquel recalled dejectedly.

Sara was encouraging. "That's just because you haven't learned how to fight them yet, Raquel," she said. "Sombras aren't scared of warriors who don't know how to fight."

"So how *do* I fight them?" Raquel asked, getting impatient.

Sara pointed to the Book. "You interrupted me before I could finish," she said with a laugh. "This is what the rest of the passage says:

Stand firm then, with the belt of truth buckled around your waist, with the breastplate of righteousness in place, and with your feet fitted with the peace that comes with being ready to share the Book of Light with others. In addition to all this, take up the shield of faith, with which you can extinguish all the fiery darts of the evil one. Take the helmet of salvation and the sword of Espíritu, which is the Book of Light. And speak to the King in the power of Espíritu on all occasions with all kinds of thanks and requests. With this in mind, be alert and be persistent in your requests for all warriors everywhere.

Having finished reading the passage, Sara laid the Book open on the countertop and looked up at Raquel.

"So I fight them with the King's armor?"

"Yep."

"And the King will give it to me?"

"Yep," Sara said again.

Raquel looked at her reflection; the belt was still there. "How am I supposed to fight those creatures off with a *belt?*" she wondered.

Sara laughed. "I take it the belt of truth is the only piece of armor you have so far?"

Raquel nodded.

"Don't worry, Raquel, the rest will come. The belt of truth is the foundation piece for the rest of the armor," she explained. "You have to establish truth before you can establish anything else. In the meantime, you can use the Book of Light itself to fight them off. Remember what I read just now? '*The sword of Espíritu, which is the Book of Light.*' The Book of Light is our sword."

"What about you?" Raquel asked. "Do you have all of the armor?"

"I sure do," Sara nodded assuredly. "I can't see it anymore, but I know it's there. Every morning before leaving the house, I ask the King to suit me up in His armor. I also ask Him to send His criados to keep watch over me."

Raquel was amused. Sara really *did* take this seriously!

"But the best defense we have against sombras is not the King's armor or even criados—as handy as they are to have around. Our best defense is the Prince Himself. Just mention the Prince by Name, Raquel, and sombras will flee. They *hate* hearing His Name."

Raquel nearly jumped out of her skin when an obnoxious bell sounded, announcing the end of lunch. The sound echoed off the restroom walls so loudly that both Raquel and Sara covered their ears. Raquel sighed. "And *I* hate hearing *that!*" she chuckled.

Sara laughed, closing the Book of Light and handing it back to Raquel. "That's probably what the Prince's Name sounds like to them!" she said.

Raquel laughed and allowed Sara to put an arm over her shoulder as they exited the restroom. As they went their separate ways—Raquel to the eighth grade wing and Sara to the seventh—Raquel found herself extremely grateful to have Sara as a friend.

Chapter 15

The Run

Raquel couldn't keep her mind on school for the remainder of the day. Every shadow made her jump; she kept wondering if she would run into anymore sombras. This was *not* what she signed up for when she decided to become a warrior!

After last period, she hurried to her locker. She was still distracted when someone said her name; she jumped a foot. She turned to see Gabe standing there. He was laughing at her reaction.

"Boy, *somebody's* jumpy today!" he said, an impish grin on his face.

Raquel blushed. "Oh, hi, Gabe," she said timidly.

"Hi," Gabe said smoothly, leaning cavalierly against his locker with crossed arms. "I'm still waiting on you to take me up on my offer."

"Your offer?"

"Now don't tell me you've already forgotten about your agreement to meet me after school."

"Oh, no, I didn't forget," said Raquel quickly. Was he wanting to do something with her today? On such short notice? She'd already made plans for after school today, and her mom was expecting her to ride the bus. If she missed the bus again, her mom would be ticked.

"Let me guess," Gabe said, reading her expression. "You have to call your mommy first and ask if it's okay, am I right?"

Raquel didn't like his insinuation. Why was he speaking to her like this—as though she were a child? She was in the same grade he was.

Raquel must have been glaring at him because Gabe suddenly took offense. His dark eyes flashed and he stood erect. "Of course, if you're not interested, I can always find somebody else..."

"Oh, no," she said quickly, then stopped. Standing behind him—sword in hand—was Relámpago. He wasn't looking at her or Gabe; in fact, he didn't seem to be looking at anything in particular. He was just standing there, but his presence alone was enough to make her throat dry up. He looked serious, and Raquel remembered how Sara had said that criados would keep watch over her. But *here?* Even at *school?* How *annoying!*

Gabe followed her gaze and naturally saw nothing unusual. "Um, Raquel," he said in a condescending drawl. "What are you looking at?"

"Huh?" Raquel said, glancing back at Gabe. "Did you say something?"

She gasped when she watched as a couple of students walked *right through* her guardian criado as though he weren't even there!

Gabe chuckled. "You look like you've just seen a ghost," he teased.

Raquel stood with mouth agape—not believing the absurdity of the situation. "Not far off," she murmured, eyes still on Relámpago.

"Look," Gabe said, glancing at his watch, "I've gotta go, Raquel."

"Oh, yeah," she said, trying to concentrate on him and not on the criado behind him.

"We'll get together another time... that is, if I decide you're not insane."

She laughed awkwardly—watching as Gabe made his way down the hall. Once Gabe was a safe distance away, Raquel glared up at her guardian criado. "What are you *doing* here?" she whispered through clenched teeth. "You don't have to follow me around *everywhere!*"

The Native American criado's expression didn't change; he continued staring into space.

"I *know* you can hear me!"

Relámpago glanced down at her, then looked away.

"What, so now you can't talk to me?"

No response.

Maybe he *couldn't* talk to her. Come to think of it, there wasn't the halo of bright light surrounding him like there had been the other times they'd spoken. And she hadn't forgotten (nor would she *ever* forget) how the students had walked right on through him as if he weren't even there. Maybe he could only talk to her once he manifested himself. At the moment, he was visible to her and no one else. This was the "Power of Paraíso" Sara had mentioned.

This realization—that she was going to be followed around by this guy until who-knows-when—hit her like a Mack truck. Why on earth did Sara view them as "handy to have around"?

"You're gonna end up messing *everything* up!" she said exasperatedly, turning to march down the hall. She looked behind her; he was following closely behind—stopping whenever she stopped. "Just *go away!*" she shouted up at him. He followed her all the way to the buses and then disappeared. *Thank goodness,* she thought, only to realize after getting off at her house that he had been riding along on top of the bus the whole time.

"How was your day?" asked her mom as soon as she walked through the door.

Raquel was in no mood to talk. "Oh, just peachy," she said, glaring up at her guardian criado behind her as she marched through the kitchen.

"I went to the store after work."

Raquel stopped dead in her tracks, causing Relámpago to nearly run into her—although she knew she wouldn't have felt it even if he had.

"Really?" she said, walking briskly over to the breakfast bar and taking a seat, grateful for a diversion. "Did you pick up some English muffins?"

"I did," her mom nodded, licking the cream cheese she was spreading on her bagel from her finger. "You want one? I won't be fixing supper for a while."

Raquel smirked. Two bagels in the same day… *and* cream cheese! Her mom was so dumb: the carbs would go straight to her hips. Raquel was glad she was too smart for that. "No thanks," she responded smugly, jumping off the bar stool and trying to ignore Relámpago as he turned to follow her. "I'm gonna go for a quick run before supper."

"A quick run?" she heard her mom say, but Raquel was out the door before her mom could ask questions.

Raquel had thought ahead and left some running shoes in the garage. She quickly put them on and then set off for her 15-minute jog around the block. This would become her daily routine: running for 15 minutes every day after school… maybe 30, if 15 turned out to be too easy for her.

Something she hadn't planned on, though, as she began her run—Relámpago needing only to take large strides in order to keep up with her—was the difficulty of running on an empty stomach. All she'd had to eat all day was a bite of salad and part of a ham and cheese sandwich. Less than five minutes into the run and Raquel needed to take a breather. She sat down on the curb, trying to catch her breath—her heart racing. Relámpago, not winded in the least, stood over her to her left—not making eye contact. She looked up at him with disdain, as though her discomfort were his fault. "You might... make yourself useful," she said between breaths, "... and get me some water."

He didn't look at her, but she hadn't expected him to. Irritated nonetheless at having been ignored, she stood up again and continued her run. A minute later, she slowed down to a walk. *No, I can do this,* she thought. She picked up speed again.

The January day was chilly, but her throat felt like it was on fire; her lungs burned with every breath. She could hear her heartbeat pounding in her ears. She looked to her left; Relámpago was still there, ignoring her. She turned her attention back to the road in front of her. Objects around her—cars and houses—began to swim around her. Black dots danced in front of her eyes. The last thing Raquel remembered seeing before her legs gave out was a large hand coming between her head and the asphalt.

When she came to, she was lying on her back on top of her bed. Things still looked blurry. She blinked. She could feel a cool washrag on her forehead, and she could smell something delicious. Raquel looked around to find her mom sitting by her bed, looking sincerely concerned about her. Raquel couldn't remember ever seeing her mom look like that.

"Oh, thank goodness," she heard her mom say. "Raquel, don't you *ever* scare me like that again!"

Raquel tried to talk, but her voice came out in a whisper. "What happened?" she managed to say.

"What happened, young lady, is that I found you by the side of the road, passed out. You're lucky you didn't get a concussion!"

Things started coming back to her. She remembered seeing Relámpago's hand coming out to break her fall.

Where was he? She looked around the room; her guardian criado was standing nearby. He, too, looked relieved that she was alright. "It may not have been luck," Raquel said softly, and offered Relámpago a weak smile to show her gratitude. He smiled back.

"Here," her mom was saying, "eat some of this, Raquel."

She tried sitting up with a groan. "What is it?" she asked, feeling the aching of her scratched up knees and arms.

"It's your favorite," her mom replied. "Ravioli."

Ravioli. She didn't know how many calories ravioli had, but her mom was right: it was her favorite, and she was starving. She could practically feel her stomach gnawing on itself. When she took the bite offered by her mom, Raquel thought that nothing had ever tasted so good. Not wanting to be fed like a baby, she took the bowl and ate the rest of it on her own in record time. Her mom had included on the plate some cheese and Ritz crackers. She had never turned down cheese before, and she decided that she would not start today. She shoveled these down, as well—including an entire glass of whole milk.

"Goodness!" her mom exclaimed. "You were hungry! I knew I should have made you eat something before letting you run. Didn't you eat lunch today?"

"Of course," Raquel answered simply, not offering any extra information.

"Well, it must not have been much. Are you feeling better?"

"Yeah," Raquel said again, and it was the truth. Who knew that a little food in your stomach could do so much? She felt her strength returning already.

Raquel wanted to thank her mom for everything—for the food, for cleaning her scrapes and applying bandages, for not being angry with her for scaring her half to death—but instead she just smiled.

"You rest a bit," her mom said, "and I'll come back in a few minutes to check on you."

As soon as her mom left the room, Raquel turned to Relámpago. She may not have shown much gratitude to her mom, but the least she could do was show him some gratitude. "Thanks," she told him.

Relámpago's smile had faded. He offered her the smallest smile in return before looking away.

"You may have saved my life," she pressed, desiring a more appropriate response.

There was no trace of a smile now.

What's his problem? Raquel thought. *I'm trying to be nice by thanking him. You'd think he could at least acknowledge me.*

Relámpago stared straight ahead, expressionless.

Maybe he's mad 'cause I didn't thank my mom, she decided. Well, who cared what he thought about her? He hadn't been around long enough to know that the relationship between her and her mom wasn't exactly ideal. If he knew the kind of mom she was, then he'd understand why she wasn't bending over backward to thank her mom for doing what was her motherly obligation anyway.

She reached for the remote control and turned on her TV. She found an exercise program and decided to watch it; maybe she could pick up on some weight-loss tips. It didn't take long for her to become painfully aware of the perfect bodies of those in the workout program. The women had flat stomachs and made the exercises they were doing look like a breeze. Raquel's heart began to sink; she hadn't been able to keep up her running for a measly 15 minutes. What was her problem? It must be that she wasn't in shape enough. Well, that settled it, then: she would just have to work out more. She could do some of these exercises that the ladies on TV were doing right here in her bedroom without even going to a gym. It was very likely that her mom wouldn't allow her to go on anymore after-school runs, so she'd have to figure out a way around it. Doing simple exercises like these in her bedroom would be the solution to that problem.

Raquel looked down at her own stomach. It looked nothing like the women's on TV. She was painfully aware of how it bulged out—especially in a sitting position. Then she remembered the food she'd eaten: the ravioli... the cheese... the crackers... the whole milk. Her heart began to flutter. What had she been thinking? That was *way* too much food! Why had she eaten it all? How many calories had she eaten in just this one meal? It had to have been off the charts!

Why on earth had she thrown away all her hard work on just one meal? The words from the website rang in her head: *No more than 400-500 calories per meal... The absolute maximum amount of saturated fat that anyone should eat per day is 20 grams.*

Raquel felt her fear increasing. She could practically feel the food in her stomach being turned into fat even as she sat there. She couldn't let that happen; it was like poison inside of her. *She had to get rid of it!*

Panicking—hoping she wasn't already too late—Raquel rushed to the bathroom, locked the door behind her, and threw herself at the toilet. She raised the lid and stuck a finger as far back into her throat as she could. Her gag reflex had always come easily for her, and she found it quite simple to heave her entire supper into the toilet, her throat and mouth burning. After vomiting several times to make sure it was all out, she sat back against the cold tile floor—a horrible taste in her mouth but with an overwhelming feeling of relief. She hadn't given her supper the chance to turn into fat! Her mom had tried to trick her into eating, but she had been too smart for her!

She looked up. Relámpago was standing over her with a pained expression on his face.

Chapter 16

The Diet

Raquel needed to study up some more on dieting, so she waited until her mom had gone to bed and then slipped downstairs. The last time she'd tried to research her diet, Relámpago had shown up and been a distraction. Here he was again tonight, but at least he wasn't being a distraction. In fact, she could hardly see him at all as he stood guard over by the wall since the halo of light wasn't surrounding him and since she'd left the light off—hoping this time that Relámpago wouldn't turn it on. It didn't look as though he planned to.

Relieved, Raquel turned to the computer and started her search. She found a website that said that drinking soda was really bad for you because of all the sugar. She knew that already, but what she didn't know was that drinking diet soda was just as bad because of the artificial sweeteners. *Well, there go my Diet Cokes,* she thought with a sigh. She learned that it's healthy to drink 48 ounces of water a day, which came out to six 8-ounce glasses. By substituting a glass of water for Coke, she would save herself from 97 calories.

It also said that "four mindless bites" of dessert a day results in the gaining of a pound by the end of the month.

Well then, I'll just cut out desserts altogether, Raquel decided.

"Get in the habit," it said, "of only eating food that has been portioned. Know exactly how many calories you're eating." It suggested keeping track of your calorie count by writing down everything you eat every day. "Keep a calorie journal," it said.

I can do that, Raquel thought. *I can keep a log right here on the computer.* She knew her mom wouldn't see it because she rarely used the computer anyway, and she could save it under a file where her mom wouldn't find it.

"You're on the right track," it said, "if you're burning 200-500 calories per day through both dieting and exercise." It suggested an exercise tip she hadn't thought of: walking up and down stairs. Doing that for 10 minutes burned 100 calories! Of course, how she would pull that one off without her mom asking her a million questions, she didn't know.

She did another search and found a site that gave the exact number of calories in just about any food. There were 150 calories in a cup of grape juice… which was the exact same number of calories as there were in a can of soda. Raquel felt her heart sink; she *loved* grape juice, but it was just as bad for her as soda was! A McDonald's hamburger and small fries together were 480 calories! *No more fast food for me!* she decided. At least apples weren't too bad: only 47 calories, and English muffins only had 63. She couldn't believe that sweetened cereal had 155 calories, and unsweetened cereal wasn't much better: still 106 calories. It would be an English muffin or an apple for breakfast from now on.

Raquel wondered how many calories she'd saved herself from that evening. Ravioli had a whopping 229 calories! A serving of Ritz crackers had 79 calories, and only *one slice* of cheddar cheese had 113 calories! How many slices had she eaten tonight? At *least* seven or eight! And a cup of whole milk had 146 calories! She grabbed a calculator and did the math: Her supper had come to a grand total of *1,245 calories!* That was more than *double* the number of calories that should be eaten for a meal! Raquel felt proud of herself for getting rid of it.

Her stomach growled. With her supper in the toilet, all of her hunger pangs were coming back; she felt just as hungry as she had after her run. *I can't give in,* she told herself. *If I eat something now, it will ruin what I'm trying to work for. I have to use self-control; I have to be in* control *of my stomach and not let my stomach control* me!

Her stomach growled again. Maybe she'd done enough research for one night. Reading about all this food was probably making her hungry.

Before shutting down the computer, Raquel created a spreadsheet and titled it "Calorie Counter." She entered today's date and typed in the ham and cheese sandwich she'd had for lunch. She looked it up on the calorie-counting website and found out it had 352 calories! Thankfully, she'd only taken a few bites, so she entered the number 176. From now on, she would keep track of every day's meals in this way. Satisfied with her progress, Raquel shut the computer down and went to bed.

She awoke the next morning to a rumbling stomach. Raquel smiled. An empty stomach meant that she was losing weight!

She stepped on the bathroom scale. She would weigh herself every day to keep up with her progress. She was smiling until she looked in the mirror; there was that metal belt again! How was she supposed to monitor her waistline if she couldn't even *see* her waistline! *I don't need the mirror anyway as long as I've got the scale,* she thought victoriously,

She spent extra time in front of the mirror getting ready for school; Gabe was losing interest in her and she couldn't let that happen. Today she would make her move, and she wanted to make sure she looked extra good for him.

Her mom greeted her in the kitchen. "English muffin?"

"I'll get it," Raquel told her, heading for the pantry.

"How are you feeling?"

Raquel was surprised at the compassion apparent in her mom's voice. "Fine," she said quickly.

"Do you still hurt from yester—"

"I said I'm fine, Mom," Raquel interrupted.

She looked up at her mom; she looked hurt. Raquel felt bad. Why was she being rude to her mom after all she'd done for her yesterday? Come to think of it, though, why was she even *worried* about it? Wasn't this *always* how she treated her mom?

"I mean... well, what I meant to say," she said shyly. "Thanks, Mom."

It wasn't much of a thank-you, but it made her mom smile. "You're welcome," she said.

Feeling embarrassed, Raquel quickly grabbed an English muffin out of the bag, put the rest back in the pantry, and headed out the door.

All the way to school (Relámpago flying alongside the bus), Raquel's heart raced as she tried to think of what she would say to Gabe. It wouldn't be convenient trying to talk to him with Relámpago standing nearby, but she would just have to ignore him. It's not easy ignoring a seven-foot-tall guy with wings, but she knew that there was nothing he could do to come between her and Gabe short of manifesting himself and she was pretty sure he wouldn't choose to do that in the middle of the junior high school hallway.

From a distance, Raquel saw Gabe putting his books in his locker. Her heart jumped and her pulse quickened. He was *so* handsome! She couldn't lose him. She'd been sure to wear clothes that she knew he'd like, and had even found a bit of her mom's perfume to put on.

It was now or never. After yesterday, she *had* to make a good impression.

She approached him slowly, her heartbeat like a drum in her ears. When he didn't notice her right away, she did the combination on her lock and opened her locker. The noise got his attention. He looked at her, and Raquel's heart sank when she saw him glare at her and then look away; he was still angry at her for blowing him off yesterday. Well, she would show him that she had no intention of blowing him off today.

"Hi, Gabe," she said in a sing-song voice.

Gabe stopped what he was doing and looked at her.

Raquel smiled seductively. "I hope you're not still mad at me."

A smile spread slowly across his face, indicating that that all was forgiven. His eyes roamed from her face to the rest of her body. "I'm glad to see you're not insane," he grinned.

Raquel could see Relámpago standing behind him—students passing through him as they walked the hallway. She couldn't allow herself to get distracted today, not if she wanted to keep from losing Gabe. "Insane for you," she said with a smile.

This got the desired response. Gabe laughed and slammed his locker closed—removing the barrier between them. He took a step toward her and leaned against his locker, his muscular bicep right next to her face. "Is that an invitation?" he asked, his face inches from hers.

She glanced up at Relámpago. His eyes flashed with indignation. But this was *her* life; she didn't care what he thought. Raquel looked back at Gabe. His face was beautiful—his dark brown eyes and black hair. Her heart was beating at an alarming rate. She ignored the warning inside of her to keep her distance. "You bet it is," she told him.

Gabe leaned in toward her and kissed her gently on the lips. Raquel felt life coursing through her just like the other day he touched her. Butterflies danced in her stomach and her heart pounded. She felt light-headed like she had right before she fainted the night before. She closed her eyes when Gabe's lips pressed harder and his hand went to her waist.

A voice in her head warned her to back off, but she didn't listen. What could be wrong with this?

She reached up to put an arm around him and felt his muscles. Instinctively, she drew him in closer. Both of his hands were now around her waist, and she could feel his strength. She felt safe and protected in his arms… and she felt loved. She put both of her arms around him.

"Alright, you two, break it up," a commanding voice said. "Save it for after school."

Raquel and Gabe looked up to see the hall monitor passing by. He was large and his orders were always respected. Raquel and Gabe let go of each other, and Gabe took a step back. Once the hall monitor was a safe distance away, Gabe leaned in close. "What do you say we take him up on his offer?" he grinned.

Nothing could have deterred her. "I'll see you after school," she said, her voice quivering.

Gabe gave her a triumphant smile, grabbed his books, and started down the hallway, looking back at her over his shoulder. His grin made her heart melt.

It was several seconds before Raquel was able to catch her breath. Several students passed by her—some of them snickering, some of the girls turning a blind eye to her. It was obvious they were jealous.

Raquel's head slowly returned to earth, the warning bell helping to bring her back. She quickly put her stuff away and grabbed up the needed books. Concentrating on the rest of her day would not be an easy task. Not with Gabe waiting at the end of it.

For the next few weeks, Raquel met with Gabe at the lockers every day before and after school. Life suddenly had meaning for her; he made her feel alive.

She continued watching her diet closely—never allowing herself more than 400 calories per meal. At the end of every day after her mom was in bed, she entered the information on the calorie chart she'd created. She watched in exhilaration as the scale continued to plummet. Once, when the scale indicated a gain rather than a loss, she had gone to the bathroom and thrown up her supper. Deciding that she hated vomiting—both the burning and the taste—she cut back even more on what she would allow herself to eat, determined to never see the scale go up again. Every time her stomach growled, a feeling of power came over her; she was in charge of her body and not allowing it to dictate what she did.

After she got home from school each day she turned her TV on and worked out to an exercise program. It seemed like one was always on TV. If she couldn't find one, she worked out anyway... doing the exercises she'd learned from the show. Sometimes her mom would go out and Raquel would take the opportunity to go for a jog around the block or—if the weather was bad—a walk up and down the stairs. The more she exercised, the more she felt her muscles tightening and she watched as her stomach size decreased. She was starting to look more and more like the women in the video! She found that she felt tired all the time, but she attributed this to all the exercising.

Her mom asked her if she was losing weight. Raquel was overjoyed that she'd noticed, but her mom looked worried rather than pleased. She would point out that she could see her collarbone, and to Raquel this was like music to her ears. But she soon tired of her mom's constant nagging and succumbed to wearing sweatshirts around the house to get her mom off her back. She actually didn't mind too much since she was noticing that she was starting to feel cold more easily than she used to. But once out of her mom's sight, it was back to tank tops and tight jeans (which, incidentally, weren't nearly as tight as they used to be).

She smiled at her reflection in the mirror; she was looking more and more like the models in the magazines!

The belt of truth kept showing up in her reflection, as well, but she was learning to see around it.

Chapter 17

Tentación

One night, as Raquel was doing her usual entering of daily calorie intake on the computer, she noticed something odd: She found that her mind kept drifting off the task at hand and onto finding other ways to lose weight. She was happy with the weight-loss program she was on; why would she research other options? But the thoughts wouldn't go away so she decided she might as well. She typed "weight-loss options" into the search engine. The first site to come up was one about supplements. She clicked on it. It was all about diet pills... guaranteeing to help you "drop two sizes in two weeks."

Raquel's heart leapt in her chest. Was that really possible? Was it possible that she'd been working hard to lose weight for all these weeks, and there was a magic pill that would get rid of the fat in just two weeks? She should have researched this earlier!

Thrilled about this revelation, she immediately began looking around for a pen to write down the information. As she did, she saw a quick flick of a dark shadow out of the corner of her eye. She turned her head; nothing was there.

What had she seen? The only light in the room was from the computer, so it was probably just her imagination. Still, she thought she'd be more comfortable with more light. She swiveled in her chair to go turn on the overhead light. As she did, she watched as a dark shape quickly stepped out of view behind her. Raquel turned quickly in the direction the shadow had gone. Again, the shadow eluded her, but she had just barely caught sight of something.

Her heart pounded in her chest. She hadn't forgotten her encounter with the sombra at school.

She jumped out of her chair and spun around. A dark shape scrambled to remain at her back, but she had seen the sombra! She looked over her shoulder and screamed: A massive shadow loomed over her with razor-sharp teeth, and it had her head in the grip of its claws!

Raquel screamed again and struggled to escape from it, but the sombra held her firmly in its grasp. She tried swinging at it but her arms went right through the creature—just like the students had walked right though Relámpago.

Relámpago! Where was her guardian criado?

Her eyes darted quickly to where she'd seen Relámpago standing guard in the past. She let out a shriek when she caught sight of his predicament: He was presently pinned to the wall by two more of the dark shadows—both of them extremely strong. Relámpago was no match for the two of them on his own; he was struggling to free himself and yelling something to her, but she couldn't hear him. Why didn't he manifest himself so that she could hear him?

"King, what's he saying?" Raquel heard herself yell.

A bright light suddenly encompassed Relámpago, and the sombras turned their faces away to reveal jagged teeth—no doubt crying out in pain from the brilliant light. But they held fast to Relámpago, never loosening their grip on him.

"Raquel!" her criado was shouting, continuing to struggle under the sombras' firm grasp. "Talk to the King! Ask Him for—"

One of the sombras didn't let him finish—punching Relámpago in the stomach so hard that he doubled over.

"Ask the King for *what,* Relámpago?" Raquel shouted.

The Native American criado started to say something, but the second sombra seized him by the throat with a clawed hand and began to squeeze.

Raquel screamed again. What was she supposed to ask the King for? She felt so helpless.

"King!" she cried out in desperation. "Help Relámpago!"

The sombras' heads jerked toward Raquel with what she imagined to be horrified expressions and began to violently beat their wings in an attempt to strengthen their hold on Relámpago—crushing him into the wall. But not for long. Suddenly possessing additional strength, Relámpago tore loose from the sombra that held his throat, lifted it into the air with one arm, and threw it half-way across the room. Wasting no time, the other sombra quickly reached for Relámpago's face with a clawed hand. With lightning-fast movement, Relámpago caught the sombra's wrist and—with a mighty yell—wrenched himself free from the sombra's hold on him, picked it up as though it were a rag doll, and hurled it through the air—sending it colliding with the other sombra. Both sombras were attempting to right themselves, but Relámpago had already drawn his sword and was rapidly advancing. Grabbing both sombras by the tops of their heads with one hand, he sent his giant sword slicing through the shadows in one singular fluid motion. The sombras promptly faded.

Her guardian criado spun around to face her—a fierce expression on his face. Raquel was alarmed until she remembered the sombra that still stood behind her, holding her in its clutches. Raquel shrieked as the sombra released her from its grip and began backing away from her—hunched over like a frightened animal, face toward the criado. Raquel looked back at Relámpago. He was staring down the sombra—breathing heavily from the exertion he'd expended.

Why didn't he attack? Was he too tired?

Relámpago directed his mighty sword at the sombra. "You are finished with her, Tentación," he informed it.

The sombra said something in return, though she couldn't hear it. All she could see was the creature's gigantic fangs.

"Your days are numbered," the criado said quickly in return. "The girl's eyes have been opened; she will listen to your lies no longer."

The dark shadow said something else.

Whatever it said must have enraged Relámpago because a fire leapt into his eyes. He began advancing toward the shadow. "I could cut out your tongue right now—"

The sombra quickly unfurled its wings and shot up—disappearing through the vaulted ceiling.

Relámpago watched it go, then looked down at her. With the room finally cleared of sombras, the fire in his eyes slowly subsided. Sheathing his enormous sword, the Native American criado collapsed onto the couch—his massive chest heaving. He looked at her with an expression of relief and gratitude. "Thank you," he said simply.

Raquel stood there, mouth agape. *He* was thanking *her?* "Thank *you,*" she said with a smile.

He returned the smile then looked away, still breathing heavily.

Raquel had so many questions she didn't know where to start. "Why didn't you kill that last sombra like you did the first two?" she wondered. "Were you too tired?"

Relámpago chuckled in his deep voice. "No, little warrior," he said, sitting up straighter. "With the King's added strength, criados can fight off sombras as long as is required. But Tentación would sooner war with words than with physical weapons, so I was meeting him on his own ground." His smile faded a bit and sadness filled his eyes. "Besides this," he said, looking at her somberly, "I do not have permission to destroy him as long as his victim grants him permission to remain."

Raquel felt her stomach drop. "His victim?" she said nervously. "You mean *me?"*

Relámpago nodded.

"I'm giving that thing permission to hang around?"

"Yes, Raquel."

"How?"

Relámpago looked at her purposefully. "You chose to listen to him, Raquel," he said. "Tentación's thought did not originate with you, but you owned it when you chose to believe it and take action on it. Tentación has no power when he is ignored."

Raquel collapsed onto the computer chair. She was silent for a moment. "What did that creature want with me?" she asked softly, shuddering to think of its claws in her head.

"What thought was in your head when you noticed his presence?" Relámpago asked her.

Raquel remembered, but she didn't feel like sharing it with her criado. One look at his piercing brown eyes, though, and she knew that he already knew—no good denying it. "I was considering buying diet pills," she told him.

The criado smiled. "*'Then you will know the truth,'*" he said, "*'and the truth will set you free.'*"

"Why would the sombra want me to buy diet pills?" Raquel asked, confused.

Relámpago sighed and leaned forward, his arms resting on his knees. "Raquel, it is the King's deepest desire to fulfill you," he told her, "to give you life more abundant. The enemy comes only to steal and kill and destroy. That is his ultimate purpose. He cares nothing for you as the King does." The criado paused and closed his eyes. "Help me, King," she heard him whisper. After a few moments, he opened his eyes again and looked at her. They shown with a renewed vitality. "Let me ask you a question, Raquel," he said. "Do you think it wise to lose any more weight?"

Raquel was appalled by the question. What she did with her own body was none of his business. Where did he get off asking her such a personal question?

Still, this was Relámpago she was talking to; arguing with him did no good. She would have to find a way to answer his question without really answering it. She thought for a moment. "I think the King wants me to look good," she said smugly.

The criado's eyes pierced her like lasers—burning a hole in her. She looked away, knowing she hadn't fooled him, that she hadn't answered the question. She was silent for a few moments, hoping he would continue the conversation, but apparently he was waiting for her to properly respond. She glanced back at him; his eyes were still on her and she looked away again.

Finally resolved that she had no choice but to come up with a better answer, she said, "I mean…" She paused. She felt her face burning. The truth was in his eyes: *She shouldn't lose any more weight*. But Raquel couldn't accept that. She *wouldn't* accept that.

"I don't *know,* Relámpago!" she cried, her face hot. "Just… *leave me alone!"* She covered her face with her hands, hating herself for the tears that were finding their way to the surface.

"You know the truth, don't you?" she heard Relámpago's gentle, resonant voice say.

She shuddered.

"You know that you should discontinue the diet."

"I *can't,* alright!" she cried, looking up at him through her tears. "I want to look good, *okay?* Is that such a crime?"

"You desire beauty more than you desire life, Raquel," her guardian criado replied calmly, his voice compassionate but unrelenting. "In the end, you will destroy both."

"*Everybody* goes on diets!" she shouted. "It *is* possible to be on a diet *and live!*"

"And it is possible to be on a diet and die," Relámpago countered.

Raquel shook her head. How could she make this winged man understand? This wasn't Paraíso; things were different here. Here, looks were everything. It meant the difference between happiness and misery—success and failure. *Thinness equals beauty*. Wasn't that what all the TV commercials said? Wasn't that what all the magazine articles portrayed? Wasn't that what all the computer websites claimed?

Seeing that his words were not reaching her, Relámpago let out a heavy sigh and leaned back against the couch. He studied her for several seconds with his probing eyes. "Rest assured, Raquel," he said resolutely, "that Tentación will be back. As long as you choose to believe his lies, he will return. I will be powerless to protect you."

"I thought that was your job," she sniffed bitterly, not looking at him.

"There is only so much I can do," the criado informed her. "I am able to guard you physically, but you must guard yourself, Raquel, in every other way. *'My child, pay attention to what I say. Listen carefully to my words. Don't lose sight of them. Let them penetrate deep into your heart, for they bring life to those who find them, and healing to their whole body. Guard your heart above all else, for it determines the course of your life. Avoid all perverse talk; stay away from corrupt speech. Look straight ahead, and fix your eyes on what lies before you. Mark out a straight path for your feet; stay on the safe path. Don't get sidetracked; keep your feet from following evil.'*"

He waited for her to respond, but Raquel continued to look away.

"'The King does not look at the things man looks at. Man looks at the outward appearance, but the King looks at the

heart.' The Book of Light is full of love and life-giving words, little warrior," Relámpago told her. "It is *here* you will find the meaning of true beauty."

Chapter 18

Valentine's Day

Raquel hated Relámpago's words, and she hated Relámpago for trying to control her life. Is this what the King was like? Did he want to control her, too? Then she wanted nothing to do with him.

He must have wanted something to do with *her,* though, because he wouldn't leave her alone. Relámpago's words kept ringing in her ears, and just when Raquel had managed to forget, she'd look in the mirror and see the belt of truth. She was a warrior—there was no escaping it. Wouldn't the King *ever* give up on her? Wouldn't there come a point when he would finally leave her alone? She wasn't loving him back; why was he still loving her?

Love. The only *real* love she knew about for sure was between her and Gabe. Now *this* was love! It was a physical thing she could feel every time he kissed her. It didn't leave her feeling satisfied, but at least it was real. At least Gabe didn't think she looked anything less than beautiful. Relámpago had said it himself: The King didn't care if she was beautiful or not.

But Gabe cared, and he was taking every opportunity to show it. Valentine's Day was around the corner, and he told her to expect big things. As it turned out, he was telling the truth. When the day arrived, she found a note in her locker gushing his love for her—telling her how beautiful she was and how lucky he felt to have her in his life. Now *these* were life-giving words!

Later in the day, she found a gorgeous pink corsage attached to her locker. *Be my date for prom night,* she read.

Raquel had never felt more elated. There would be a seventh and eighth grade prom at the end of the school year, and out of the whole school he was inviting *her!* Her next class was English, but she ran instead to the nearest restroom to try on the corsage. Looking in the mirror, she pinned the pink flower over her heart. It was beautiful; she felt like a princess.

Then, in her reflection, the corsage disappeared as a metal breastplate covered her torso. Raquel gasped, taken by surprise. The breastplate was shiny and silver with a cursive letter "R" where the corsage had been. Raquel couldn't remember what the "R" stood for.

The belt and now the breastplate: gifts from the King. But she preferred to look at her corsage instead. She looked down and was shocked to see that the corsage was not visible; the breastplate covered over it. Her hands flew to her torso and her heart began to race as Raquel found herself able to feel the cold metal beneath her fingers. It was not merely in her reflection; she was actually wearing it! The belt was around her waist, as well—overlapping the breastplate.

The first thought to cross her mind was how she was going to go the rest of the school day dressed in armor, but this thought quickly vanished when she looked and saw the enormous black shadow standing nearby. It stood hunched over the way Tentación had—its long, curved claws ready to attack.

Raquel screamed, but she knew that she couldn't count on Sara to come to her rescue this time. Sara was nowhere nearby; she was in the seventh grade wing.

Tentación took a calculated step toward her and stopped—no doubt wanting to get her reaction. He got a reaction, alright. Raquel jumped and let out another blood-curdling scream. Tentación was unresponsive but continued to stare her down. Raquel felt herself break out into a cold sweat; there was nothing she could do to escape the creature. Relámpago was not here to fight it off, or if he was he was choosing not to show himself. With chills, she recalled his words: *"Tentación will be back. As long as you choose to believe his lies, he will return. I will be powerless to protect you."*

She was on her own this time.

The creature took another step toward her. Raquel could feel her heart pounding beneath her breastplate. Tentación seemed to be playing with her—enjoying watching her writhe helplessly before him. *Just like a cat playing with a mouse,* Raquel thought with a shudder.

Suddenly, a verse from the Book of Light popped into her head: *Temptation comes from our own desires, which entice us and drag us away.* Raquel whispered the verse aloud to herself.

Tentación had begun to take another step toward her, but as soon as she said the verse he stopped. Raquel noticed. Was he afraid of the Book of Light? Sara had said that the Book of Light was like a sword. Is this what she meant?

Raquel tried hard to think of another verse, but her mind was frozen. It had been over a month since she'd read from the Book of Light; nothing was coming to mind. And she couldn't use it as a reference because she'd left the Book at home; she couldn't remember the last time she'd brought it to school. She wished now that she had it with her.

The sombra noticed her hesitation and began advancing toward her quickly. Raquel shrieked and only had time to raise her hands in terror before the creature sunk its claws into the top of her head.

An image of Gabe flashed across her mind. She could see him smiling seductively at her with his dark brown eyes and black hair. He was reaching toward her to touch her cheek.

Why was she thinking of Gabe at a time like this? Was the sombra putting the thought into her head?

Raquel struggled to get loose, but Tentación's hold on her was firm. She looked over her shoulder at him; he seemed to be laughing down at her—his snake-like tongue darting about.

Suddenly, a new thought flew into her mind: Gabe was leaning toward her and pressing his lips against hers. She could feel the rush it gave her as though it were actually happening. She could feel his strong hands around her waist.

A return to reality revealed that the creature still loomed above her. She looked up at it and it shoved its claws in with a renewed fervor.

Now Raquel saw herself at the prom. Gabe was gently pinning the pink corsage on her dress, grinning at her. He reached over and squeezed her leg.

Raquel caught her breath. The thought brought a rush of adrenaline, but it somehow carried a sense of foreboding, as well. The feeling felt right, but somehow it felt wrong, too. It felt dangerous. *Mark out a straight path for your feet; stay on the safe path*. Relámpago's words echoed her in mind.

Tentación instantly recoiled—releasing her head and taking to the air, landing a safe distance away from her. Raquel stood staring at it, breathing heavily. What had caused the creature to react this way? Was it the words from the Book of Light?

Raquel repeated the verse aloud. "'*Mark out a straight path for your feet; stay on the safe path,*'" she quoted timidly.

She watched in amazement as the large shadow dropped to the floor—cowering like a frightened animal and hissing at her through clenched teeth. It looked ready to pounce at the slightest hint of weakness—wings outstretched and curved claws ready to attack.

But Raquel wouldn't give it that chance. "Get away from me!" she shouted.

The shadow didn't move except to continue its heavy breathing.

"You have no power over me, Tentación, as long as I don't believe your lies!"

The dark shadow remained where it was.

"I'm a warrior of the King!"

At the mention of the King, the creature made a move to leave and then seemed to think better of it and remained where it was.

"You can't hurt me because the King protects me!"

The sombra was gathering its strength to leap at her. She needed to think of something quick; how could she make it leave? What were sombras afraid of most?

The Prince!

Raquel recalled Sara's words: *"Our best defense is the Prince Himself. Just mention the Prince, Raquel, and sombras will flee. They* hate *hearing His Name."*

Well, it was time to find out.

With a great flapping of wings, Tentación came flying toward her. Raquel only had time to call out the Prince's Name before falling on the floor in terror before her attacker.

But it was time enough.

Raquel couldn't believe the effect that one simple word had on this creature. As soon as the Prince's Name crossed her lips, the sombra halted in midflight—opening its wings like a parachute to stop itself—and fell to the floor in a heap no more than two feet away from her before scrambling to the far side of the room. Once there, it remained on all-fours breathing heavily, and Raquel couldn't tell whether it spoke or hissed at her before existing through the wall.

With the creature gone, Raquel threw a hand over her racing heart. She felt the cold metal of the breastplate and smiled. She was a warrior. And for the first time she appreciated the fact.

The belt and breastplate slowly faded, leaving her hand to rest against Gabe's corsage. She recoiled at the touch. She remembered the image that Tentación had placed in her mind of Gabe pinning it on her at the prom—and what he had done afterward. A chill swept through her; the thought frightened her, though she hardly knew why. All she knew was that she felt an overwhelming sense of foreboding.

Raquel's hands flew to the corsage—yanking it from her shirt and throwing it to the floor as though it contained poison. She slowly backed away from it.

What was she *doing?* Didn't she *want* to go to the prom with Gabe? "What's the matter, Raquel?" she heard herself ask. "Are you going to throw away the best thing that's ever happened to you?"

Moving slowly and cautiously, she bent over and with trembling hands picked up the pink flower. Her heart raced in her chest as she held it—whether from fear or excitement she didn't know. All she knew was that she couldn't throw it away. Not yet, anyway.

At the end of the day, she was at her locker when she felt two strong hands grab her around the waist. It startled her so much that she let out a cry.

She heard Gabe's laughter behind her. "A little jumpy, aren't we?"

Embarrassed, she turned around to face him. He looked just the way he always did—playful smile, dark hair framing his face, gorgeous brown eyes—but somehow he looked different to her, too.

He leaned in to kiss her.

Raquel gasped and backed away from him.

Puzzled, Gabe looked at her strangely. "What's wrong?" he asked. "Are you mad at me about something? Didn't you get the Valentine's Day note I left in your locker and the corsage?"

Raquel suddenly felt like a jerk. "Oh, yeah, I got it," she said softly, wiping her sweaty palms on her jeans. "Thank you, Gabe, it's beautiful."

He smiled and moved in closer. "You *will* accept my invitation, I hope."

"Invitation?"

He searched her eyes. "The prom?"

"Oh, of course," Raquel said nervously.

"You do want to go with me, don't you?"

"Of course I do."

Gabe looked at her curiously. "You don't sound too sure," he said. He sounded mad about it.

I can't lose him, Raquel thought. "Of course I'm sure," Raquel said, draping an arm over his shoulder.

Gabe smiled and took her by the waist again—pulling her toward him and kissing her on the lips. All of the old feelings were still there, but Raquel wasn't fully enjoying it the way she usually did. As his kiss became more forceful, Raquel felt herself becoming more and more afraid rather than more excited. She pulled away from him and took a step back.

"Why are you acting so weird?" he demanded, looking at her with disdain.

Butterflies fluttered in her stomach. *Don't lose him, Raquel!* "I—I've just had a rough day, that's all," she said.

"Isn't this making it better?"

"No. I mean—" she added quickly, "It's just... I have so much homework and everything..."

"How can you think about homework at a time like this?" Gabe asked incredulously. "How can you *think* at all?"

His question confused her. Was Gabe asking her not to think? Did he want her only to *feel* but not to *think?*

Gabe didn't like the way she was looking at him. "What's your problem?" he asked angrily. "Here I try and make Valentine's Day special for you, and this is the thanks I get?"

"I already told you thank you, Gabe," Raquel said defensively. "What more do you want me to say?"

"Can't you hear yourself?" he said, his voice level rising. "You're acting insane!"

"I am not," Raquel insisted, her voice level rising to meet his. "And I don't appreciate being referred to as 'insane'!"

"Then don't act like it!"

"How am I acting 'insane,' Gabe? Just because I don't want your hands all over me?"

He gave her a startled look as though she had slapped him. Then his face turned red and the look was replaced by one of fury. He slammed his locker closed. "You can find somebody else to go to the prom with," he said coldly and started down the hall.

Don't lose him, Raquel!

Raquel slammed her own locker closed and ran after him. "Gabe, wait," she called. "I'm sorry, I didn't mean it."

"I think you did," he said without turning to look at her.

Raquel caught up to him. "I told you... I've just had a rough day, that's all."

He didn't look at her.

"Please, Gabe, I want to go to the prom with you."

"Why?" he asked in a raspy voice. "You've made it clear that you don't want 'my hands all over you.'"

Raquel knew that she should end the conversation right here and just walk away, but instead she heard herself say, "What, you mean like this?" and took his face in her hands, kissing him fiercely on the mouth.

Gabe stopped dead in his tracks, unable to catch his breath. When Raquel pulled back to see his reaction, she knew his invitation still stood.

Chapter 19

Supper

It was official: She would be Gabe's date for the prom! She couldn't believe it!

All the way home, Raquel concentrated on this fact and not on the mixed feelings she'd had as she kissed Gabe. What was there to be scared of? So what if the sombra had put images in her mind of Gabe; did that mean Gabe was a bad person? Maybe Tentación had just been trying to confuse her. If so, it was working. She felt sure that she could shake the feeling of danger that she'd had when she was with him today. Things would be better tomorrow; she was just shook up because of the sombra incident. She had no regrets of accepting his invitation to the prom; in fact, it made her pulse race with excitement just thinking about it!

Her mom was still at work when she got home, so she grabbed some grapes out of the fridge for a quick snack before going for a jog around the block. (She now knew better than to run on an empty stomach.) When she got back, she immediately stepped on the scale: She'd dropped a pound since that morning. Raquel smiled; she was on the right track.

With the prom only a little more than two months away, she decided she'd better cut down on the calories even more. She decided to limit herself to 200 calories per meal rather than the 300-calorie plan she'd been on. She couldn't risk gaining weight and having Gabe choose someone else to go with.

Her mom came home carrying a load of groceries. "Raquel, could you help me carry in the groceries, please?" It was more of a command than a request. After bringing in several loads of groceries, Raquel helped her mom put them away. It was torture looking at all that food knowing that she couldn't eat most of it. But at the same time, it gave her a feeling of power: She was strong enough to keep from eating it.

She put the groceries away in silence, and when she was done she gave her mom a quick smile before heading for her room.

"Don't go too far," her mom called after her. "I have a special supper planned for us tonight."

Raquel felt her stomach do a somersault as she turned to look at her mom. "Oh, yeah?" she said nervously.

Her mom was smiling. Raquel was surprised; her mom was rarely happy about anything. "Well, it's Valentine's Day, isn't it?" she said with a grin, continuing to take groceries out of the sacks. "We're going to celebrate tonight."

What was this all about? Did her mom somehow know about her new diet plan and was trying to sabotage it? Since when did they have a "special supper" together? Normally, they ate separately, her mom in front of the TV and Raquel in her room. This allowed her to eat as much—or as little—as she pleased. What would she do if she had to eat in front of her mom?

"You know, Mom," Raquel said, hoping that she sounded casual. "I'm honestly not all that hungry tonight. Thanks for the thought, though."

Her mom looked hurt. She must have been planning this "special supper" all day.

Raquel thought fast; there had to be some way around this. "Since it's Valentine's Day, Mom," she said quickly, "there was a party at school with all kinds of chocolate, and I filled up on that so I'm really not hungry at all." It was a stupid lie; she hadn't had Valentine's Day parties at school since she was in elementary school.

But her mom bought it. "Oh," she said quietly. She began to put the groceries away more slowly.

Raquel's heart sank. Was she actually feeling guilty about lying to her mom, or was it that she couldn't stand to see her mom looking so sad? Either way, something made her say with a sigh, "Okay, Mom. I'll eat supper with you."

Her mom's face immediately brightened. Raquel was glad she'd given in.

Until suppertime. Her mom had gone all out. She'd bought lasagna, breadsticks, salad, Coca-Cola, and even a chocolate cake... none of which Raquel was allowed to eat except for the salad (as long as it didn't have dressing). One serving of lasagna alone was 385 calories! She could eat a breadstick and some salad—a breadstick was 70 calories and salad was 30—but that was the absolute most she could have since the grapes she'd had earlier had 100 calories: That fulfilled her 200-calorie limit right there. And of course the Coke and chocolate cake were *completely* off limits.

As she sat at the dining room table with her mom, Raquel began to wonder how she was going to pull this off. She knew she couldn't leave; her mom looked so proud sitting there. She would be crushed if she decided to get up and leave now.

The aroma was overwhelming. There were few things Raquel liked better than lasagna, and the smell of it was making her mouth water. Maybe she could eat just one bite.

No, Raquel! she reprimanded herself. *Remember your diet plan! You don't want to get fat, do you?*

Would one meal *really* make her fat? Surely she could splurge just this once.

No, she shouldn't risk it. She knew what the scale would read after such a large meal, and she didn't like having to throw it up. No, she would have to figure out a way to keep from eating while at the same time appearing as though she were.

Her mom looked across the table at her and smiled. Raquel tried her best to smile back. She reached for her fork, but then her mom surprised her by bowing her head and closing her eyes. "Thank you for this food, Lord," she prayed. "Please use it to nourish our bodies. Amen." She looked back up at Raquel with a smile and proceeded to eat.

Raquel was shocked. She'd never seen her mom pray before. When did *this* start?

Use this food to nourish our bodies. What a laugh. The only thing food was good for was making you fat!

Raquel took her fork in hand and did all she could to stall for time. "So... did you have a nice Valentine's Day, Mom?" she asked.

Her mom looked up at her, chewing a bite of lasagna. "It was okay," she said with a smile. "How was yours?"

"Oh, it was great!" Raquel said excitedly, hoping she didn't sound overly excited.

"What made it so great?" her mom asked, taking another bite. "The Valentine's Day party?"

Raquel found herself not wanting to lie to her mom. "Actually," she said, clearing her throat and cutting a piece of her lasagna, "I got asked out to the prom." As soon as the words had escaped her lips, Raquel felt all the blood rush to her face. Now her mom would ask her a million questions about Gabe.

"Wow, that's exciting," her mom said with a smile. "I didn't even know your school was having a prom. Congratulations."

"Thanks," said Raquel, cutting the piece she'd already cut into smaller pieces.

"What the boy's name?"

Raquel continued looking down at her plate and cleared her throat. "Gabe," she said softly.

"That's a nice name. Is he cute?"

Raquel looked up from her plate. Her mom was smiling. Strangely, Raquel didn't feel as though her mom were prying; she was just making conversation. Raquel giggled, blushing again. "Yeah, he's cute," she said, smiling down at her plate.

Her mom took another bite. "Did he *kiss* ya?" she asked playfully, her mouth full of food.

Raquel tried to stifle laughter and it came out as a snort instead. She'd never talked with her mom so freely before about her private life... or *anything,* for that matter. She kind of liked it.

Raquel gave a quick shrug. "Maybe," she said, her smile giving her away.

"Oooh, Raquel's in *love,"* her mom cooed.

Raquel snorted again.

"Did he getcha a big ole box of chocolates?"

Raquel smiled, cutting off a big piece of lasagna. It smelled so delicious she considered taking a bite. No, if she took one bite she wouldn't be able to stop herself from eating more. *Just concentrate on the conversation, Raquel,* she told herself. "No," she answered, "but he gave me a corsage for the prom."

"What color?"

"Pink."

"Oh, how pretty."

Raquel couldn't believe this; she and her mom were actually *talking!*

When her mom looked down at her plate, Raquel stabbed the big piece of lasagna she'd just cut and hid it in her paper napkin.

"Do you know yet what you're gonna wear?" her mom asked, looking up at her, chewing a bite of salad.

Raquel was jealous; her mom was eating her salad with Ranch dressing. Raquel *loved* Ranch dressing, but it had 73 calories.

She took a small bite of her breadstick. It tasted *so* good! *Too* good, in fact. She quickly decided that it had to have more than 70 calories, so she wouldn't eat it. "I don't know," Raquel shrugged, stabbing a forkful of tasteless salad. "I was thinking I could buy something new."

Her mom took another bite of lasagna. "What about the dress your dad gave you?" she asked.

At the mention of her dad, Raquel felt her stomach turn. "Can we not talk about Dad, please?" she said.

Her mom's chewing slowed, and she looked at Raquel with a hurt expression.

Raquel didn't care. Her dad had succeeded in tearing their family apart, and she wanted nothing to do with him.

Her mom mechanically speared some of her salad onto her fork. "Alright," she said quietly.

Raquel squirmed in her chair. She cleared her throat. She had to think of something else to say to keep the conversation going; as long as she kept talking, she had a good excuse not to eat. She tried to change the subject. "So, did *you* get a big box of chocolates for Valentine's Day?" she asked her mom, knowing she didn't.

Her mom smiled slightly. "No," she said softly, then hesitated. "But I got a phone call from your dad."

Raquel dropped her fork onto her plate with a clang. "Mom, I thought I just got through telling you I didn't want to talk about *dad!*" she said angrily.

"Well, you asked, Raquel."

"I asked if you got *chocolates!*" she said, picking up her fork. Raquel could feel her face turning red. "That's all I asked!"

"Why don't you like for me to talk about your dad, Raquel?" asked her mom in an uncharacteristically calm voice, which only enraged Raquel more.

"Um... hmm, maybe because he *cheated* on you?" she said, spitting out the words with disdain.

She expected her mom to fight back—the way she always did—but instead she hung her head and picked at her food with her fork.

Why was her mom acting this way? Why did she have to bring up Dad at all? The conversation had been going so well up till now.

Her mom was sitting there in silence; Raquel felt like she had to say something. "Can't you just let him go, Mom?" she asked, frustrated with her mom for being so weak. "Why do you let him control you like this?"

She looked up at her. Raquel was shocked to see that her mom had tears in her eyes. "I love your dad, Raquel," she said simply.

"*Why?*" Raquel asked, determined to make her point despite her mom's tears. "Why do you still love him after all he's done to us?"

"It was a one-time thing, Raquel," her mom said sternly, "and I've forgiven him."

"Why?" Raquel demanded again. "So that he can just cheat on you again?"

Anger filled her mom's eyes; this was more the mom she knew. "Everyone makes mistakes, Raquel," she told her. "I still love your father, and he still loves me... and *you*."

"Then why did he leave us?"

She looked down sorrowfully. When her mom answered, her voice broke. "Because I told him to."

"And you had a *right* to kick him out, Mom!" Raquel insisted. "Anyone who cheats on his wife—"

"I cheated on him, too, Raquel," her mom interrupted.

Raquel gasped. No, it couldn't be true.

"Not physically," her mom added quickly, "but in other ways. I cheated him out of happiness and peace and…" Her voice trailed off. "Believe me, Raquel," she continued, "your father is doing me a great kindness by wanting to give me a second chance."

Raquel couldn't believe what she was hearing. "You would actually consider getting back together with someone who… gave his love… to someone else?" she asked incredulously.

Her mom looked at her determinedly. "Your father has never given his love to anyone other than me," she told her. "Your dad has always loved me. It's *me* who hasn't given my love to *him.*"

"You actually believe that?"

"It's true, Raquel."

"Then why did he go and sleep with someone else?"

"Love is not about that, Raquel," her mom stated emphatically. "It goes beyond sleeping with someone. It's a commitment to care for someone no matter what happens."

Raquel couldn't wrap her mind around what her mom was saying. She was making the word "love" sound so complicated, but really love was very simple: It was something physical. She felt it whenever Gabe touched her. When her dad had cheated on his mom, he had given his love to someone else, which meant that he no longer loved *them.* That's what it all came down to.

Raquel shook her head contemptuously. "Wow, Mom," she said, smiling smugly. "He's sure got you fooled."

Her mom's face turned red and she dropped her fork onto her plate. "Now you listen to me, young lady," she said, grabbing a tight hold of her napkin. "You will *not* say another word against your father, do you understand?"

Raquel smiled triumphantly. This was the mom she was more familiar with; she knew how to fight *this* mom.

But strangely, she didn't feel like fighting. Just the thought of hurting her mom gave her a sick feeling in the pit of her stomach. *Why?* Was it because she was a warrior now? Was the King beginning to change her heart?

Raquel sighed, put the napkin on her plate that hid the lasagna, and scooted back from the table to go scrape the uneaten food into the trash. "Fine, Mom," she said. "Have it your way."

Chapter 20

Love Song

Raquel didn't feel like doing homework. She turned on the TV in her room, but she soon discovered that she didn't feel like exercising, either. Besides, she didn't have the energy to work out; she'd only eaten one bite of salad and one bite of breadstick for supper.

Unable to concentrate, she finally turned the TV off and fell down on her bed—staring up at the ceiling. Why did her mom have to bring up her dad? Didn't she know that it always led to arguing? Was her mom trying to fix everything? You can't fix something like that. Her mom was wrong about her dad loving them; love that's been given away to someone else is gone for good. There was no turning back for her parents, and it was cruel of her mom to give her reason to hope. The damage had been done; there *were* no second chances.

For some reason, words from the Book of Light came to mind: *Man looks at the outward appearance, but the King looks at the heart.*

Why had she thought that? Was the King wanting her to read the Book?

She ignored the thought; just because a thought enters your head doesn't mean that someone is putting it there. Still, the thought wouldn't go away, so heaving a great sigh she threw herself into a sitting position and tried to remember where she'd put the Book of Light. It had been so long since she'd read it...

It was over on her dresser hidden beneath fashion magazines. She got up and brought it back to her bed—leaning back against her pillow with a sigh and opening the book, forgetting to be careful. The book's light hit her eyes and it stung, but after a few seconds the effect was gone and she found herself able to look down at the page without any trouble at all. Was she starting to adjust to the Book?

She began reading on the page she'd turned to:

If I speak in the tongues of men and of criados, but have not love, I am only a resounding gong or a clanging cymbal. If I have the gift of prophecy and can fathom all mysteries and all knowledge, and if I have a faith that can move mountains, but have not love, I am nothing. If I give all I possess to the poor and surrender my body to the flames, but have not love, I gain nothing.

Raquel couldn't believe the coincidence; she'd just gotten through talking with her mom about love, and now here she was reading about it in the Book of Light. Did the King direct her to this chapter?

She continued reading:

Love is patient, love is kind. It does not envy, it does not boast, it is not proud. It is not rude, it is not self-seeking, it is not easily angered, it keeps no record of wrongs. Love does not delight in evil but rejoices with the truth. It always protects, always trusts, always hopes, always perseveres. Love never fails.

Raquel paused. The Book had just defined "love": Patient. Kind. Not envying. Not boastful. Not proud. Not rude. Not self-seeking. Not easily angered. Not holding grudges. Not delighting in evil. Rejoicing with the truth.

Always protecting. Always trusting.

Always *hoping?* Always *persevering?*

Never failing?

This was the definition of love?

There was nothing whatsoever about the *physical* aspect of love. Why hadn't it mentioned *that?*

Raquel looked down at the page again:

When I was a child, I talked like a child, I thought like a child, I reasoned like a child. But when I grew up, I put childish ways behind me. Now we see but a poor reflection as in a mirror; then we shall see face to face. Now I know in part; then I shall know fully, even as I am fully known.

And now these three remain: faith, hope and love. But the greatest of these is love.

Raquel sat there staring down at the page—for how long, she didn't know. *Now I know in part; then I shall know fully, even as I am fully known. And now these three remain: faith, hope and love. But the greatest of these is love.*

She was "fully known" by the King? And yet He *loved* her? Why? She'd just spent the last month ignoring Him!

This was what *real* love looked like—loving someone when they don't deserve it? Did she love her dad that way? Did she love *anybody* that way? What about Gabe? He certainly didn't love *her* that way. She remembered the expression on his face when she told him she didn't want him touching her. He would have given up on her right then if she hadn't run after him.

Does *true love* act that way?

Her mind and heart raced with so many conflicting feelings.

She *wanted* Gabe. She *needed* him!

But did she, really? Did she want to be with someone who didn't love her back? If the Book's definition of love was the real one, did Gabe love her at all? Was he patient? Was he kind? Was he *anything* on that list?

Raquel's head hurt. She placed the Book of Light on the bed without closing it and laid her head down on her pillow. She felt drowsy. She smiled at the open Book beside her—her eyes closing on the dancing beacon of light.

When she awoke, night had fallen. The Book of Light was still open and bright next to her.

No longer tired, she got up and went downstairs. Her mom had probably gone to bed hours ago. She considered getting on the computer, but the only thing she used the computer for these days was entering her daily calorie count, and she didn't feel like doing that.

She turned on the overhead light, sat down on the couch, and sighed. What was she supposed to do now?

The family's grand piano sat in the far corner. She hadn't used it since moving here. She used to play on it all the time; her dad had insisted that she take piano lessons all throughout her childhood. He was an accomplished musician, and he wanted her to be, too. She used to *hate* practicing but had actually grown to enjoy it. She was pretty good, although she knew she wasn't as good as her dad.

She thought she might like to play on it again.

Standing, Raquel walked over to the large black piano and took a seat on the bench. She didn't think she would wake her mom up; her bedroom was at the far end of the house.

She began to feel nervous. It had been a while; would she remember any of her old songs? She had several pieces memorized, but she was afraid that nothing would come back to her.

There was only one way to find out. She placed her fingers on the keys and began to play.

A feeling of ecstasy rolled over her; her fingers were remembering the notes! It was as though she'd never stopped playing. Her fingers danced over the keys like skillful dancers—her upper body flowing with the rhythm.

Raquel closed her eyes and let the music carry her away. Her thoughts drifted back to the many piano recitals she'd taken part in over the years. She used to hate them; nothing ever made her more nervous than playing in front of people. But she remembered them with fondness, too: Her parents had always been there to cheer for her. Her dad would drop everything to be sure and be in attendance for her recitals. That had always meant the world to her. She had forgotten.

She hit a wrong note and she opened her eyes to correct it. As she did, she noticed a dark shadow standing over by the computer.

Her heart leapt in her chest. She looked down: the belt and breastplate had materialized. When she looked to her left, she saw that Relámpago had materialized, as well.

"Keep playing," he told her, his tone serious and his eyes on the sombra.

"What?" Raquel asked in amazement.

"Keep playing," the Native American criado repeated without diverting his attention from the shadow.

"You do realize there's a sombra in the room, right?"

Relámpago said nothing as he slowly walked around behind her and then to her right—placing himself between her and the shadow. "Keep playing," he said simply, "and sing."

And sing? She could play, but she couldn't sing!

"I *can't* sing, Relámpago," she informed him. "And even if I *could,* do you really think this is the best time to be singing?"

For the first time since he'd begun speaking to her, Relámpago turned to look at her with a smile. "It is the *perfect* time for singing," he said. His eyes sparkled mischievously. "Would you enjoy torturing a sombra tonight, little warrior?"

Raquel didn't understand, but she had to admit she liked the idea of torturing a sombra.

"What songs do you know?" he asked her, turning back to face the sombra.

"Can't you just attack it with your sword, the way you did last time?" Raquel wondered.

"Do you know any love songs to the King?" Relámpago asked, undeterred.

Love songs *to the King?* "No," she said, keeping a watchful eye on the sombra.

"That's alright," said the criado, taking a few more steps toward the sombra. "I know enough for the both of us."

The sombra was beginning to look nervous; it took a step back.

"How is singing going to make it go away, Relámpago?" Raquel asked insistently.

"You will see. I recommend that you take a hold of something, little warrior," he told her without turning to face her. "I cannot be responsible for what my wings do when I am praising my King."

Raquel grabbed a tight hold of the piano.

Tilting his head back toward the ceiling and lifting his mighty arms high above his head, the Native American criado began to sing. He sang in another language—the most beautiful sound Raquel had ever heard. His voice was deep and rich. She sat there spellbound.

Immediately upon singing, the criado's wings fluttered once and then began to flap incessantly. The longer he sang, the more powerful the beating of the wings became. She soon realized what a good thing it was that he had advised her to grab a hold of something, because she found herself nearly being blown off the piano bench. Before too long, the flapping became so forceful that the criado's feet were no longer on the floor but rather hovering above it. And still he didn't stop. He continued on—the singing and beating of the wings becoming stronger until he was slowly rising to the ceiling.

From the moment the singing began, the sombra had dropped to the floor—throwing its clawed hands to the sides of its head and opening its mouth—no doubt howling in an attempt to drown out the singing. It wasn't having any difficulty bracing itself against the windstorm created by the criado's wings, but bracing itself against the power of the singing was proving difficult for it. It refused to even look at Relámpago, and it had seemingly forgotten all about Raquel. She watched in amazement as the muscular shadow sat hunkered on the floor like a frightened child. A couple different times during the song, the sombra flinched as though it had just been hit over the head; Raquel wondered if Relámpago had used the Prince's Name. Unable to take any more, the sombra finally slunk away into the shadows—unable to find the strength to use its wings.

Sensing the sombra's absence, Relámpago stopped singing and began to lower himself—keeping his eyes and arms raised until his feet touched the floor. Raquel found herself wishing for the singing to continue.

With one final flutter of his wings, the Native American criado slowly lowered his arms and turned to face her—eyes shining and a corner of his mouth turned upward in amusement. "Works every time," he chuckled.

"That was *incredible!*" Raquel breathed.

Unable to stop grinning, Relámpago seemed hesitant to remain on the floor. With a flap of his enormous wings, he took a seat on the grand piano. "Not so incredible as when warriors sing," he told her, smiling down at her.

"I seriously doubt that," Raquel laughed.

"When criados sing," he said, "it does not mean as much as when warriors sing."

"What do you mean?" Raquel asked.

"Warriors have been *forgiven,*" he explained. "Criados have not since they have done nothing that necessitates forgiveness. For this reason, the King would much prefer to hear love songs sung to him by His warriors; it means more coming from them." Relámpago smiled. "Criados are familiar with the greatness of the King, but warriors are even *more* familiar."

"You think I know the King better than *you* do?" Raquel asked incredulously.

"You have experienced a portion of His love, little warrior, that no criado will ever have the privilege of experiencing. You have experienced His *grace*." Relámpago's eyes were so bright that Raquel blinked. "*'For the King so loved the world that He gave His one and only Son, that whoever believes in Him shall not perish but have eternal life.'*"

Raquel smiled up at her criado. "That's from the Book of Light, isn't it?" she said.

Relámpago nodded. "The King loves you so much, Raquel, that I cannot speak of it. Not without creating a windstorm, that is."

Raquel laughed.

"Above all else He desires that His warriors love Him back."

Raquel was surprised to find herself actually *wanting* to love Him back. "How can I do that?" she asked shyly.

Relámpago's grin widened. "By loving others, little warrior," he said, "and by giving the gifts He's given you back to Him. *'Therefore, as the King's chosen people, holy and dearly loved, clothe yourselves with compassion, kindness, humility, gentleness and patience. Bear with each other and forgive whatever grievances you may have against one another. Forgive as the King forgave you. And over all these virtues put on love, which binds them all together in perfect unity. Let the peace of the Prince rule in your hearts, since as members of one body you were called to peace. And be thankful. Let the word of the Prince dwell in you richly as you teach and admonish one another with all wisdom, and as you sing psalms, hymns and spiritual songs with gratitude in your hearts to the King. And whatever you do, whether in word or deed, do it all in the Name of the Prince, giving thanks to your Father the King through Him.'"*

Raquel waited for him to continue, and was a little disappointed when he didn't. Placing her fingers on the keys of the piano, she looked up at her guardian criado with a smile. "I can't sing," she informed him, "but I can play."

And she began to play—this time for the King.

Chapter 21

The Point of No Return

Raquel had the weekend to think over all that had transpired here lately. What a Valentine's Day this had turned out to be—full of so many ups and downs that Raquel felt like she was on a giant roller coaster. She'd been elated when Gabe invited her to the prom, and less than 24 hours later she was wondering if he even loved her at all. She'd been enraged when her mom had brought up her dad, and now she was starting to care about him again. She'd decided that the King wasn't worth her time, and now she couldn't get His Book off her mind.

What was going *on* with her?

These conflicting thoughts and emotions were maddening. What should she do about Gabe? Should she go with him to the prom or not? If not, it was only fair to tell him so that he could ask somebody else.

Ask somebody else? Are you *crazy*, Raquel?

She was beginning to think so.

Would the King want her to go with him?

Who cares what the King wants! Just go *with him!*

Raquel was growing tired of the endless conversations going on in her head. Which thoughts should she listen to? Which voice spoke the truth?

By Monday morning, she'd reluctantly decided that she shouldn't go with Gabe. She didn't think he felt for her the Book of Light's definition of love. Or if he did, he had a strange way of showing it.

But what excuse would she give?

The thought plagued her as she neared the lockers. Did she have what it took to do this? Was she even convinced she *should* be doing this?

Don't back down now, Raquel. "Then you will know the truth, and the truth will set you free."

But what is *the truth?* Raquel wondered. *I wish I knew…*

She felt Gabe's hands around her waist, and she shivered.

"Hey, sexy lady," he said, leaning in close and kissing her on the neck. "Did you miss me this weekend?"

It's now or never, Raquel, she told herself. She turned to face him.

This was going to be harder than she thought. His smile melted her heart the way it always did.

C'mon, Raquel, you can do this! Stay strong!

She opened her mouth to speak to him, but before she could get a word out he was kissing her full on the lips. Oh, what his kisses did to her! She felt herself relax as a gentle warmth rushed all through her body. When he cupped her face in his hands and kissed her harder, Raquel found herself wanting more, not less.

No! She had to turn him down! He didn't love her!

Or did he? She should try to find out for sure before turning him down. Otherwise, it wouldn't be fair to him.

"Gabe," she said, after he had allowed her to come up for air. "There's something I wanted to ask you."

His hands reached behind her back, accidentally brushing her front along the way. A shiver shot down her spine.

It *had* been an accident...right?

"Gabe," she started again, as he pulled her toward him. "How do you feel about me?"

"You *know* how I feel about you, baby," he said, brushing a strand of her hair behind her ear.

She felt so warm here next to him. Her whole body felt alive. "Do you *love* me?" she asked.

"Of course I do," he said softly, kissing her again.

Her pulse raced. Maybe he *did* love her! This certainly *felt* like love.

But, at the same time, there was a gnawing feeling in the pit of her stomach that wouldn't leave her alone. *He's using you,* a voice said. *He doesn't love you.*

She looked at him, his hands on the small of her back. How could the way he was looking at her be anything *but* love?

"Why?" she asked.

"Why?" he said, confused.

"Why do you love me?"

He laughed and she could feel his body shaking against hers. "I love you because of what you do to me," he said. "Whenever I hold you, I feel alive."

I feel the exact same way! Raquel thought.

But why does he love you, *Raquel?* the nagging voice persisted. *Is he truly loving you or loving the way you make him feel?*

Raquel decided to find out. "I feel the same way," she told him. "But what do you love about *me?*"

"I'm not following you," he said, gently kissing her neck.

He sure wasn't making this easy. "I mean, what do you love about me that's different from other girls?"

"Other girls?" he asked, genuinely alarmed. "There *are* no other girls, baby."

She wasn't sure how to put what she was trying to say into words. "I mean," she said again, "what do you love about me that you don't love about anyone else?"

"I told you," he said, leaning to kiss her on the lips again. "Only you make me come alive."

Back off from him, Raquel!

The warning in her head was so clear and straightforward that she took a step back.

"What's the matter, sweetheart?" he asked. He looked hurt.

Ask the question again, Raquel.

"What do you love about *me,* though," she asked, her voice trembling.

"I don't understand your question," he said, clasping her hands in his. "I love you for *you.*"

"But what *about* me do you love, Gabe?" she inquired, feeling her courage increasing.

Gabe truly seemed at a loss for words. She expected him to say something like, "You're sweet" or "You're funny" or "You're smart." After all, they'd been together for over a month now; surely there was *something* nice he could find to say about her.

She watched him smile his seductive smile. "You're the most beautiful girl in school," he told her.

A month ago, that would have flattered her. Now she found herself asking, *Is that all?*

"But what about the *inside* of me, Gabe? Do you care about what's on the *inside*?"

Now he looked offended. His eyes flashed. Then he quickly recovered and he tried to smile, but Raquel could tell it was fake. "Of course I do," he said, his voice raspy.

"Then tell me, Gabe," she said, pulling her hands out of his grasp. "Tell me what you love about me."

He opened his mouth, and then closed it again.

He couldn't think of anything!

He doesn't love you because he doesn't know *you,* she heard the voice say.

This reality hit her like a bucket of ice water.

Raquel stood there speechless. The shock and hurt must have been evident on her face, because Gabe reached for her hands again. "What's wrong, baby?" he asked. "What did I say?"

Raquel tried to laugh, blinking back tears. "It's what you *didn't* say," she told him.

"What didn't I say?" he asked, holding her hands tightly in his. "I'll try and make it right."

She shook her head. "Don't you see, Gabe?" she said, seeing him for the first time through rational thought rather than emotions. "You don't know what you love about me because you don't really *know* me."

She expected for him to be offended and perhaps even push her away, but what she didn't expect was for him to draw her gently to him and wrap his arms around her—holding her close. "Then let me get to know you," he whispered in her ear.

A barrage of conflicting thoughts and emotions flowed through her. She didn't expect him to answer this way, and so she wasn't prepared for it. She knew she should back away from him; the voice in her head was telling her to do just that.

But she found that she couldn't. She was enjoying this too much. She needed to feel his strong arms around her as much as she needed air to breathe. She imagined what life would be like without him—without having him here every day at school to tell her how beautiful she was. Without feeling his electrifying touch. She couldn't imagine it. She didn't want to.

When Gabe took her face in his hands again and kissed her gently on the mouth, her lips tingled and she felt her heart flutter in her chest.

She felt the pang in the pit of her stomach, too, but she ignored it.

She couldn't resist him. She just couldn't. She was powerless to do so. She took his face in her hands and kissed him voraciously.

She didn't see the sombra standing directly behind her—her head caught in its grip like a vise.

Chapter 22

Tough Love

"You certainly seem happy today," Sara observed at lunch.

Raquel couldn't hide the excitement she felt; it was like a million butterflies were swarming inside of her.

She also felt sick when she thought of how she was disobeying the King, but one thought of Gabe made the sick feeling go away.

"I am," Raquel said with a grin, taking a seat next to her friend at the lunch table.

"This wouldn't have anything to do with Gabe the Babe, would it?" Sara asked, flashing her a knowing smile.

Raquel returned the smile. "It might."

"And what has your knight in shining armor done this time?" Sara laughed, taking a bite of her burger.

Raquel opened her bottled water. Her school lunches these days consisted of bottled water, the occasional skim milk, dressing-less salad, and fruit. Today, the fruit she'd chosen was sliced peaches. Peaches had the least number of calories of all the fruits: only 35. Now that her date with Gabe was officially on, she needed to work extra hard at keeping the calories off.

"Oh," said Raquel, taking a swig of her water. "He might have given me a nice surprise on Valentine's Day."

"And what surprise is that?" Sara asked, still chewing. "A cute little stuffed bear and chocolate?"

"Better than that," Raquel said smugly, picking up her fork. "An invitation to the prom!"

Sara's expression suddenly became clouded.

What was this reaction? Was she jealous?

Yes, she probably was. After all, hadn't Sara told her from the beginning that she was interested in Gabe?

But rather than gloating over the news, Raquel found herself feeling bad about hurting her friend. "I'm sorry he didn't ask you," she said quickly, even though she really wasn't. "It's just... you know, our lockers are right next to each other, and everything— "

"Oh, I'm not jealous," Sara told her plainly. "It's just that—I don't know, when you told me that... it's like I got a funny feeling in the pit of my stomach."

Raquel had taken a bite of salad, and upon hearing Sara's words she nearly choked.

"Are you okay?" Sara asked, putting a hand on her back.

Raquel nodded—feeling her blood boil. Did the King have to follow her *everywhere?* So now He was speaking to her through her *friend?*

"I'm fine," she said clearing her throat, even though nothing could have been farther from the truth. She was relieved when Sara finally removed her hand from her back. Raquel tried hard to think of a way to change the subject, but nothing was coming to mind.

"Do you really feel comfortable going to the prom with Gabe?" Sara wanted to know.

Raquel was so mad she could hardly see straight. *Why was the King trying to control her life?* "Why wouldn't I?"

she asked, trying to sound nonchalant—focusing on the salad in front of her.

"I don't know," Sara admitted. "I mean, he seems like a nice guy, and everything…"

"He is," Raquel said shortly.

"But I just have a funny feeling about you going to the prom with him."

Raquel turned and looked at her. "You sure it's not jealousy?" she asked maliciously, no longer concerned about hurting her friend's feelings.

"I told you, Raquel, I'm not jealous," she said matter-of-factly, not in the least bit disgruntled. "I just have this feeling."

"You sure it's not a feeling of love for *my* boyfriend?" Raquel asked, choosing to rub salt in the wound. "Can you honestly admit to me that you haven't had a crush on 'Gabe the Babe' since you laid eyes on him?"

"You *know* I've always had a crush on him, Raquel; I've told you that before. That's not the point."

"Then what *is* the point, Sara?" Raquel demanded, turning to glare directly at her. "Why *shouldn't* I go to the prom with him, huh? Answer me *that!*"

"I don't *know,* Raquel. Do *you* think you should go to the prom with him?"

The question caught Raquel off-guard. She fumbled for the words, and then finally spat out, "Of course I do! He asked me to go with him! Why on earth should I turn him down?"

"Do you trust him?"

"What kind of a question is that?"

"Just answer the question, Raquel," Sara stated calmly, further infuriating Raquel.

"I don't have to answer anything!" she blurted out. "I don't have to answer to you or to anyone else! You're not my *mother,* Sara!"

"You have to answer to the King, Raquel."

At the mention of the King, Raquel thought she would explode. "Leave *the King* out of this!" she demanded. "I'm sick and tired of you, Sara, always bringing the King into our conversations!"

"I'm not always—"

"Don't interrupt me!" she blurted out. "I wasn't finished! It hurts to hear the truth, doesn't it, Sara? It hurts to find out that you're living a lie... that you're nothing but a hypocrite! How can you sit there, look me in the face, and tell me you're not jealous about Gabe? That's the *only* reason you don't want me going to the prom with him!"

"I never said I don't want you going to the prom with him, Raquel," Sara told her. "I just think you should talk to the King about it before you make your decision."

"Why?" Raquel demanded. "Are you trying to control my life just like the King is?"

"Now hold on a minute, Raquel," Sara said, placing a hand over her friend's. Raquel jerked it away. "I think you're being unfair to both me *and* the King. Neither one of us is trying to 'control your life.' We both want what's best for you. You've known me for a long time, Raquel; you know I have your best interests in mind."

"And just because you do, that automatically means the King does, too?"

"The King *loves* you, Raquel."

Raquel turned her face away.

"Is that what this is all about? Has the King already told you you're not supposed to go with him?"

"Why don't you tell me?" Raquel said in a snarky voice. "If you and the King are so close, why don't you ask *Him* what He told me!"

"If He doesn't want you to go with him, Raquel, then there must be a reason. How well do you really know Gabe?"

"Better than you," she replied smugly, "and I hope to get to know him even better on prom night!"

The color drained from Sara's face. "What do you mean, Raquel?"

"What do you *think* I mean?" Raquel shot back.

Sara paused for a moment. "You wouldn't give yourself away to him, would you?"

Raquel lowered her voice to a near-whisper. "What I choose to do with *my* own body is *my* business, Sara!"

Sara seemed speechless. It was the first time Raquel had ever seen her this way, and she gloated over the fact.

"Raquel," Sara said slowly, finding her voice again. "You don't know what you're saying. You would give yourself away to someone you hardly know?"

"I've known him for over a month," Raquel informed her, "and it will be nearly four months by prom night."

"That's not long," Sara told her. "And I'm going to be honest with you, Raquel, because you're my friend and I care about you: If you give yourself to this guy, you'll be giving away a part of yourself that you can never get back again. Your body is sacred, Raquel. It's where the Prince Himself lives. Your body doesn't belong to you; it belongs to *Him*."

"I'll do whatever feels right, Sara," Raquel said mechanically, taking a bite of her salad.

"Whatever *feels* right is not necessarily *right*," Sara reminded her. "The King always has a reason for His commands, and one of His commands in the Book of Light is to save yourself for your husband. I don't claim to totally understand all the reasons why, either, but I do know that the King commanded it and I trust Him."

"Good for you," Raquel said flatly, taking a drink from her water bottle.

"Have you thought about the practical implications of what you're planning to do, Raquel? What if you get an STD or STI? What if you get pregnant?"

"We'll use protection," Raquel said with a smirk, taking a bite of her salad. She was already imagining her night with Gabe.

"There's no protection you can use that works 100% of the time, Raquel. What if it doesn't work and you get pregnant?"

"I'll cross that bridge when I come to it."

"You can't wait till prom night to start thinking about this, Raquel. You need to start thinking about it *now.*"

"Oh, I am," Raquel said, chewing her food slowly while staring off into space.

"Raquel, listen to me: If you *did* happen to get pregnant, do you really think you're ready to raise a child?"

"I could get an abortion."

This got the desired response: Sara gasped, giving Raquel a feeling of power; she had a comeback for all of Sara's questions.

After she'd gotten over the initial shock, Sara asked weakly, "You would kill your own child?"

"It's not a *child*, Sara," she said derisively. "Everybody knows that a fetus is just a blob of tissue."

"It's more than that, Raquel," Sara said, tears springing to her eyes. "It's a human life."

"Says who?" Raquel asked, then quickly added, "And don't say 'the King.'"

When Sara didn't say anything else, Raquel looked at her with a haughty smile, taking another bite of salad. Could it be that the girl with all the answers was finally speechless?

Sara looked at her friend. "I did a report on abortion earlier this year," she said, obviously holding back tears. "Would you like to know what I learned?"

"Fire away," Raquel laughed, taking another stab at her salad.

"By the third week—that's before you even *know* you're pregnant, Raquel—science has found that your baby already has a brain and a heartbeat."

Raquel stopped chewing and looked at Sara.

"By the fourth week, the baby has a tongue and well-developed eyes that already have color. By the fifth week, brain waves can be detected. By the sixth week, the baby's fingers can be seen, and by the seventh week..." Sara paused and took a breath. "By the seventh week, the baby is sensitive to touch. In other words, Raquel, it can *feel pain.*"

Raquel forgot all about her salad. She stared at Sara in silence. She'd never heard any of that. She'd always heard an unborn baby was just a blob of tissue. That didn't sound like a blob of tissue to her.

Suddenly, words from the Book of Light came to mind: *Temptation comes from our own desires, which entice us and drag us away. These desires give birth to sinful actions. And when sin is allowed to grow, it gives birth to death.*

Raquel swallowed and turned slowly back to her salad. "I'm not going to get pregnant," she said quietly, no longer feeling like eating.

"If you did and you chose to have an abortion, the King would forgive you," Sara assured her. "His mercy is very great. But you would have trouble forgiving *yourself,* Raquel. You'd be carrying the emotional and maybe even physical scars around with you for the rest of your life. Do you *really* want that to happen?"

"I'm not going to get pregnant," Raquel reiterated.

"The only way to make sure of that is abstinence."

Raquel sat rearranging her salad with her fork. "You sound like my mother," she said disgruntledly. Actually, that wasn't the case at all. Her mom hadn't spent a moment of her life talking to her about *any* of this.

"It's true, Raquel," Sara insisted.

Raquel had heard enough. *"I'll* decide what's true, Sara," she said, and quickly left the lunchroom.

Chapter 23

The Day of Evil

Over the next several weeks, Raquel found herself divided. Half the time she spent wanting to continue losing weight and continue dating Gabe, and the other half of the time she spent wanting to do neither. The King had already let her know in no uncertain terms that He wanted her to do neither, and she found herself wanting to please Him because she knew He loved her; she could feel it even though it wasn't a physical love. But pleasing the King meant giving up what was most important to her: Her dieting and her dating. She didn't know how she could live without them in her life.

But she was beginning to wonder how she could live *with* them. More and more, whenever Gabe kissed her, her heart was beating more with fear than with happiness. And every time she skipped a meal, it panged her to know that she was hurting the King.

She couldn't live like this forever.

She continued reading the Book of Light, and the King led her to some verses that seemed to speak directly to her situation:

I don't really understand myself, for I want to do what is right, but I don't do it. Instead, I do what I hate. But if I know that what I am doing is wrong, this shows that I agree that the King's law is good. So I am not the one doing wrong; it is sin living in me that does it. And I know that nothing good lives in me, that is, in my sinful nature. I want to do what is right, but I can't. I want to do what is good, but I don't. I don't want to do what is wrong, but I do it anyway.

"I can *so* relate," Raquel told herself.

It was a comfort knowing that she wasn't the only one who had gone through this. Apparently, people had been wrestling with themselves over right versus wrong for quite a while.

Of course, knowing this didn't make her situation any easier. She *still* wanted to date Gabe, and she *still* wanted to be thinner.

So she continued to do both.

And she continued to come under attack.

She was reclining on her bed one evening, thumbing through the latest issue of her fashion magazine, when Gabe suddenly came to mind. In her mind, she saw his handsome body and she imagined him shirtless with his muscular arms wrapped around her. She was enjoying the vision until she looked down and noticed that not only was the belt of truth around her waist and the breastplate of righteousness covering her torso, but some silver shoes with the letter "P" carved on the sides were on her feet. The shoes of peace.

She was admiring the shoes when something hit her fashion magazine and burned a hole directly through it—hitting her in the stomach. She let out a cry and looked down just in time to see some few remaining sparks.

What in the world...?

She looked up: A sombra stood on the other side of the room. In its curled fingers, it held some kind of ball made out of fire. Before she'd had time to study it for very long, the creature reared back and sent whatever it was holding directly her way.

Raquel screamed and only had time to raise her hands to her face before being hit by the object. It hit her in stomach again—knocking the wind out of her but not doing any further damage because of the belt and the breastplate.

What was the creature throwing at her? *Fireballs?*

She looked up quickly: The sombra had another one ready to throw.

Raquel panicked. She looked around for the Book of Light. *Where was it?*

She spotted it over on her dresser.

She jumped off the bed just as another fireball was hurled her way and barely escaped another hit. She looked behind her: the ball of fire had burnt a hole in the wall.

Dashing over to her dresser, Raquel grabbed up the Book of Light and held it to her face as another fireball came flying her way. It hit the Book of Light with such force that Raquel lost her balance and fell across her dresser—sweeping all of her fashion magazines onto the floor along with her. She looked up from the floor to see the muscular sombra advancing toward her quickly. Still holding the Book of Light (which was seemingly unharmed by the sombra's fire), Raquel fumbled with it with trembling hands and yanked it open, directing its light at the sombra.

The beacon of light's effect on the sombra was immediate. As soon as the light touched it, it fell to its knees—temporarily immobilized. Raquel sat up straighter and aimed the Book directly at its head; the sombra fell backward as though suffering a punch to its face.

The Book of Light really is *like a sword!* Raquel thought excitedly.

While the sombra was down, she took the opportunity to get quickly to her feet. Had she killed it? She decided to find out. Using extreme cautious, she slowly approached the giant mass lying on the floor—the Book of Light held tightly in her grasp by her side. The creature lay sprawled on its back with its wings outstretched below it. Raquel was enthralled; she had never seen a sombra this close before!

She looked down at its face. Of course she couldn't see its expression, but she knew it must be dead since it wasn't moving.

She loosened her grip on the Book of Light.

The sombra's massive head suddenly shot up—its mouth wide open! Raquel shrieked and lost her grip on the Book of Light; it fell to the floor facedown. She tried to grab it but the sombra grabbed a hold of her leg and pulled her feet out from under her. She rolled quickly onto her back and looked up; the sombra was leaping toward her! She fell flat on her back—the sombra's enormous weight on top of her. She struggled to get free but she was no match for the strength of this creature.

She looked up at it; it seemed to be leering at her—knowing that it had trapped her.

Raquel struggled beneath its weight. She tried to reach for the Book of Light but a clawed hand shot out and pinned her arm to the floor. She looked up at it in terror.

Why wasn't it destroying her? Surely it could if it wanted to. She was at its mercy; why wasn't it using its claws to shred her to pieces?

Was the King protecting her? Could the sombra only do as much as the King allowed?

The thought gave her courage. "I'm not afraid of you!" she shouted up at the shadow, wishing it were true. *"Get off of me!* In the Name of the—"

Before she could say "Prince," the sombra released her arm and a clawed hand came darting toward her face. Raquel quickly dodged it and—with her arm now free—reached quickly for the Book of Light. She grabbed it up and aimed it at the sombra—the light propelling the mighty shadow off of her.

She was unable to hold the Book steady and the sombra managed to escape the beacon of light. It came flying back at her with a vengeance. Raquel screamed and blocked her face with the open Book. She never felt the creature land on top of her. When she opened her eyes and peered around the Book, the sombra was on the opposite side of the room in a heap.

Raquel scrambled quickly to her feet. She needed a battle plan. How could she make the creature leave? Relámpago had sung, but she didn't know any love songs to the King; and besides, she didn't exactly feel like singing at the moment.

She remembered what had made the sombra leave last time: quoting the Book of Light. She'd been studying it lately, so she did in fact have a few verses memorized.

The sombra was now on its feet. It stood hunched over, the way Tentación had stood before. Was this Tentación?

"'*Temptation comes from our own desires,*'" she shouted at the creature, "'*which entice us and drag us away. These desires give birth to sinful actions. And when sin is allowed to grow, it gives birth to death.*'"

Upon hearing the words from the Book of Light, the sombra threw clawed hands to the sides of his head and howled to reveal a long snake-like tongue. Yep, it was Tentación, alright.

Raquel searched her mind frantically for another verse. She was still holding the Book of Light in her hand but she knew she didn't have time to look anything up. "'*Look straight ahead,*'" she shouted, "'*and fix your eyes on what lies before you. Mark out a straight path for your feet; stay on the safe path. Don't get sidetracked; keep your feet from following evil.*'"

These verses proved particularly painful for the sombra to hear. It not only covered its ears and howled, but it also hunkered on the floor in anguish.

Raquel was amused. How could such a big, strong creature be so easily defeated?

Tentación was quickly recovering. Raquel tried to think of another verse from the Book of Light she could use as ammunition, but her mind was blank. She watched in horror as the sombra rose again to its full height, creating another flaming ball of fire with its hands. Before Raquel had a chance to react, the fireball had hit the Book of Light and sent it sailing out of her hands. She quickly scrambled after it, but Tentación was too fast for her. It rushed toward her with a beating of its wings and knocked her to the floor. She fell facedown, and Tentación flipped her over onto her back in a single movement. It pinned her down and sat staring down at her.

What would the creature do? Would it try and claw her face again?

Surprisingly, the creature didn't do anything at first. It merely sat there—breathing heavily. What could the creature possibly be thinking? She couldn't read its expression, because there was no expression to read.

She watched as its head jerked away from her face and traveled down her torso, then jerked back up at her face again. The sombra reached a clawed hand to her face; Raquel gasped and threw her free hand up to cover her face. Tentación's clawed hand hovered momentarily over her face, then traveled down to her torso. His hand remained there—hovering over her breastplate. His hand closed and then opened again as though he longed to touch her but couldn't. He was within inches of her armor, but he seemed afraid to come in contact with it.

Raquel was appalled when she realized what it longed to do. "Get your slimy hand off me, Tentación!" she shouted up at it.

The sombra instantly turned its attention back to her face—reaching for her with long, curved claws. Raquel only had time to yell out the Prince's Name, but it was time enough. Tentación took to the air—Raquel feeling an overwhelming sense of relief at the sombra's release of her. He landed over on her bed on all-fours, breathing heavily. Relámpago was right: This sombra didn't give up easily.

But neither did she. More enraged than she was afraid, Raquel got to her feet and marched over to the Book of Light—picking it up from near her dresser where Tentación had knocked it out of her hand. She aimed the light directly at the creature. Tentación flew quickly to another corner of the room like a frightened sparrow, avoiding the light.

"Leave *now,* Tentación!" she yelled at him. "In the Name of the Prince!"

The sombra shot through the ceiling.

Exhausted, Raquel collapsed onto the chair next to her dresser. She looked in the mirror—never so relieved to be covered in armor. She watched as the armor that covered her slowly faded while remaining constant in her reflection.

"Thank You, King," she breathed, still trying to catch her breath. "Thank You for protecting me."

Raquel felt a peace flood over her, and she knew that the King was in control. For the first time, Raquel found that she was *glad* that the King was the One in control.

Chapter 24

The Dress

On a Saturday morning, Raquel's mom surprised her by suggesting they go to the mall together. Her mom never wanted to go anywhere with her. "I can help you pick out a prom dress," she told her. This surprised Raquel even more—especially considering that she figured her mom would stick doggedly with the idea of her wearing the dress her dad had given her. Raquel took her mom up on the offer.

The town was not large, but it was large enough to have a nice shopping mall. Raquel frequented it often—as often as she could find someone to go with. Sara had gone with her several times even though Sara had told her that she really didn't enjoy shopping all that much but enjoyed spending time with Raquel.

It would be so different going with her mom. Not that she'd never been shopping with her mom before, but she could count the number of times on one hand. What would they talk about the whole time? Not her dad, she hoped.

She went to her room and changed, then came back downstairs to meet her mom. Her mom was watching TV, and the moment she turned to look at Raquel her jaw dropped.

What was wrong? Was there a sombra standing behind her, or something? Raquel turned to look but nothing was there.

"Raquel!" her mom said frantically. "You're so thin!"

It was then that Raquel realized her terrible mistake; she'd always worn baggy clothes around her mom to cover up her weight loss, but she'd forgotten and changed into a tank top that revealed her bony wrists, elbows, and shoulders.

"I'm fine, Mom," she said quickly, blood rushing to her face. "C'mon, let's go."

Her mom jumped off the couch and practically sprinted over to her. She grabbed a hold of one of her arms and held it out—examining it as though she were a doctor. She felt of her shoulder blades and collarbone like she had some kind of disease. "You're not fine at all!" she exclaimed, a terrified expression on her face. "You're *way* too thin! Haven't you been eating?"

Raquel didn't like her mom touching her, and she couldn't stand her mom's pitying look. "Of *course* I've been eating," she said, irritated, starting for the garage. "Now let's go!"

"Raquel!"

"I said *let's go!*" she hollered over her shoulder.

She considered dropping the whole deal and just staying home, and she would have done just that if it weren't for the prom dress her mom was going to buy her. She kept a jean jacket hanging in the laundry room; she grabbed it up before jumping in the car.

Neither one of them said a word on their way to the mall, which was fine with Raquel. She didn't want to hear what her mom had to say. *It's* my *body!* She kept reminding herself. *Nobody can tell me what to do with* my *body!* She tried to forget what Sara had told her about her body belonging to the Prince.

When they got to the mall, Raquel soon forgot all about this when she stepped inside the mall's large department store. The place was crowded—not only with people but with criados and sombras, as well! Powerful, winged criados of all different nationalities were standing guard next to unsuspecting humans, and sombras were doing what they do best: *attacking* unsuspecting humans. One stood with its claws sunk deep inside a woman's head as she admired a piece of clothing. Raquel watched as the woman smiled and took the article of clothing to the dressing room to try it on, followed closely by the sombra.

Somewhere else, a little boy was fighting with his mom; apparently, he didn't want the shoes his mom was wanting to buy for him. Noticing the fight, a sombra flew swiftly over to her—sinking in its claws. As soon as the sombra arrived on the scene, the mother lost her temper and started shaking the boy—telling him to shut up. Raquel and her mom passed by them before she could find out what happened next.

She saw a man under attack, although to the casual observer one would never have known it. He was professionally dressed in a business suit and tie, and his behavior fit the part as he meandered around the store with a sombra hanging out of his head. Raquel marveled at how easy it was to be under attack without even knowing it. And sombras, it seemed, were no respecters of the high-class and well-dressed; *any* human was fair game.

Raquel was also careful to note several who were *not* under attack. An elderly woman who walked the store alone had a large criado by her side, so no sombras were messing with her. A high school-aged boy, also with a criado by his side, seemed to be protected from nearby sombras. Raquel watched as a couple sombras slowly approached the boy—moving in from different directions. His guardian criado was keeping a close eye on both of them, and when the shadows got too close for comfort he drew his sword. At that point, the sombras backed off and wandered away—no doubt in pursuit of someone else to attack.

The entire store was a virtual battle ground: sombras attacking and criados warding them off. Of course, there were some situations that were a little less clear-cut. Some people were being guarded by a criado, but when a sombra approached he did not drive it away. He allowed it to get close to the human he was guarding, a pained expression on his face. Raquel watched as the sombra approached cautiously—mindful of the criado's sword—but when the criado made no move to draw his sword, the sombra sunk its claws in. The sombra seemed to be mocking the criado.

Why had the criado allowed the sombra to attack? Maybe for the same reason that *her* criado allowed sombras to attack: Living in disobedience to the King. Or maybe the King gave permission for sombras to attack His warriors sometimes in order to test them and make them stronger.

Raquel looked over her left shoulder at Relámpago. He looked so solemn; she supposed he had to be solemn in a place like this where so many sombras roamed about.

"This looks like a nice place to look," Raquel heard her mom say.

Raquel took her eyes off the criados and sombras long enough to look in her mom's direction.

"Do you like any of these, Raquel?"

Raquel looked at the dresses her mom was referring to. They were pretty, but she didn't think they were pretty enough for prom night. "I was thinking of something maybe a little fancier," Raquel told her.

She expected her mom to put her foot down and give her a speech about how she was being unappreciative, but instead she smiled and said, "I know just the place. There's a new shop that opened in the mall not too long ago that specifically sells wedding and prom dresses. Let's go have a look, shall we?"

Raquel was taken aback; this was not the same mom she'd grown up with. Either her mom had changed or *she* had. Or both.

She was amazed to find herself actually enjoying being here at the mall with her mom. Since she'd put on the jean jacket, her mom hadn't given her anymore grief about her appearance; maybe she'd forgotten all about it. Or if she hadn't, she was being considerate enough to keep her thoughts to herself.

As they left the department store and began to make their way to the shop her mom had mentioned, Raquel was amused by what she saw some criados doing. There was a group of them standing and singing like a group of Christmas carolers in the middle of the walking area. In fact, Raquel and her mom had to walk *directly through them* in order to pass by! She couldn't hear what they were singing, of course, but she could imagine their majestic voices echoing off the walls. She wondered if they were as good as Relámpago. Relámpago must have been able to hear them because she watched as her guardian criado patted one of the criados amiably on the shoulder as he passed by and said a quick word to him.

Once they reached the dress shop, Raquel began to look around. Now *this* was more like it; she'd find the *perfect* prom dress here! She was prepared to do all her own looking, but she didn't anticipate how involved her mom wanted to be. *What the heck,* Raquel decided. *If Mom wants to be a part of this, why not let her?* She allowed her mom to make suggestions—even if her suggestions made her want to puke, and Raquel told her so. Her mom was surprisingly good-natured about it and even laughed, saying, "What, are my clothing tastes not *hip* enough for ya?" Raquel laughed at her mom's usage of the word "hip"—her laugh coming out in a snort—which set them *both* to laughing.

Raquel and her mom carried several dresses to the dressing room for her to try on. They'd found a beautiful emerald green dress with spaghetti straps, a strapless purple dress with sequins all over it and a big bow on the side, a knee-length pink dress that was low-cut, and a strapless white dress that had beautiful folds and was covered in lace. Raquel tried all of them on—exiting the dressing room after each one to get her mom's opinion. She left the jean jacket on each time and appreciated her mom for not saying anything about it.

"I like the pink one," was her mom's final analysis. "You said the corsage that Gabe gave you was pink, so the pink dress would go well with it."

Just hearing Gabe's name flooded her with mixed emotions. She tried not to think about him, but instead focused on the white dress she was wearing. "I don't know," Raquel said pensively, looking down at it. "I think I like this one best."

"We have expensive taste, don't we?" her mom smirked. The white dress was the second-to-the-most expensive one out of the ones she'd chosen.

Raquel shrugged. "We can afford it," she reminded her.

"True," her mom said, walking over to her to get a better look. "Doesn't mean we have to spend it, though, does it? But I'd say prom night is important enough to splurge."

Raquel smiled.

"It *is* beautiful, Raquel," her mom said, examining it. "You look like a princess with this on."

Raquel blushed. She couldn't remember the last time her mom had complimented her. She was amazed to find herself wondering if her dad would like it.

"I think we should get it," her mom said.

Raquel's smile turned into a grin. "Really?"

"Absolutely, girl!" she said, fluffing out the dress's folds. "Lucky Gabe doesn't know what he's in for!"

Raquel's throat felt dry; she swallowed. "Yeah," she said softly.

Chapter 25

The Secret

They left with the dress and her mom headed in the direction of the food court. "Let's grab a bite to eat before we head home," she suggested. "Then I won't have to fix supper tonight."

Raquel heard her heart begin to pound in her ears. How could she turn her mom down? What excuse could she give? It wouldn't make sense to tell her that she wasn't hungry; they'd been shopping all day without eating anything. Her mom already had suspicions of her not eating; if she told her she wasn't hungry, it would just heighten her suspicions. She couldn't hide her food in her napkin like she had last time—her mom would surely notice.

She would have to throw it up. She hated having to do that, but it was the only option she had.

Of all the places in the food court, her mom had to choose the place with the most grease. It was admittedly one of Raquel's favorite places to eat—or at least it *had* been before her diet—so she figured her mom was probably trying to do her a favor. As it was, though, it felt like torture.

"The usual?" her mom asked her when the lady asked for their order.

Raquel tried to smile. "Sure," she said weakly. *The usual* was a fried chicken sandwich, french-fries, and a Coke. Nothing but grease and sugar.

For some reason, some verses from the Book of Light came to mind: *Joyful are people of integrity, who follow the instructions of the King. Joyful are those who obey his laws and search for him with all their hearts.*

Joyful. She would be *joyful* if she didn't have to stay here and eat!

When their food was ready, her mom carried the tray over to a nearby table and sat down, unwrapping her usual favorite: a chicken salad sandwich. It was a small table; her mom would see everything she did. Hiding her food was definitely not an option this time—especially since a chicken sandwich wasn't eaten with a fork and therefore couldn't be cut up and hid anywhere.

"*Bon appétit," her* mom said, watching her like a hawk.

Raquel stalled for time by slowly removing her straw from the plastic wrap and sticking it in her Coke. Then she carefully opened her napkin and laid it in her lap—even though she usually never bothered to do this.

"I'm gonna go get some ketchup," she said, quickly scooting away from the table.

"I already got some," said her mom with her mouth full, pointing to the ketchup packets on the tray.

"Oh," Raquel said, and reluctantly scooted back to the table.

With trembling hands, she took a ketchup packet, opened it, and slowly began to squeeze ketchup onto her fries. She shuddered at the thought of how many calories were in the ketchup alone.

She looked up at her mom; she was watching her. *Did she know?*

She slowly lifted her grease-filled chicken sandwich from the tray. Her heart was beating so loudly, she wondered if her mom could hear it. She hadn't bothered putting any mayo on the sandwich like she normally did, but she hoped her mom wouldn't notice.

Her mom was still watching her. She had no choice but to eat.

She took a bite.

She'd forgotten how good these grease-filled sandwiches were; it was like biting into a little piece of heaven. But at the same time, she felt dread well up inside of her: the fried chicken and bread would turn to fat in her stomach in no time.

It's alright, Raquel reassured herself. *I can throw it all up in the restroom afterward.*

She chewed slowly, counting at least twenty chews before swallowing. She felt like she was putting poison into her body; she was scared to death of what she was doing to herself. *It will make you fat!* she kept hearing in her head. *It will make you fat!*

She finished chewing and took another microscopic bite.

"Something wrong with your sandwich?" her mom asked, looking at her curiously.

Raquel shook her head.

"You're not devouring it the way you usually do."

It was no use; Raquel had to eat normally in front of her mom or else she would catch on. She began eating quickly—the sooner she got this over with the better. Maybe if she ate fast enough, the food wouldn't have time to digest before she had a chance to throw it up.

"That's more like it," her mom nodded approvingly. "That's the Raquel I know."

Her mom continued talking, but Raquel didn't hear a word of it. All she could hear was her heart beating like a drum in her ears, the sound of her chewing, and the voice in her head telling her over and over again, *This is making you fat! This is making you fat!*

As soon as she'd finished her sandwich, Raquel jumped up from the table. "I'll be back in a minute," she said. "I've gotta go use the restroom."

"But you haven't even touched your fries," her mom called after her.

But Raquel was already on her way. "I'll finish them when I get back," she yelled over her shoulder. She couldn't wait another second to get this stuff out of her. She could practically feel it beginning to turn into fat.

She raced to the restroom and threw open the door. *Wouldn't you know there'd be a line!*

Raquel groaned loudly and several of the women turned and looked at her. An elderly lady with gray hair and shining blue eyes looked at her compassionately. "An emergency, huh?" she smiled.

Raquel didn't respond, but rather began pacing back and forth, her hands balled into fists at her sides. *I have to get it out of me! I have to get it out!*

"If you want to go ahead of me, sweetie, that's fine," the elderly lady said.

"Thank you," Raquel said hurriedly, cutting in front of her—not that this helped all that much. There were still two more people in front of her, and every stall was full, so she would have to throw up surrounded by an audience. *Oh, that's just* great! *Why did I eat that stupid sandwich??*

"My name is JoAnna," the lady continued, oblivious to her plight. "What's yours, sweetie?"

What was *wrong* with this lady? Couldn't she see that she didn't feel like talking? "Raquel," she replied through gritted teeth.

"Beautiful name," the lady went on. "I have a granddaughter about your age."

That's great, Raquel thought, then felt a wave of relief as the line moved forward; there was only one person ahead of her now.

"Are you here shopping by yourself today?"

"I'm with my mom," she answered shortly, fidgeting by bouncing up and down. She could feel the food bouncing up and down in her stomach.

"Oh, how fun! Have you—" the lady started to ask, but two more stalls opened up and Raquel dashed into the one closest to her. She didn't care if she had an audience or not; *she had to empty her stomach!*

She locked the stall door, fell to her knees beside the toilet, grabbed a wad of toilet paper and used it to lift the lid—not wanting to touch a public toilet seat. She stuck her finger down her throat and threw up her sandwich, wincing at the awful taste and at the burning in her throat. She gagged herself several times before she was satisfied that she'd gotten it all. When she found herself dry heaving, she wiped her mouth with toilet paper, lowered the lid, and flushed the toilet. She tried to look nonchalant as she left the stall.

She walked over to the sink and began washing her hands. She felt someone's eyes on her; she turned to see the little old lady staring at her with a horrified expression on her face.

She knows! Raquel's mind screamed.

Raquel avoided the lady's eyes as she hastily exited the restroom.

"Your fries are probably cold by now," her mom informed her as she returned from the restroom.

Raquel couldn't care less about her fries. All she could think about was the fact that her secret was out.

"Raquel? Are you okay?"

Raquel forced herself to smile at her mom, even though she felt like screaming. "Yeah," she said, her voice cracking. "I'm fine."

"Do you want to eat your fries before we go?"

Heck, no! "Naw, they're probably cold anyway."

"Well, of *course* they are! You took too long—"

"Let's go, Mom," Raquel said quickly, pushing back her chair.

"Excuse me."

Raquel turned; the old lady from the restroom was standing behind her! Her jaw dropped.

"Yes?" her mom said. "Can we help you?"

The lady was looking at Raquel—her bright blue eyes full of sympathy. "I don't mean to bother the two of you," she said, turning to her mom, "but my name is JoAnna. Could I perhaps speak with you for a moment?"

Absolutely not! "C'mon, Mom, let's go!" Raquel demanded, jumping up from her chair and shoving it under the table.

"Just a minute, Raquel," her mom said, looking at JoAnna. "What do you want to speak with me about?"

Raquel began to panic; she had to protect her secret at all costs. "Mom, *let's go!*" she yelled.

"Calm down, Raquel! This lady wants to speak to me about something—"

"We have to go home *now!!*"

By now, several people in the food court were staring.

"I'm so sorry," said her mom embarrassedly, pushing out her chair and standing. "I don't know what's gotten into my daughter, but I guess we'd better go. You know how teen-agers can be!"

"Yes, I have a granddaughter about her age, and she has a problem that I wanted to talk to you about..."

"Mom!" Raquel yelled.

"Your granddaughter has a problem?" her mom asked.

"Yes, and it relates to your daughter—"

"*Mom!!* Let's go *NOW!!*"

"I'm really sorry," said her mom as Raquel grabbed a tight hold of her arm and started pulling her toward the mall exit.

Chapter 26

The Confession

The whole way home, Raquel sat in complete silence—even as her mom lectured her on rudeness and ungratefulness. And the look on Raquel's face might have been taken by her mom to be remorse but in actuality it was fear. *Someone had discovered her secret.*

Sure, it was just a stranger. Just an old lady who Raquel probably would never see again. But what if she did? What if her mom ran into her while shopping or while at the grocery store? She would tell her everything! She would tell her how she'd heard her daughter throwing up in the bathroom, and that's when the interrogation would begin. Her mom would ask her a million questions until she finally got it out of her that she'd been throwing up her food and practically starving herself to keep from gaining weight.

Practically? Was she merely *practically* starving herself? Or was it *actually* happening?

The lady had called it a "problem." Was it?

It was far-fetched for Raquel to think of what she was doing as a "problem." It was a *good* thing to be beautiful, right? A *good* thing to lose weight? *Food* was the problem!

Right?

When she got home, she went up to her room and sat down on her bed, opening the Book of Light—not even noticing that the light from the Book no longer hurt her eyes. She needed answers, and this Book seemed to be right a lot of the time. Just maybe it would have something to say about this… "problem."

She began reading where her eyes fell:

Do not let sin control the way you live; do not give in to sinful desires. Do not let any part of your body become an instrument of evil to serve sin. Instead, give yourselves completely to the King, for you were dead, but now you have new life. So use your whole body as an instrument to do what is right for the glory of the King.

She read the first part again: *Do not let sin control the way you live.* Was she letting her diet control the way she lived? Was she letting food control her? It seemed like such a silly concept…

But the more Raquel thought about it, it didn't seem so far-fetched after all. Didn't her whole day revolve around counting calories? Wasn't she *constantly* thinking about food? Could it be that she really was letting food control her?

She kept reading:

Sin is no longer your master, for you no longer live under the requirements of the law. Instead, you live under the freedom of the King's grace.

The word "freedom" made her think of the verse that Relámpago had quoted to her: "*Then you will know the truth, and the truth will set you free.*"

But set her free from what? Was she a prisoner? She looked down at the Book again:

Don't you realize that you become the slave of whatever you choose to obey? You can be a slave to sin, which leads to death, or you can choose to obey the King, which leads to righteous living.

"Which leads to death." Raquel couldn't stop focusing on that phrase. She didn't *feel* like she was close to death. In fact, it made her feel alive every time she rejected food.

But was she slowly killing herself?

Raquel got up and walked over to her dresser mirror. The metal belt and breastplate in her reflection covered up her torso, but she could still see her arms. They *did* look very thin. And for the first time since her diet, she didn't automatically associate the word "thin" with "beautiful." In fact, maybe she was a little *too* thin. Was that possible?

She looked down at the magazine covers. The pictures on the magazines were telling her one thing, while the Book of Light was telling her another. Who was she supposed to believe?

She went back to her bed and looked down at the Book of Light again:

For the wages of sin is death, but the free gift of the King is eternal life through our Lord, the Prince.

"Eternal life." She suddenly thought of that moment in Paraíso when she'd talked to the Prince and told Him she'd decided to follow Him. Espíritu, the Great Horse, had taken to the air in celebration. He loved her, and so did the King.

They could be trusted.

The King's *Book* could be trusted.

Then that settled it. She had a problem and it needed to be fixed.

But how?

Raquel realized that she would need to start by telling someone her secret. This realization terrified her, but she also realized that the problem was too big for her. It had taken over her life, and she wasn't strong enough to solve it on her own.

Who would she tell? Not her mom—her mom would freak.

What about Sara?

She got her first opportunity the next time they met in the lunchroom. Raquel could feel her heart racing, but she knew that sharing her secret was the right thing to do. *King, give me strength.*

"Sara, I have something I need to tell you."

"Aren't you going to get a lunch?"

Raquel realized that she had sat down at the table without going through the lunch line. "Um, no," she said, squirming on the bench. "I'm not hungry." And for the first time since Raquel could remember, this statement was actually true.

"Is something wrong?"

"Yeah."

Sara put down her fork and gave Raquel her full attention. "What is it?" she asked.

Help me, King....

Do not let sin control the way you live; do not give in to sinful desires. Do not let any part of your body become an instrument of evil to serve sin.

The words from the Book of Light flooded her mind.

Instead, give yourselves completely to the King, for you were dead, but now you have new life. So use your whole body as an instrument to do what is right for the glory of the King.

Help me to do what's right...

"Raquel?"

Sara was still waiting for an answer. "I have a problem," Raquel said quietly, not making eye contact.

"What kind of problem?"

Raquel wiped her sweaty palms on her jeans. *Instead, give yourselves completely to the King*, she quoted to herself. "With eating."

"With eating?" Sara asked, confused. "You have a problem with eating?"

...for you were dead, but now you have new life. "Yes."

"You mean you don't like the school's food?"

Raquel chuckled. "That too," she said, breaking a smile. "I wish that's all it was."

"What else is it?"

So use your whole body as an instrument to do what is right for the glory of the King. "I have a… disorder. An eating disorder."

Sara didn't say anything. Raquel looked up at her. "What kind of eating disorder, Raquel?"

Raquel looked down at the table again. She picked at the edge of it with her fingernail. Could she say the word? She knew what it was called, but could she say it? She tried to speak and the word got caught in her throat.

Sin is no longer your master, for you no longer live under the requirements of the law. Instead, you live under the freedom of the King's grace.

She cleared her throat and tried again. The word came out in a squeak. "Anorexia."

She heard Sara catch her breath.

"…and bulimia."

Putting names to the monsters that had taken over her life had a strange effect on her; she felt her eyes well up with tears. They spilled over onto her cheeks and then just kept falling. Raquel couldn't help it. She felt so weak. But at the same time, she felt free, too.

Sara scooted over and put an arm around her friend. "We're gonna get you help, Raquel." There was a fierce determination in her voice. "You hear me? We're gonna beat this!"

Her friend's compassion was overwhelming; Raquel's tears turned into sobs.

"I'm not going to let anything happen to you! We're going to get you the help you need! Are you willing to do whatever it takes?"

Raquel nodded through her tears as Sara continued to hold her.

"Ok, then. I'm going to research places that can help you. You know you can't beat this on your own, right?"

Raquel nodded again.

"Do you know how brave you are, Raquel, for telling me?"

Raquel laughed, sending more tears streaming down her face. "I don't feel brave," she said.

"To tell someone a secret like this, are you kidding? It takes an *incredible* amount of courage!"

"I couldn't have done it without the King," Raquel said, choking through her sobs.

Sara gave her a squeeze. "He comes in handy for times like this, doesn't He?"

Raquel laughed, looking at her friend. As usual, Sara's eyes were shining that familiar light. "He sure does," Raquel said with a grin.

Chapter 27

The Recovery

True to her word, Sara returned the following day with a list of locations that were specifically for helping people in Raquel's situation. "This looks like a really good place," she said, pointing to the first place on the list. "It has the option of attending up to six days a week for three hours each day. The days' sessions start at 3:30, so you would be able to go after school."

Sara went on to explain more about this place. She would eat supper with other girls who were dealing with the same problems she was; everything she ate would be monitored. They would make *sure* that she was eating a certain number of calories, and she knew it would be more than what she was used to. Just thinking about this scared Raquel half to death. But, then, that's what she needed to be doing, wasn't it—*eating?* Even so, the thought made her feel sick to her stomach.

"They'll also have specialists there for you to talk to," Sara went on, "people who specialize in helping people with anorexia and bulimia."

Raquel nodded. Sara had gone to so much trouble for her. Raquel could have done all this research herself, but it would have been like researching how to cure yourself from cancer. Sara had saved her the agony.

"Hang in there, Raquel," Sara said with a smile. "Spring is almost here. And in just a couple months, summer vacation!"

Raquel returned the smile, thankful for a friend who knew how to look on the bright side.

Raquel took the information home to show her mom. Having already talked about it with Sara, Raquel found it less difficult to work up the courage to speak to her mom. She took the news harder than Raquel expected. She cried and blamed herself—saying that she should have known what was going on. Raquel told her that she had purposely kept it a secret, but that didn't stop her mom from blaming herself.

She called the place at the top of the list and set up an appointment for them to come in. They went in that week and Raquel was impressed with the friendliness of the staff. The staff was equally impressed with her for seeking help for her eating disorder on her own. Raquel admitted that she was scared to be there, but they said that was normal; it would take some time for her to get used to the daily routine. They said openly that the program would be difficult for her at first, but that if she gave it some time she would be on the path to recovery. That was the path Raquel wanted to be on, so she said okay.

She began attending the following Monday after school. It was a beautiful facility—not as beautiful as her home, of course, but it had a nice family feel to it. She met the other girls who were there, most of them teenagers like her. They all had the same problem she had, so she found that she felt comfortable around them.

She couldn't believe that there was actually an exercise session; she thought she would be encouraged *not* to exercise. But the instructor said that there was a right and a wrong way to exercise, and they were going to learn the right way. Besides, the lady told them, exercise is good for the body; it's only when one exercises too long or too much that it becomes harmful. The instructor also said that it was normal for girls their age to have a little extra fat; they were at an age when their bodies were changing, so this was nothing to worry about. She also brought up the subject of magazine models; apparently, the pictures were oftentimes modified to make the women appear slimmer than they really were. Raquel wished she'd known that three months ago.

The dreaded part of the evening arrived when supper was served. She was given half of a grilled chicken sandwich on wheat bread without any condiments, some canned corn, a small apple, and a cup of 2% milk. Raquel stared at her plate, calculating the numbers in her head: the total came to around 450 calories which was within the recommended range of calories per meal, but to Raquel who had limited herself to only 200 it looked like an inordinate amount of food. She couldn't remember the last time she'd eaten a meal this large. She looked up at the other girls; some of them who were new like her looked just as scared as she felt, but those who had been there longer had already begun to eat.

Here, there would be no skipping meals. No asking if she could eat alone so that she could not eat at all. No hiding food in her napkin. And no throwing it up afterward.

Here, there would be no lying.

Raquel's heart was beating so fast she thought it would explode, but somehow she managed to get it all down. It took a while, but it took some of the other girls just as long or even longer. Raquel actually felt a sense of accomplishment when she looked at her empty plate.

It had been difficult, but she had done it!

As soon as supper was over, they had a group activity—no doubt to try and take their minds off the food in their stomachs. Raquel enjoyed the activity; it helped her to get to know the girls a little better. When her mom arrived at seven o'clock to pick her up, she wanted to know how it went. Raquel had mixed feelings, but overall she was glad to be there. She *needed* to be there.

As they were leaving the facility, a large man stood with his back to them, holding the door open. "Oh, thank you, sir," her mom said, smiling up at him as they passed by.

"My pleasure, ma'am," the man said.

Wait a minute; she recognized that voice. Raquel looked up to see Relámpago standing there—wingless and in every-day clothes!

"C'mon, Raquel," her mom called excitedly. "I want to hear all about what happened!"

Relámpago gave her a wink before she rejoined her mother—half in a daze.

As soon as she got home, Raquel dropped her backpack beside her dresser and looked at herself proudly in the mirror: *She'd done it!* She'd eaten a regular meal! It hadn't been easy, but she'd done it, anyway!

She collapsed onto her chair in ecstasy. *"I did it!"* she shouted, arms high above her head.

She felt the King's peace envelop her. He was proud of her, too.

Raquel basked in the joy of His presence, admiring the armor in her reflection. She noticed for the first time a new piece of armor: a large shield that hung from her left shoulder. She jumped to her feet to get a better look. The shield was magnificent—shiny and silver reaching almost to the floor with a large calligraphic letter "F" covering the surface of it. "The shield of *faith!*" Raquel cheered.

The thought came to her that it wasn't too late; she could still throw up the supper she'd eaten.

Where in the world did *that* come from?

She got her answer when in her reflection she saw a blinding ball of light come zooming toward her from behind.

At the same exact moment, she lost her balance and lurched to the left as an unexpected heaviness—the shield of faith now manifested—pulled her over with its weight. It was a good thing it did, too, because the fireball aimed at her from Tentación would have hit her in the head.

Raquel restored her balance and turned to face him, unafraid; she had the shield of faith now!

"I won't give in to your lies ever again, Tentación!" she yelled at the monstrous sombra. "You're finished!"

The large black shadow reared back, sending another fireball her way, but Raquel blocked it with her shield. The shield was a little too heavy for her, but she knew that this was due to a lack of strength on her part—not a lack of consideration on the King's. If she were her normal strength she would be able to hold the shield with no trouble at all, but her eating disorder had weakened her. "Give me Your strength, O King," she breathed. "Give me the strength to stand."

Another fireball came sailing her way, and she was just barely able to lift the shield in time to protect her face before feeling the powerful impact of the sombra's fiery dart. She stumbled backward, but was able to keep her balance and steady herself.

All of this armor was weighing her down. She wasn't sure how much longer she could hold up, and Tentación seemed to know it. He began pacing from one side of the room to the other, like a cat playing with a mouse.

It suddenly occurred to her to use the Book of Light. She thanked the King for the suggestion and immediately began rummaging through her backpack where she'd begun carrying it with her to school. Tentación figured out what she was doing and hurled another ball of fire at her. It hit her in the chest and she fell backward—hitting her head on the desk. She was rubbing the back of her head when she looked up and saw the giant sombra moving rapidly toward her. Before she had time to react, it had sunk its claws deep into her head.

Gabe will not love me now, she thought. *I'll get fat, and he'll ask somebody else to the prom.*

"Get away from me!" Raquel yelled up at him. "I'm not going to listen to your lies!"

I have to get out of this new eating program before it's too late...

"No!" Raquel yelled, interrupting the thought. "Get off of me in the Name of—"

Tentación released her before she could finish and flew fuming to the far side of the room.

Raquel hurriedly turned her attention back to her backpack and—finding the Book of Light—yanked it out and stood to her feet, aiming its light at the sombra. It was still fuming from having been made to release her and the light caught it off-guard. The light hit Tentación square in the face and knocked him off his feet.

While he was down, Raquel searched her memory banks for backup. "'*The King blesses those who patiently endure testing and temptation,*'" Raquel quoted to the creature. "'*Afterward they will receive the crown of life that the King has promised to those who love him.*'"

Tentación tried to stand but could not find the strength to do so.

"'*And remember,*'" continued Raquel, undaunted, "'*when you are being tempted, do not say, "The King is tempting me." The King is never tempted to do wrong, and he never tempts anyone else. Temptation comes from our own desires, which entice us and drag us away.*'"

The massive sombra was slowly and painfully getting to its feet, its clawed hands clutching the sides of its head in an attempt to tune her out.

But Raquel would not be tuned out. "'*These desires give birth to sinful actions,*'" Raquel said, taking a few steps toward the creature. "'*And when sin is allowed to grow, it gives birth to death.*'"

The sombra roared at her—showing her its fangs and serpent-like tongue.

"I'm not afraid of you anymore, Tentación," she calmly stated. "You don't own me. I'm not going to allow your lies to be a part of my life *anymore*. I belong to *the King* now; I'm *His* child. The King makes me feel beautiful because He loves me, and His love is all I need. I don't *need* you anymore. Your lies only lead to death, but the King's truth leads to life and joy and happiness."

Tentación was breathing heavily—probably more from rage than from exhaustion.

"Leave now," she said, holding up the open Book while pointing its light away from him. "Unless you'd like to hear more."

Tentación had heard enough; he took off.

As soon as he left, her armor disappeared and—with the shield gone—she lost her balance again and fell to the floor, laughing hysterically at herself.

"Oh, well," she said with a sigh, still laughing. "At least I had the strength to stand while he was here!" She looked up at the ceiling. "Thank You, Father."

Filled with indescribable joy, she interlocked her fingers and pulled a leg toward her, resting her chin on top of her knee. She sat in silence—simply enjoying the King's presence.

Glancing over at the open Book, she dragged it closer and looked down into the light to see what else the King had to say.

Chapter 28

Esther

Sara couldn't wait to hear about Raquel's first day at the treatment center. Raquel told her what it was like—that she both liked it and hated it at the same time—and Sara listened to her without interrupting or judging. It was going to be hard, Raquel said… probably the hardest thing she'd ever had to do.

Sara gave her plenty of encouragement. "You can do it, Raquel!" she exclaimed. "I'm so proud of you!"

"Thanks," Raquel replied, sincerely appreciative of her friend's kindness. "I'll just have to take it one day at a time, I guess. That's all I can do, right? *'Therefore do not worry about tomorrow, for tomorrow will worry about itself. Each day has enough trouble of its own.'*"

"Hey," Sara said exuberantly, "you've been reading the Book of Light!"

"Yeah," she admitted. "It's pretty addicting."

Sara laughed. "It sure is! And speaking of the Book of Light, I found a really cool section in there last night. I think the King led me directly to it; He wanted me to share it with you."

"What is it?" Raquel asked curiously.

"It's a true story about a girl named Esther. Have you read it before?"

Raquel shook her head.

"Esther was a girl who lived a long time ago, and she was probably about your age. She was also like you in another way: She was beautiful."

Raquel blushed. "Outward beauty isn't everything, Sara," she told her, smiling.

"True!" Sara responded, her eyes shining. "It's so cool to hear you say that, Raquel!"

"I'm still trying to believe it," Raquel admitted.

"Saying it comes first, *then* believing it," Sara reminded her.

Raquel returned the light she saw in her friend's eyes. "I'm glad you're my friend, Sara," she told her. "You've got a beautiful heart."

Now it was Sara's turn to blush. *"Anyway,"* she laughed, "back to the story of Esther. So Esther was this beautiful girl; she must have been *really* beautiful because—out of all the other girls in the kingdom—King Xerxes chose *her* to be his queen!"

"King *what?*" Raquel laughed. "Weird name!"

"I know," said Sara, laughing too. "There's a *lot* of weird names in the Book of Light."

"Esther became a queen when she was only thirteen years old?" Raquel asked incredulously.

"We don't know for sure," Sara admitted, "but she was probably about that age. Girls married young back then."

"I'll say!"

"So anyway, King Xerxes... let's refer to him as the 'X-man,' shall we?"

Raquel started cracking up. Sara was so glad to see her friend finally enjoying life.

"So the X-man," Sara continued with a grin as Raquel continued to laugh, "decided that Esther would be his queen, and the Book of Light says that Esther got a *whole year* of beauty treatments!"

"Whoa!" Raquel said, still laughing. "It's good to be queen!"

"Actually, that was even *before* she became queen," Sara said, "so just *imagine* what life was like *after* she was queen!"

"Nice," Raquel grinned, nodding.

"And the X-man was *extremely* rich! Esther was allowed to wear whatever clothes and jewelry she wanted to from the king's palace! She had fallen into the lap of luxury."

"Lucky girl."

"But she hadn't always been so lucky. Her mom and dad died when she was young, so she was an orphan."

"Oh," Raquel said, her face falling.

"Before living in the palace, she lived with her older cousin Mordecai, who raised her. And even after she started living there, Mordecai stopped by the palace every single day to check on her."

"That's so cool."

"Yeah," Sara nodded. "And Esther didn't forget about Mordecai, either—even after she became queen. She kept following his rules just like she did at home."

"What rules?"

"She had been taught to keep her nationality a secret."

"Why?"

"Because Esther and Mordecai were Jewish," Sara explained, "and Jews were treated badly—not only in this story but pretty much all throughout history."

"That doesn't seem fair," Raquel frowned.

"That's because it's *not* fair," Sara agreed. "But at that time in history, warriors of the King were mostly Jewish—and the Prince Himself was Jewish when He lived on the earth—so they often came under attack by sombras (and by humans under the influence of sombras). Even today, Jews are still persecuted... just for being Jewish."

Raquel looked enraged at the injustice.

"So Esther followed Mordecai's directions and didn't tell anybody that she was Jewish," Sara said, then added to try and lighten the mood, "...even her husband, the X-man."

Raquel smiled.

"Shortly after Esther became queen," Sara continued, "Mordecai became a guard at the palace gate. One day, while he was on duty, he overheard a conversation between two other guards talking about how they planned to murder the X-man. Mordecai told Esther about it, and Esther told the X-man—being careful to give credit to Mordecai for the information. So Mordecai helped save the X-man's life, and he was later rewarded for this. Then, this dude named Haman got promoted to a really high position in the palace, and everybody was told to bow down to him whenever he went by. But Mordecai refused to bow down to him."

"Why?" Raquel wondered.

"The Book of Light doesn't say," Sara said. "Maybe because Mordecai was a warrior of the King and had decided that he would never bow down to anyone other than the King. Or maybe he just somehow knew that Haman was a major creep."

Raquel laughed again. "Why was Haman a 'major creep'?"

"Because when he saw that Mordecai wouldn't bow down to him and he found out that Mordecai was Jewish," Sara told her, "he decided to kill not only Mordecai but also every other Jew in the kingdom."

"What?" Raquel exclaimed. *"Why?"*

"Because he was a major creep," Sara said with a shrug. "And because—and this is my opinion—it goes back to the whole thing about people being influenced by sombras. This was a perfect opportunity for Mentiroso to destroy the King's warriors."

"Who's Mentiroso?" Raquel wondered.

"He's the leader of the sombras; all of the other sombras answer to him. He's the most powerful sombra, but never forget, Raquel, that the King is more powerful still. Mentiroso can only do as much as the King allows him to do."

Raquel nodded thoughtfully.

"So Mentiroso put the idea in Haman's head to kill the Jews. When the Jews heard that their lives were in danger, they cried out to the King for help."

Raquel smiled wistfully. "I'll bet He helped," she said.

"You bet He did," Sara nodded, "but not in the way you'd expect. One thing about the King is expect the unexpected."

"So what happened?" Raquel asked eagerly.

"Well, Esther heard that Mordecai was depressed and it made her worried so she sent a servant out to the palace gate to ask him what was wrong. Even though Esther lived in the palace, she hadn't heard the bad news yet about Haman's plan to kill her people, the Jews. Mordecai told the servant about Haman's plan and asked Esther to go to the X-man and plead for their lives. Esther sent a message back to Mordecai telling him that no one was allowed to see the X-man unless they were invited by him. If she went to him uninvited, the X-man could have her killed."

"She's *married* to the X-man, right? He would kill his own wife?"

Sara nodded. "A king could do whatever he wanted," she said. "So Queen Esther's life would be in danger if she approached the king uninvited, and Esther reminded Mordecai of that. But Mordecai's response to Esther has gone down in history as being famous."

"What was it?" Raquel wanted to know.

"Mordecai said that if she didn't ask the X-man to spare the Jews, she would be killed along with all the other Jews. And he said, '*Who knows if perhaps you were made queen for just such a time as this?*' In other words, "Maybe the King put you in the palace at this specific time in history so that you would be able to save the Jews' lives.'"

"Wow."

"So the Jews would all die unless Esther came to their rescue. And the only way she could come to their rescue was by risking her own life by approaching the X-man uninvited."

"Did she do it?"

Sara smiled. "She told Mordecai to get all the Jews in the kingdom—the warriors of the King—to pray to the King, asking Him to help her. Then after three days, she went to the X-man uninvited, and the King answered the prayers of His warriors... Esther's life was spared! *And* she saved the life of every single Jew in the kingdom, too!"

"Wow," Raquel breathed. "She was so brave!"

"You're pretty brave yourself, Raquel," Sara replied. "Just like Esther walking in to ask the X-man for help, you walked into the treatment center to ask for help."

Raquel shook her head. "I went there to ask for help just for myself. Esther asked for help for an entire race of people! I'm nothing like Esther."

"By helping yourself, you were helping others too, Raquel," Sara said with a smile. "One life touches so many others. By walking into the treatment center, you saved not only your own life but also the lives of your family members and friends... especially me."

Raquel's eyes welled up with tears. She let all her defenses go and pulled Sara to herself in a tight embrace. "You're such a good friend, Sara," she said.

Chapter 29

Austin

Sara's heart was full to overflowing. The King truly did marvelous things. She knew He would save Raquel's life just like He saved Esther's so long ago because Raquel was asking the King for help. "Thank You, King," she whispered, "for hearing us when we come to You for help. Give Raquel courage as she attends this treatment center. Don't let her stop attending, Father. Let her keep going so that she can get the help she needs for her eating disorder."

On her way to her next class, Sara heard someone shouting in the hallway. There was a lot of noise in the school hallway, as usual, but somebody was shouting above all the other noise. As she got closer, she could tell what they were shouting: "I'm lost!"

She thought that was a strange thing to be shouting; the school year was practically over… how could they not know where their class was?

She tried to see who it was, but there were so many other kids in the hall that she couldn't see who was yelling. Then she heard it again: "I'm lost!" The voice was getting louder, so she must be getting closer. Some kid just kept screaming over and over again, "I'm lost! I'm lost!"

Then she saw who it was: A boy was standing in the middle of the hallway with kids passing by him on either side—completely ignoring him or, even worse, laughing at him. He looked like a regular seventh grader, so why was he acting like this? If he was lost, why didn't he ask a teacher or another student for directions instead of standing in the middle of the hallway yelling "I'm lost" over and over again?

Someone else must have been wondering the same thing because another boy got up in his face. "If you're lost, why don't you ask for directions?" the kid demanded. "Why stand here in the middle of the hallway and look like an idiot?"

A small crowd had now gathered, and they were enjoying the show. The boy who was lost wasn't saying anything now; he was looking around terrified at the laughing kids and especially at the boy who was right in his face. "What class are you looking for?" the kid demanded.

"I'm lost," the boy merely repeated.

"I know you're lost, stupid," said the other kid, eliciting another peal of laughter from the crowd. "I'm trying to *help* you, dummy. Tell me where your class is and then you won't be lost anymore, get it?"

"I'm lost."

"You're such an idiot," he laughed. "Are you retarded, or something?" He knocked the boy's books out of his hands. The crowd cheered.

Enraged, Sara started toward the kid. She didn't know what she would do or say once she got there, but she knew that she couldn't just stand by and let this boy get picked on.

But before she could reach them, a tall African-American boy stepped up to the kid. He was over a foot taller than him and had some muscles to show off, so needless to say he got the kid's attention. "Leave him alone," he said in a gruff voice.

"Hey, man," the kid said, the color draining from his face. "I was just helping him find his class."

"Knockin' the books outta his hands ain't helpin' him," the taller boy told him. "Pick 'em up."

The kid looked around at his audience. His fear was quickly turning to pride. "If you wanna help him," he said, staring up at him, "then *you* pick—"

Before he could finish, the African-American boy grabbed the other by the front of his shirt and yanked him toward him so that they were nose-to-nose. "You pick 'em up or you be hurtin'," he informed the kid.

Before the kid even had time to react, the hall monitor appeared from out of nowhere, grabbed both boys by the arms, and began to escort them down to the office. "Let's go," he said coldly. The first kid rebelled and tried to get away, but the hall monitor's grip was firm. Sara noticed that the African-American kid—although he was as tall as the hall monitor himself—went willingly without a fight.

With the perpetrator gone, the crowd began to disperse. The lost kid hadn't moved; he was still standing in the middle of the hallway looking as lost as ever. He bent down slowly to pick up the books that had been knocked out of his hands.

Sara made her way over to him. She bent down and helped him gather his books. "I'm sorry that kid was mean to you," she said kindly. "Don't worry though; he probably won't bother you again."

The boy stared at her with wide eyes and an open mouth.

Sara smiled. "Here ya go," she said, handing his books back.

The boy looked down at the books, taking them from her, then back up at Sara. He smiled.

"Are you still lost?" Sara wondered, standing to her feet. "Maybe I can help you find your class."

The boy rose slowly to a standing position, looked at Sara, and again repeated, "I'm lost."

Sara raked a hand through her hair, unsure of what to do to help him.

"Where are you trying to get to, Austin?" asked a girl, stepping forward. "Let me see your schedule."

Understanding filled the boy's eyes as he quickly opened a binder, pulled out his school schedule, and handed it to the girl. The girl quickly glanced over the schedule. "Your next class is room 118," she informed him. "It's just right there, Austin. You're standing right next to it."

"I'm lost," he repeated.

"C'mon," she sighed, pulling him toward the room. "You're gonna make me late for my class—you know that, right?" She stuck her head into room 118. "Excuse me," she said to the teacher sitting at her desk. "Is Austin in your next class?"

"Yes," the teacher replied, not looking up from the work she was doing on her desk.

"Well, he's out here yelling that he's lost."

The teacher looked up and then over at one of the students sitting at a desk. "Carl!" she said angrily, "Get out of Austin's desk!"

A boy who apparently was Carl started cracking up as he moved quickly from one desk to another. "Austin, your seat is available now," she said wearily. "Go sit down."

The girl appeared frustrated with the teacher. She looked at Austin with a compassionate expression. "It's okay now, Austin," she told him. "Go sit down."

The boy obeyed, taking a seat at the desk that Carl had been occupying. Sara was glad to see that the boy didn't look humiliated; he merely sat down and got his books ready for class to start. Carl and his friends rolled their eyes and whispered insults at him under their breath. The teacher didn't seem to notice or care.

The girl turned away from the classroom and headed quickly down the hall. Sara caught up with her. "Thanks for helping him," she told the girl.

"Oh, it's no problem," the girl said distractedly, obviously concerned about being late for her next class. "That's not the first time I've had to help Austin."

"Why did he keep yelling that he was lost?" Sara wondered.

"Austin has autism," she said.

"What's autism?" Sara wondered.

The girl stopped her frantic rush to class and turned to Sara. She didn't look frustrated, just bored as though she'd explained this to so many other people before and was getting tired of it. "It's a communication disorder," she said quickly. "Austin has trouble with words—both speaking and understanding certain phrases... but don't let him fool you; he's actually really smart."

"How do you know about him?"

"His family has lived on my street for years," she said. "I've been asked to watch him a lot."

"Why was he shouting that he was lost? He seemed to know right where his desk was."

"Oh, he knew alright," she nodded. "But Carl (I'll deal with him later) was purposely sitting in his desk so that Austin wouldn't have anywhere to sit."

"Couldn't Austin have just sat down in a different desk?"

The girl shook her head. "Nope. A lot of people with autism like routine, and if you throw off their routine they don't know what to do. Their brain is a lot like a computer; once the data has been entered, they're 'programmed' to do things a certain way. Austin saw the other desks, but since they weren't his he wasn't going to sit in them."

"So why didn't he just tell the teacher that someone was in his desk?"

"I told you," the girl sighed, "Austin has a communication disorder. He can only say what he's been taught to say.

His mom taught him to say 'I'm lost' whenever he can't find where he's supposed to go." She shrugged. "I guess she taught him to say that so if he ever wandered away from their house and someone started questioning him, he would be able to tell them he was lost so they could help him get home. Well..." she said, "I've gotta go," and she hurried on down the hall and into one of the classrooms.

Sara figured she'd better head for her own classroom. She made it just as the tardy bell sounded.

Throughout the entire class period, Sara couldn't get Austin out of her mind. What would it be like to have a communication disorder? What would it be like to know that you needed help but to not know how to ask for it?

Then it hit her like a ton of bricks: That's how Raquel used to be. She knew she had an eating disorder, but she didn't know how to get help for it. Sara imagined Raquel standing in the middle of the hallway screaming "I'm lost" just like Austin—with everyone passing her by.

She shuddered. That's how it had been; Raquel had been screaming "I'm lost" internally, but people had been passing her by—oblivious to her cries for help.

How many other girls were screaming out for help every day as they walked the school hallways? How many other Austins and Raquels were there?

Chapter 30

Carteis

At the end of the school day, Sara was waiting outside for her bus to show up when she saw the African-American boy who had come to Austin's rescue. He was sitting off by himself against the wall. He was a big kid; he looked like he was definitely into weight-lifting. He had really dark skin and wore baggy clothes—just like most of the other boys at this school. His arms were resting on his knees and he was staring off into space… actually, *glaring* was more like it. He'd probably gotten a detention for fighting and wasn't exactly thrilled about it. If only the hall monitor had known that he'd been fighting for a good reason—in order to defend Austin. Actually, would that have made any difference?

Go and talk to him.

Sara had learned to recognize the King's voice. She laughed. "No way," she whispered. "Look at him, Father! He's *huge!* He might beat me up just for getting close to him!"

Go speak to him.

It was no use; Sara knew that she could ignore the King, but that eventually she'd have to give in if she was going to have any peace. She sighed. "What do I say?"

I'll give you the words to say.

"Okay."

Sara tried to appear nonchalant as she wandered over to him. At first he didn't seem to notice her, but as she got closer he suddenly looked up at her sharply.

"Hey," Sara said nervously. "What's up?"

He predictably didn't respond but continued to glare at her.

"I think it was really nice what you did for Austin today."

"Who?" he yelled angrily, his voice just as mean and gruff as she remembered.

Sara cleared her throat. "Austin, the boy in the hallway—"

"Whatever," he interrupted, looking away.

Sara took a deep breath and let it out slowly. *You said you'd help me, remember?* she reminded the King.

I can do all things through the Prince who strengthens me.

Sara smiled and thanked the King for the reminder.

"Mind if I have a seat?"

When the boy made no move to respond, Sara went over to the wall and sat down beside him—ensuring a safe distance between them. The boy jerked his head in her direction. "What you doin'?" he demanded.

"Just sittin'."

"Not there, you're not!"

Sara was feeling braver than before, so she had courage enough to chuckle and say, "Don't worry… I don't bite."

The boy glowered at her another moment and then looked away.

"I'm sorry you got in trouble with the hall monitor. You were just trying to help."

"What's it to you?" the boy shouted, turning to look at her.

He was so much bigger than her; she cowered under his glare. "I—I just meant..." she stammered.

The boy scrambled to his feet so quickly that it startled her. He grabbed up his backpack and walked several feet away, throwing it down and collapsing heavily onto the ground against another section of the wall.

Sara sighed. "Now what?" she whispered.

Keep trying.

Hesitantly, Sara stood and walked over to him slowly. "What you *want?*" he demanded before she had even reached him.

For some reason, she found that she wasn't afraid of him. She knew it was the Prince giving her strength. "I wanted to meet you."

"How come?"

"My name is Sara."

"So?"

"What's yours?"

"Why you care?"

"I just—"

"Just go away!"

Sara was used to dealing with her dad. Her dad used to be hard to talk to, too, so this was not unfamiliar territory for her. She didn't give up trying to talk to her dad, and she wouldn't give up now, either. "You mind if I sit down?"

"Yeah, I mind!"

She sat down anyway.

"You deaf? I said I mind!"

"You haven't told me your name yet."

"If I tell you my name, will you leave?"

"Maybe," Sara smiled. "Maybe not."

"You annoyin', you know that?"

"Yeah, I know. I've been told that before."

For the first time, the boy cracked a smile. He even chuckled a little. "You said yo' name is Sara?"

He *was* listening! "That's right," she nodded.

"Carteis," he said, indicating himself with his thumb.

"Nice to meet you, Carteis!"

Sara extended a hand. At first, the boy stared at it, then he looked up at her. With a sigh, he took her hand and shook it. *Whoa, what a grip!* Sara was afraid he was going to squeeze her hand off. "You're pretty strong," she said between clenched teeth.

"Oh, sorry," he said, releasing her hand. He really did sound sorry.

"That's okay," she said, rubbing her hand. "At least I still have one good hand."

He snorted. "You funny."

"I try," she said with a smile. "You sure are big for a seventh grader."

He smirked. "Comes in handy sometimes."

"Yeah, like today! That was awesome how you came to that boy's rescue!"

Carteis shrugged but Sara could tell that he was proud.

"Do you even know Austin?"

"Nope," he said. "All I know is...hate to see kids picked on."

"Bet nobody picks on *you!*"

Carteis had been smiling up till this point, but now his face fell. "You don't know nothin' about me!"

Sara realized that she'd said the wrong thing. "I'm sorry," she said. "You're right...I don't."

"So don't go making 'ssumptions 'bout me based on the way I look, got it?"

Sara nodded. "I didn't mean to," she said sincerely. "I'm sorry, Carteis. You're right."

Carteis seemed surprised at the apology and turned away.

"I don't like it when people make assumption about me, either," Sara offered.

Carteis blinked.

"It doesn't matter what people think about us, anyway. All that matters is what the King thinks."

"The King?"

Sara nodded. "He said in His Book of Light, *'I have told you these things, so that in me you may have peace. In this world you will have trouble. But take heart! I have overcome the world.'*"

Carteis smiled. "You got peace?"

"Sure! Don't you?"

"How you s'pposed to have peace in this dang world?" Carteis snorted. "Wit' people judgin' you all the time?"

"When He lived on the earth," Sara told him, "the Prince said, *'The thief comes only to steal and kill and destroy; I have come that they may have life, and have it to the full.'*"

"Who's 'they'?"

"Whoever chooses to follow the Prince."

Carteis studied her, a strange expression on his face.

"Oh, sorry, Carteis," she said, jumping to her feet. "That's my bus, I've gotta go. I'll talk to you later!" And she ran to get on the nearby bus that had just pulled up.

Chapter 31

The Stand

When you choose to follow the King, that doesn't necessarily mean that things are about to get easier; sometimes, it means just the opposite. But being a warrior means that you always have the King on your side to help fight your battles for you. Raquel was now finding this out for herself.

Sombras, it seemed, didn't choose their moments to attack arbitrarily. Everything seemed pre-planned... right down to the second of the attack. They seemed to know when her moment of weakness would come, and they seemed to be able to wait for it. Raquel very rarely found herself being attacked when she was feeling sure of the King and His power. It was usually moments of doubt when she wasn't sure whether or not the King was even there or when she doubted His love for her. It was at these moments that the enemy chose to send fiery darts of despair and hopelessness her way. Sara was right: sombras were good fighters.

Raquel was learning how to be a good fighter herself. She was learning to recognize her own weaknesses so that she would know her moments of vulnerability. She continued to be caught off-guard, but the number of times was becoming fewer and fewer. She was learning where and when she could expect a sombra to show up.

A time when she could almost undoubtedly expect a battle with sombras came after her daily trip to the treatment center. This didn't surprise her; Mentiroso didn't want her believing that food was good for her rather than bad, so naturally he would send the sombras under his authority to try and convince her to stop going to the center. The lies came in varying forms, but they were always lies: *They're trying to control your life... You don't need their help; you can beat this on your own... How can you know for sure that what they're telling you is true?* These were the most effective fiery darts: the ones that came in the form of a question. They always made Raquel want to stop and answer them. The questions were still lies, though, so she was learning to ignore the questions along with everything else.

She kept the Book of Light handy in her moments of doubt. She was finding that it really was one of her best defenses against the enemy; sombras *hated* hearing what the Book had to say—probably since the words came directly from the King Himself. Without the Book of Light, Raquel would have no weapon with which to fight them off. Not only did the Book provide her with the life-giving assurance she needed, but the words themselves had power. It really did seem as though quoting the Book had the effect of fingernails on a chalkboard to the sombras. She didn't know what she would do if she ever managed to get caught without the Book of Light around.

Then one night she got the chance to find out. She had just gotten home from the treatment center and left her backpack downstairs since she hadn't had any homework. She'd forgotten that the Book of Light was in there, too.

She knew she was being attacked when the familiar lies started: *The center is not helping you... It's not too late to quit... What's so wrong with exercising?*

Against her better judgment, she stopped to think about the question. What *was* so wrong with exercising? It was good for the body, right?

But not excessive exercising.

Raquel immediately recognized the voice of the King. It was that still, small voice that did not come abrasively and loudly as the other voices did. It came gently but steadfastly; there was no mistaking it.

Also against her better judgment, she began to argue with the King. "What if I exercise just a *little bit,* tonight?"

Silence.

"Wouldn't it be okay if I exercised just for fifteen minutes tonight? I could practice some of the stuff they're teaching us."

Again, silence.

Raquel felt herself growing frustrated; she didn't like it when she couldn't hear the King's voice—she took it to mean He was ignoring her.

"Fine!" she exclaimed, reaching for the remote control. "If I'm not gonna get any help from You, I'll get a little help from the TV!" She turned it on and quickly found an exercise program. It was the first time she'd turned to an exercise program since attending the center.

She didn't notice the sombra's claws in her head until half-way through her 15-minute workout. She panicked and ran over to her dresser, but the Book of Light wasn't there. She saw the sombra in the mirror's reflection towering above her; she imagined that it had a vicious grin on its face. She had her armor on, but it wasn't doing her much good at the moment since her head was unprotected.

She did a quick search for her backpack; she'd left it downstairs. Without a second thought, she threw open her bedroom door and raced down the stairs—the sombra easily keeping up with her while keeping its claws firmly planted in her head. When she reached the living room, she flipped on the light and froze: There was an ambush waiting for her! Her backpack lay next to the couch where she'd dropped it, and several sombras stood guard around it.

They had planned all this out?

The sombras stood still, waiting for her to approach. She'd already forgotten about the sombra standing behind her.

It's my own fault, she found herself thinking. *I should have brought it upstairs with me. Why was I so stupid? Better yet, I should have just left the Book at home.*

This last lie was a mistake on the sombra's part. Raquel knew better than to leave the Book of Light at home; there were just as many sombras at school as there were at home. She'd been convinced that these thoughts were her own up until hearing this, but now she knew that the sombra standing behind her was initiating them.

"Leave me alone!" she yelled, spinning around to glare up into its dark face. "I *know* you're the one saying that stuff!"

A fireball hit her so hard that she fell over. She'd forgotten about the other sombras, and as soon as her attention was elsewhere one of them had taken the opportunity to send a fiery dart her way. Thankfully, she'd turned to the right so that the shield of faith on her left shoulder had effectively shielded her. Day by day since attending the treatment center, her body was growing stronger, so she now found that she could stand under the weight of her armor without any trouble. Of course, fireballs could still knock her down.

Raquel stood quickly to her feet. She was mad now. "Get out of my house! *All* of you!" she commanded.

The sombras looked at each other; they were probably laughing at her.

"In the Name of the—"

Two of the sombras came swarming toward her—wings beating violently. She let out a shriek. "Help me, King!" she shouted.

She watched in awe as the two sombras were yanked off their feet by Relámpago who had a tight hold of their wings—one in each hand. He pulled them back so hard that they landed on their rears before they'd even realized what had happened. As soon as they saw who had a hold of them, they immediately began floundering around like chickens—trying to get to their feet with the help of their wings but their wings were still held tightly in Relámpago's grasp. They attempted to slash him with their claws, and when one of them got too close for comfort Relámpago released them and they rushed to the safety of the other sombras like frightened buzzards.

Every sombra in the room was now focused on her guardian criado rather than on Raquel. This was good for her, naturally, but not so good for Relámpago. In a movement as swift as lightning, her guardian criado drew his immense sword from its sheath and held it out before him with both hands. The sombras took a step back at this gesture, but none of them seemed willing to leave. Not without a fight, anyway.

For several seconds, nothing seemed to be happening. It was something of a standoff as the sombras continued to stand their ground around the backpack and Relámpago continued to hold his sword out to them. Finally, one of the sombras spoke; she could see its mouth move. Relámpago responded to it but she couldn't hear him, either, since he wasn't manifested. Then her guardian criado jerked his head in her direction. He was looking at the sombra holding her in its grip. She looked up at it—watching as a forked tongue danced about. *What was it saying?*

Raquel looked back at Relámpago and tried to read his lips: he used the word "Tentación" so she knew this was who held her captive. Tentación would try to talk his way to a victory, Raquel knew. But she also knew that Relámpago was not easily defeated with words any more than with blows. He could hold his own against her captor.

But couldn't she help him? After all, she was one of Paraíso's warriors! She had all the power that Relámpago possessed if only she would apply it. "'*Finally,*'" she quoted aloud from the Book of Light, "'*be strong in the King and in his mighty power. Put on the full armor of the King so that you can take your stand against the enemy's schemes.*'"

Relámpago's eyes shifted from Tentación down to her. A smile slowly spread across his face; she smiled back him. He looked back up at Tentación and said something else. Raquel noticed that she no longer felt oppressed. She looked back; Tentación had released her.

Now free from the sombra, she ran forward quickly to get away from him—not realizing that she was running straight toward the flock of other dark shadows over by the couch. She also didn't realize that the sombras were scattering upon her approach until she looked around and noticed that they had all dispersed to separate corners of the room. *Had she really just scared them away?*

Relámpago was laughing heartily. He said something, and one of the sombras must have taken offense because it sent a fireball blazing his way. Relámpago readily blocked it with the flat of his blade and then—propelled by his powerful wings—flew straight into the sombra, impaling it with his sword before it even knew what was happening.

This seemed to signal the start of the fight: The other sombras in the room all rushed at Relámpago. Raquel watched incredulously as the Native American criado slashed one before it could reach him and grabbed another by the top of its head and rammed his sword into its stomach. The next sombra to attack was more of a challenge for him; it grabbed a tight hold of Relámpago's right arm (the arm that held the sword) and sunk its claws in. Relámpago cried out in pain and grabbed onto the sombra's other arm as it attempted to scratch his eyes out. It was now a power struggle between the two beings; they seemed to be matched equally in strength. Raquel watched as both the criado and the sombra struggled for dominance. With the shadow's claws in his arm and no use of his sword, the criado appeared to be on the losing end.

But Raquel could help him!

Suddenly remembering, she looked around at her feet for her backpack. It was next to the couch—right where she'd left it. She quickly unzipped it and pulled out the Book of Light. She stood back up, aimed it at the sombra, and opened it wide.

The powerful light slammed into the back of the sombra and sent the creature colliding with Relámpago. It was momentarily stunned but quickly recovered and soon a wrestling match ensued—both criado and sombra rolling around on the floor. One moment, the criado would be on top, then the sombra. Raquel forgot all about the Book of Light she held in her hands and stood mesmerized at the brawl. The sombra's claws finally became too much for Relámpago to handle and he dropped his sword. Before he could retrieve it, the sombra had heaved Relámpago over onto his back with his arms pinned to the floor. The look on Relámpago's face scared her; she had never seen even a trace of fear on the criado's face, but he looked afraid now.

Which enraged Raquel. Remembering the Book of Light in her hands, she aimed it directly at the monster's head—just as it was about to come at Relámpago's face, teeth bared. The light struck it so hard that the creature was thrown off of the criado. Arms now free, Relámpago reached for his sword and sent it slicing through the air—and slicing through the sombra.

All of the sombras were now gone.

Except for one. Tentación still stood in the doorway to the living room having watched all of this unfold—not coming to the defense of the other sombras but having chosen instead to stand back and watch them die rather than get involved.

Relámpago got to his feet as quickly as he could—clearly in pain. But he was determined to defend Raquel to the death.

"It's okay, Relámpago," Raquel said, surprised at how calm her voice sounded. "You've done enough. It's my turn now."

She turned and faced Tentación. "I was a fool to listen to you," she told him. "You won't catch me off-guard again. You tempted me to exercise because you know very well that too much exercise will start me losing weight again." The words were hard to say, but she kept going. "Well, I don't *want* to lose any more weight, okay? I've got a new agenda now, and it doesn't include *you!* I *know* that I'm already beautiful tonight—I don't need to lose weight to make that happen!"

Raquel's words seemed to be revitalizing Relámpago… and weakening Tentación.

"You would have me on a slow downward spiral toward death, but you're *done* trying to make me lose weight, Tentación, do you hear me? *Done!*"

Tentación was backing out of the doorway, but Raquel wasn't about to let him leave without ensuring that he felt a little pain. "'*Temptation,*'" she quoted, "'*comes from our own desires, which entice us and drag us away. These desires give birth to sinful actions. And when sin is allowed to grow, it gives birth to death.*' But death is no longer an option for me."

Suddenly, something obscured her vision. She dropped the Book of Light and her hands flew to her face; she felt something hard covering her head. She heard Relámpago laughing and looked over at him, now manifested and surrounded by a halo of light. "I guess the King figured this was the best time to present you with the helmet of salvation," he said while sheathing his sword, eyes shining.

Then her vision was no longer obscured as the helmet of salvation and the rest of her armor vanished. She looked over at the doorway; Tentación was gone.

Chapter 32

Prom Night

She had conquered Tentación in one area of weakness, but there was yet another over which she was still allowing the sombra to have control.

Raquel didn't like to think about it. She knew what it would mean: giving up control of her relationship with Gabe and turning it over to the King. And she already knew what the King would have her do: Break up with him.

And she wasn't ready to do that. Not till after prom night. Prom was only one week away. "Just *one more week,*" she pleaded with the King. "I'll break up with him after *one more week,* okay? *Please* don't ask me to do it now; You *know* how much I've been looking forward to this. I've already got the dress, and everything."

It didn't matter what excuses she tried to use, she knew the real reason she didn't want to break up with Gabe but she also knew she wasn't about to discuss it with the King. She knew what He would say on the matter and she didn't want to hear it.

So she continued seeing Gabe at school as though nothing had changed, even though everything had changed. She wasn't the same person at all that she had been four months ago, but she led Gabe to believe that she still enjoyed his kisses as much as she had in the beginning. The truth was, she didn't. She still enjoyed them, but it wasn't the same anymore; they no longer captivated her the way they used to. Maybe it was because she wasn't seeing the love in his eyes that she wished was there. But whenever Gabe reached for her, she stuffed the bad feeling way down deep so that she could just concentrate on the physical—although the physical just wasn't enough anymore.

The physical seemed enough for Gabe. Whenever Raquel tried to ask him about his day or tell him about something going on with her, he would lean in and start kissing her and the conversation would be over. It was as though he weren't really interested in her life. Raquel tried to convince herself that this was what love was all about, but she knew better now. She'd read about true love in the Book of Light, and true love really had nothing to do with the physical.

The whole school was abuzz the Friday of prom. Everyone was talking about who was going with whom, and the staff had already begun to put some decorations up. The school cafeteria would be turned into a dance floor. Signs were hung everywhere announcing the big event, as if anyone could forget. Raquel could hardly wait for the school day to end so that the night could begin.

Her mom was nearly as excited for her as she was; she kept telling her about what a wonderful time she was going to have. Raquel felt like a hypocrite. If her mom knew what she planned to do with Gabe, she wouldn't be so excited. *Lighten up, Raquel,* she told herself. *There's nothing wrong with what you're going to do with Gabe.*

She put on the strapless white dress her mom had bought for her and looked in the mirror. The breastplate of righteousness covered her torso and her newest piece of armor, the helmet of salvation, covered her head—the visor lifted and the letter "S" inscribed on the front. For all her trouble of dressing up and fixing her hair, she couldn't see any of it. "Well, at least *Gabe* will be able to see it," she said resolutely.

Her mom helped her pin on the new corsage Gabe had given her to replace the old one. She told her she looked beautiful and even kissed her on the cheek—something she never did. She drove her to the school at seven o'clock and said she'd be back to pick her up at ten when it was over. Raquel told her she didn't need to do that; she could get a ride with a friend. She didn't tell her about Gabe's plan to borrow his older brother's car, even though he wasn't yet fifteen.

As she entered the school, her eyes got wide when she saw how the cafeteria had been transformed. Streamers and balloons hung from the walls, and a huge banner read "Welcome to Prom Night." Some popular music was playing and a DJ was already taking requests. Several other students had already arrived—the girls in beautiful dresses of different colors and the boys mostly in button-down shirts and slacks. None of them were in tuxes. She wondered if Gabe would be wearing a tux.

Not seeing Gabe, she walked over to the refreshment table. A long table had been set up with a cake already cut into slices with the pieces on individual plates, along with a large bowl full of fruit punch. Thanks to the treatment center, she was starting to develop an interest in eating again; she thought she might like to try a small piece of cake. She was reaching for a plate when she felt an arm around her waist. She jumped in surprise, then felt a warmth encompass her. "Hey, Baby," Gabe whispered in her ear, kissing her on the neck.

She turned to face him. He looked *so* handsome! Unlike any of the other boys, Gabe was wearing a tux—complete with black bowtie and shiny black shoes. He even *smelled* nice! And, as usual, he was wearing a smile that made her heart melt. *She was the luckiest girl in school!*

"Now, you weren't about to touch that cake, were you?" he said playfully, holding her close. "You want it to go straight to your waist?"

Raquel felt all the blood rush to her face. *What a jerk!*

Gabe noticed her reaction. "Hey, I didn't mean anything by it," he said quickly. "I was just playin'. Don't let it ruin our evening." He looked at her seductively. "I've been looking forward to this evening for a long time."

He was only joking, she told herself. "I've been looking forward to it, too, Gabe," she said.

"I hope you don't have after-prom plans," he said with a wink.

She felt her heart jump; he was wanting the same thing she was!

He kissed her softly on the lips. *Oh, what his kisses did to her!*

The prom was everything she'd dreamed it would be—like a fairytale come true. She danced with Gabe as he held her close, looking into each other's eyes. He was a true gentleman; he knew all the right words to say and all the right dance moves. During some of the more romantic songs, he would cup her face in his hands and kiss her tenderly on the mouth. Every time he did, she felt the warmth spread throughout her body all the way down to her toes. She wished he would kiss her harder, but she knew there were teachers watching to make sure the students were acting "appropriately." She could wait; it was just a little longer till prom would be over and then the night would *really* begin!

Around nine o'clock, Gabe asked her if she was ready to go. With a dreamy look, she said she was ready. Hand-in-hand, they walked out the front doors of the school—away from the loud music and into the silence of the night. She looked up at the night sky; spring was now here and the weather was getting warmer, but she strangely felt a chill. She shivered.

Noticing, Gabe released her hand and put a hand on her bare shoulder. "Are you cold?" he asked.

"No," Raquel said, smiling up at him. "I'm alright."

"I bet I know of a good way to warm you up," he said, smiling down at her.

She gazed into his eyes. He was so beautiful.

He'd never disclosed much about his family, but they must have been well-off because his brother's car was a red Mustang. "Nice car," she said sincerely, going around to the passenger side.

He looked at her over the roof of the car. "It will be once you're in it," he said smoothly.

She grinned and got in.

The car was very spacious with plenty of legroom. Raquel made herself comfortable. "Where are we going?" she asked with a smile.

He smiled back. "I know of a nice park where we can be alone to gaze at the moon… and do other things," he added.

Raquel ignored the persistent voice in her head telling her to *get out now.*

"Sounds good," she told him.

Gabe drove to a park near her house. It was a nice park that overlooked a lake with several benches scattered throughout where couples could sit. Gabe parked the car in a secluded spot with only one streetlamp glowing nearby.

Raquel's heart was racing in anticipation of what she was about to do; she'd been longing for this moment ever since she'd laid eyes on him.

Turning off the ignition, Gabe sat staring at her in the stillness. Then he reached over and stroked her hair. "You look very beautiful tonight, Raquel," he told her. His eyes looked strange in the light of the streetlamp.

She grinned. Gabe always made her feel like a princess.

He continued stroking her hair, then gently pulled her head toward him and kissed her on the mouth.

The verses came unwarranted and unwanted:

Mark out a straight path for your feet; stay on the safe path. Don't get sidetracked; keep your feet from following evil.

She pulled back.

"What?" Gabe asked, looking at her strangely.

"Oh, nothing," Raquel said quickly, not wanting to ruin the moment. She found it annoying that the verses had to pop into her head right now—just as she was trying to create a magical memory.

She went back to kissing him. The kissing became more intense.

How can a young person stay pure? By obeying your word.

Again, she pulled back.

"*What,* Raquel?" Gabe demanded. He was sounding frustrated now. "I thought you wanted to do this."

"I do," Raquel said, combing her fingers through her hair. "I mean, I *did*..."

"Don't tell me you're changing your mind."

"No, no," Raquel said quickly. "It's just... maybe we could do this some other time."

"Why?"

"I—I'm not sure I'm ready, Gabe."

Gabe sat back and sighed, looking at her. "Chickening out, huh?"

This struck a nerve. *"No,"* she said defensively. "I just want more time, that's all."

"More time for what? To find somebody *else* to do it with?" He sounded hurt. Raquel didn't want to hurt him.

"No, Gabe," she said sincerely. "You're the only guy I'm interested in. *Really.*"

"Then why wait?"

What excuse could she give? She remembered Sara's words. "What about STDs?" she said. "And what if I got pregnant?"

Gabe laughed as though she had made a joke. "You honestly think that's gonna happen?"

"It *could* happen, Gabe. You *know* it could."

"What if I told you I brought protection with me?"

"What?"

"I've got some right here in my pocket. They give it out free at school."

Raquel's mind was swimming. *Now* what excuse could she give? "That doesn't always work, Gabe. And even if it did, I still want to wait."

"I thought you were different from other girls, Raquel," he said, shaking his head disappointedly.

Finally, be strong in the King and in his mighty power. Put on the full armor of the King so that you can take your stand against the enemy's schemes.

Raquel felt her courage growing. "I *am* different," she informed him. "But in a *good* way."

"What's *that* supposed to mean?"

"It doesn't mean anything, Gabe. Look..." She sighed. "Gabe, you mean a lot to me. When we first met, you made me feel special, and I want to thank you for that. But..." How could she make him understand? "Things are different now."

"How are they different?"

Raquel raked her fingers through her hair. "I don't know, it's just... I used to think I needed this," she told him, "You know... the *physical* part of love. But I don't need that anymore."

"You don't want me to show you that I love you?"

"Love isn't something you can show someone in one night. It takes time."

"We've been dating for *four months*, Raquel," he reminded her. "You should let me show you that I love you."

"You've already had plenty of opportunities to show me that, Gabe."

A fire sprang into his eyes that startled her, but it was quickly replaced by softness. "Then let me take that opportunity tonight," he said, and drew her to him, kissing her passionately. Raquel felt her insides churn within her and her heart pounding like a drum.

She *did* want this! It felt *so right!*

Gabe's hand moved from the back of her head down to her shoulder and then down to her front.

Raquel felt her stomach tighten. It felt right, but it felt wrong, too.

An image flashed through her mind of Tentación on top of her with his clawed hand over her breastplate. *Temptation comes from our own desires, which entice us and drag us away.*

Raquel gasped and shoved his hand away. "Get your hand *off* me!"

There was no longer a softness in Gabe's eyes. He looked at her like an animal about to devour its prey and pulled her toward him abruptly, kissing her on the neck.

"Stop it, Gabe!" she shouted, trying to shove him away. But he was too strong for her.

"Just relax," he said. His voice was chillingly calm.

"I want to get out of here!" Raquel screamed, still struggling against him as he inched his way closer. "Drive me home *right now!*"

He seemed deaf to her. He pressed toward her until he was on top of her.

"Get off of me, Gabe!" she shrieked.

She watched as one of his hands reached down to lift her dress.

"No!" she screamed in horror. *"Prince, help me!"*

Gabe's arm was suddenly wrenched behind him as from an invisible source. Then his other arm was yanked off of her, as well—both arms pinned behind his back. "Hey!" Gabe shouted in pain and alarm. *"What the heck's going on?"*

Raquel herself didn't know what was going on until she saw Relámpago sitting on the hood of the car—reaching through the windshield with a tight hold on Gabe.

"What in the heck is going on here?" Gabe demanded, struggling against the invisible hands. Gabe's strength was no match for the criado's; he struggled to no avail.

Raquel looked through the windshield at Relámpago. He mouthed one word: "Run."

Raquel threw open the car door and ran. She stopped a short distance away and looked back: A sombra with a snake-like tongue sat on top of the car. Tentación was reaching down through the roof of the car with his claws planted firmly in the top of Gabe's head—bending his mind to do his will like a puppet master.

Tentación looked her way. Seeing that he'd lost his victim, the sombra noticed her guardian criado sitting on the hood and instantly released Gabe—flying full force at Relámpago and clawing at his face and arms. Raquel watched in terror as her criado did nothing to defend himself; he was determined to keep a tight hold of Gabe.

"Oh, King!" Raquel cried out. "Help Relámpago!"

Instantly, two other criados flew to the scene and yanked Tentación off of Relámpago. Stunned, the sombra took to the air, shouting something back at them as he left. The two criados began immediately tending to Relámpago's lacerations.

Even now, the Native American criado refused to release his hold on Gabe. She knew he wouldn't release him until she was safely home.

Chapter 33

The Ring

Raquel ran the mile and a half to her house—heart pounding with both exhaustion and terror. Tonight she'd never felt so vulnerable… or so terrified. Gabe didn't *love* her; he had wanted to *use* her. She could see that now. Why didn't she see it before?

She arrived at home out of breath, threw open the front door, and ran quickly through the living room and up the stairs—avoiding her mom as she sat on the couch. "Hey," she heard her mom call to her. "How'd it go?"

"I'll tell you tomorrow," Raquel called back. She didn't want to talk about it. Not with her mom. Not with anybody.

Alone in her room, she finally broke down into sobs—her pent-up fear causing her whole body to shake. "I'm sorry, King," she said over and over again, crying into her pillow. "I'm sorry, I'm sorry, I'm *so* sorry." He had tried to warn her and she didn't listen.

As she cried out to the King, she felt a peace envelop her like a blanket. Her sobbing subsided; she could feel the King's gentle hand upon her. He was forgiving her. Even though she didn't deserve it, He was forgiving her.

This was love.

She sniffed and turned over on her back. "I love You, King," she said with a smile. "I love You, Prince. Thank You for protecting me tonight. I love You *so much*."

She closed her eyes, repeating the phrases over and over again. And she meant every single one of them.

She woke up the following morning and found herself lying on the bed still wearing her white dress. She rose slowly and walked over to the mirror. Once again, she couldn't see past the armor, but she was okay with that today. Her armor *meant* something: it meant she was loved and protected by the King.

It was a Saturday, and there were only a couple weeks of school left. She'd attended the eating disorder program for a month now; they say it takes twenty-one days to develop a habit, and Raquel was finding that she was starting to develop some new habits. She no longer weighed herself every morning and evening, and she no longer exercised after coming home. Instead, she filled these time gaps with reading from the Book of Light and spending more time with her mom—which was something she never thought she'd find herself doing. Raquel didn't think she was the only one who had changed; her mom seemed different, too. She seemed to want to get more involved in her life. Why she had waited till now Raquel didn't know, but it was a welcomed change.

Her mom had told her some funny stories about her dad. At first, Raquel didn't want to hear them, but then she got curious. She found that, deep down, she still loved her dad—despite what he had done to tear the family apart. He was only human, after all, and everyone makes mistakes; she had seen for herself how powerful the desire for physical affection could be. Maybe she'd been too hard on him. Besides, if her mom could forgive him for what he'd done, shouldn't she?

"Your father has always been *such* a jokester!" her mom had laughed one evening during what used to be Raquel's workout time. "Once, when we were dating in college, your dad called me on the phone and disguised his voice and said, 'I thought you should know, ma'am, that a rabid dog has been spotted outside your dormitory.' I didn't go to *any* of my classes that day, I was so scared! And the jokes only got better after we were married: When we'd been married for about a month, I went to wash the dishes and got sprayed by the spray nozzle! Your dad had taken rubber bands and put them around the sprayer so that the water would automatically spray when the water was turned on!"

Her mom had recalled story after story until both Raquel and her mom were laughing so hard they had tears running down their faces. When Raquel had looked over at Relámpago, he had been laughing, too.

Raquel started recalling all the practical jokes he'd played on *her*—and that *she* in retribution had played on *him!* The ole salt-on-the-toothbrush trick never failed to get a reaction, and the lotion-on-the-doorknob trick never got old. April Fool's Day had always been her dad's favorite day of the year. She'd forgotten what a great sense of humor her dad had.

Then the conversation had taken a serious turn as her mom began to recount all the things she loved about her dad: the way he'd held her and told her he loved her—her mom having always pushed him away. Raquel had never heard her mom be so open with her before. It was obvious she was still in love with him.

Was it too late for them to get back together? It was clear her mom wanted to. She wondered if her dad wanted to, too. It *would* be kind of nice, she supposed, having him around again.

Raquel changed out of her prom dress—throwing the corsage in the trash—and into a t shirt and shorts. Now that it was May and the weather was finally warming up (and now that she wasn't trying to hide anything anymore), she wore normal clothes around the house instead of the baggy sweatshirts and sweatpants she'd worn before. She went downstairs to find her mom.

On most Saturday mornings, her mom either slept in or ran errands or simply lay on the couch watching TV. Once, she'd caught her mom reading from her own copy of the Book of Light—which had absolutely floored her. She didn't even know her mom *had* a copy of the Book of Light! Could she see the light pouring out of it? What else could she see? Raquel hadn't asked, and her mom hadn't volunteered the information, but had merely looked up at her with a smile on her face.

This morning, the living room was empty, so she figured her mom must still be in bed or out running an errand. With a sigh, she flopped down on the couch and started channel surfing. She hadn't gotten far when she heard shouting coming from upstairs. Raquel sat straight up. Seconds later, she heard footsteps thundering down the stairs. Her mom rushed into the living room looking panic-stricken, her face deathly white.

"Mom?" Raquel asked worriedly, running to her. "What's wrong?"

"I've searched *everywhere* for it, Raquel!" her mom said, her face changing from white to red as tears sprang into her eyes. "But I can't find it!"

"Can't find *what,* Mom?"

The tears were now finding their way out. *"My wedding ring!"* she sobbed.

Raquel breathed a sigh of relief. She considered saying, "Is that all?" but she knew how important her dad was to her. "I'll help you find it, Mom."

"I've already looked—" she said, then didn't finish. She ran back up the stairs, no doubt to continue tearing her bedroom apart in search of the ring.

Raquel sank slowly to the couch. If there had been any remaining doubt that her mom was still in love with her dad, it was totally obliterated now.

She wanted to help her mom. It wasn't like her mom to lose stuff. Where did she normally keep her ring? She'd only ever seen it on her finger, even after she'd ordered her dad out of the house. At night, she probably put it on her dresser. It must have fallen behind it, or something. Once, when Raquel was only three or four, she'd played "dress up" with some of her mom's jewelry—and that had included her wedding ring. The ring had wound up getting flushed down the toilet, and her mom had called the plumbing company and gone to all kinds of trouble to get it back. She wouldn't stop until she found it this time, either.

Well, there goes my Saturday, she thought drearily.

Raquel chided herself for being so selfish. Here, her mom was upstairs having a panic attack, and she was worried about *her* day?

What could she do to help? Raquel had no idea where to even begin looking.

She thought to ask the King for help. Why not? Hadn't the King helped her with bigger things than this? Was there any task too small that the King didn't have time to help His children with? He *loved* her; her problems became *His*.

Raquel clasped her hands together. "Father," she said, looking up at the ceiling. "I know in the big scheme of things, a ring is just a little thing, but I believe that You care about the little things, too, because You care about *us*. If it's our concern, then that makes it Yours, too. You know where my mom's ring is, Lord. Please, just... open her eyes, or something, and help her to see it. The Prince said in the Book of Light, *'I tell you the truth, my Father will give you whatever you ask in my Name. Until now you have not asked for anything in my Name. Ask and you will receive, and your joy will be complete.'* Well, now I'm asking, Father, in the Name of the Prince that You would help my mom find her ring."

She leaned back on the couch. There was nothing else to do now other than wait. Either that or keep asking for help; the King probably liked it when His children were persistent.

She looked over at Relámpago who stood guard near her, as usual. He offered her a small, concerned smile. Then she watched as Relámpago's face jerked skyward and his eyes remained glued to the ceiling for several seconds. Then he looked slowly down at Raquel, a smile creeping over his face. He spread his wings and—with a mighty leap and flapping of his wings—shot up through the ceiling!

Raquel sat there open-mouthed. She'd never seen her guardian criado desert her before. But within seconds he returned—sailing down through the ceiling with a great flutter of wings and took his place next to her again. His smile had now become a grin.

A moment later, Raquel heard another scream coming from upstairs.

This time, Raquel didn't wait for her mom to come down. She flew up the stairs and burst into her mom's bedroom. Her mom sat on her bed—hands clasped and head bowed.

Was she talking to the King? "Are you okay, Mom?" Raquel asked, concerned.

Her mom lifted her tear-stained face and held out one of her hands. In it was the ring.

"You found it?" Raquel asked incredulously. *"Already?"*

She clasped the ring to her chest, nodded, and began to cry tears of joy.

Raquel sat down on the bed next to her. "Where did you find it?" she wanted to know.

Her mom pulled herself together enough to talk. "I was tearing the room apart," she said. "As you can plainly see..."

Raquel looked around; the room was in shambles.

"...and I'd just about given up hope when I came and sat down here on the bed. I happened to glance over at my nightstand..." She broke down and started crying again. "... and there it was! I don't know how I could have missed it, Raquel! It's a *miracle!"*

Raquel looked over to her left at Relámpago, who donned a huge smile. She knew the King had told him where to find the ring and that the criado had retrieved it—placing it on her mom's nightstand where she would find it.

But only because she'd asked the King for help. In characteristic humility, the criado pointed heavenward—giving credit where credit was due.

"Ask and you will receive, and your joy will be complete."

As Raquel watched her mom cry tears of joy, she knew the verse was true. Sara had been right: The reason warriors don't have is because they don't ask.

Chapter 34

All Things New

Raquel knew come Monday morning that Sara would want to know all about her date with Gabe.

"Ask and you will receive..."

"King," Raquel pleaded. "I don't wanna talk to Sara about this. Please don't let her ask."

Yeah, right, she thought secretly. *What are the chances of* that *happening?*

But sure enough, as Raquel took a seat at the lunch table next to her friend on Monday—carrying her sandwich with mayo and her salad with dressing—she found that Sara wanted to talk about her own weekend and what she planned to do this summer... and basically kept a tight rein on her tongue. Never once did she bring up prom night.

Eventually, Raquel's curiosity got the better of her. "Aren't you going to ask me how my date with Gabe went?" she asked.

Sara took a bite of her sandwich and took a few moments to respond. Raquel took the opportunity to take a bite of her own. When Sara had finished chewing, she said, "I thought I'd let you bring it up if you wanted to."

"Aren't you the least bit curious about whether or not we..." Raquel didn't finish.

Sara took another bite. Strange how she was taking bites when she was supposed to be answering questions. "Yes," she answered finally. "I am."

"Then ask me," Raquel challenged.

Sara was about to take another bite, but Raquel reached over and gently put a hand on her friend's arm. Sara halted with the sandwich half-way to her mouth. "I'm glad you're enjoying your sandwich so much," Raquel smiled, "but could you possibly respond *before* you put more food in your mouth?"

Sara laughed and it came out as a snort. Both of them laughed for several seconds before Sara put her sandwich down and looked Raquel in the eyes. "The reason I didn't ask you," she said sensitively, "is because Espíritu told me not to."

Raquel felt her stomach drop. *"Espíritu* told you not to?"

Sara nodded shyly. "I know it sounds crazy," she shrugged, "but Espíritu really does speak to me. It's hard to explain, but—"

"No, I believe you," Raquel interrupted. "I just didn't know it was *Espíritu* doing the talking; I thought it was the King."

Sara smiled. "So you've experienced it too, huh?" she said.

"Well, *yeah...*"

"And the King and the Prince speak to us, too," Sara added, taking another bite.

Raquel pressed her fingers against her forehead. "Does that not blow your mind?" she asked incredulously, still in awe that the King—or Espíritu or *Whoever*—had spoken to Sara on her behalf.

Sara chuckled, still chewing. "Yeah, it does," she said, looking at Raquel in a new way.

"You're not gonna believe this, Sara," Raquel said, shaking her head, "but I asked the King for you to not ask me about prom night!"

"Oh, I believe it," she said, pointing to Raquel's sandwich. "But in your disbelief, don't forget to eat."

Raquel laughed, unoffended. For the past month now, Sara had made sure she ate her lunches—not in a pushy or condescending way, but with gentle reminders. And she'd made sure her own lunches were healthy so that Raquel wouldn't get discouraged and stop eating. Besides, Sara insisted, she needed to be eating healthy, anyway! Raquel greatly appreciated Sara for her constant consideration and encouragement. She had stayed true to her commitment to help her along the path to recovery.

Raquel took a bite of her sandwich, shaking her head. "I still can't get over that," she said incredulously.

"Get used to it," Sara laughed. "The King enjoys interacting with His kids."

Raquel looked at her and smiled. "Just like a Father," she said, taking another bite.

Sara nodded, her eyes aglow.

Raquel finished chewing and took another bite. "I've been thinking a lot about my dad lately, Sara... my *earthly* dad," she clarified.

Sara nodded again.

"My mom really does love him, Sara. And... I think I do, too."

"I've never heard you talk about your dad, Raquel," Sara observed, taking a bite of her salad.

"That's because, up till recently, I thought I hated him."

Sara's face fell. She took another bite of salad.

Raquel took a bite of her own and hesitated before continuing. "He cheated on my mom," she said, looking down at the table.

"Oh, I'm so sorry, Raquel," Sara said, clearly distressed by this news.

"It's okay," Raquel said, taking a deep breath. "I used to hate him for it. But now..." She shook her head, amazed at how the King had turned evil into good. "Now I've forgiven him," she told her.

"That's *awesome,* Raquel," Sara said, reaching for her friend's hand. "I know that couldn't have been easy."

Raquel looked her in the eyes. "It hasn't been easy for the King to forgive me either, Sara, but He did it anyway."

Sara nodded with understanding.

"Now," Raquel said, going back to her sandwich and Sara doing the same, "I find myself wanting my dad to come back. He's been separated from my mom since before Christmas."

"Does your mom want him to come back?"

"Oh, my gosh!" Raquel laughed. She recounted the incident of the lost and found ring. "You should have seen her, Sara; I thought she'd gone crazy!"

"You're right," Sara nodded. "She clearly loves your dad."

"Yeah," Raquel said, considering the statement. "I think I've finally figured out what love is, Sara. You tried to tell me once, but I didn't listen. Relámpago tried to tell me, too." Raquel laughed. "Even a chubby kid named Dante back in Paraíso tried to tell me!"

Sara smiled.

"My mom said that love is a commitment to care for someone no matter what happens."

"That sounds like a good definition to me."

"But it wasn't enough for me to be *told* what love was," Raquel said. "I had to find it out for myself. And I *did,* Sara. I found out that Gabe doesn't love me—and that he never did. *Real* love cares about what's on the inside of a person, not the outside. *Real* love is the kind of love the King has for His children—an unconditional, unselfish commitment. I know now that, even if my dad never comes back, I'll never stop loving him—'cause he's my dad."

Sara paused before speaking. "Have you asked the King about it?" she asked, her eyes shining.

"About my dad coming back?"

Sara nodded.

"Well, no..."

"You should," Sara said simply, taking a bite of salad. "You've got plenty of evidence that the King answers all kinds of requests."

"But..." Raquel tried to wrap her mind around what Sara was saying. "The King would bring my dad back... just 'cause I asked Him to?"

Sara shrugged. "You'll never know if you don't ask," she smiled. "The King doesn't always give us what we ask for, but you'd better believe He will if He already wants us to have it! Maybe the King wants your dad to come home, too—even more than you do! Maybe He's just waiting for someone to ask for it to happen. The King will move heaven and earth to answer His kids' requests."

"The King has to wait for someone to ask before He makes stuff happen?"

"Not at all," Sara said, shaking her head. "But He *chooses* to. He waits for His children to come to Him with requests. One reason, I think, is to help strengthen the Father/child relationship, but one of the main reasons is probably because it helps His warriors' faith grow. Just look what it did for yours when you asked the King to help your mom find her ring!"

"Or when I asked for you not to ask me about prom night," Raquel added.

"Exactly."

"Incidentally," Raquel said shyly, "nothing happened that night. Just so you know."

Sara didn't say a word, but her relief was obvious.

"So now," Raquel said, finishing up her sandwich. "I guess it's back to the drawing board, as far as relationships go, huh?"

"You'll meet somebody else, Raquel," Sara assured her. "You've got plenty of time. For goodness sake, you're not even in *high school* yet!" she laughed. "And look at me: I've gone thirteen whole years of my life without a boyfriend!"

Raquel looked at her curiously. "I thought you told me you were twelve," she said.

"I was," Sara smiled, "but this past weekend was my birthday."

Raquel felt her stomach turn. She'd been so selfish—caught up in her date with Gabe—that she'd forgotten all about it.

"Don't feel bad," Sara told her quickly. "I didn't expect you to remember, what with prom coming up, and everything."

"I should have remembered," Raquel said remorsefully, shaking her head. "I'm so sorry, Sara. Happy belated birthday."

"Thanks!" Sara laughed.

"I should have gotten you something."

"You *did,* Raquel," she said, giving her friend's hand a squeeze. "You got me the best present *ever!* You decided to *eat!*"

Raquel laughed, feeling tears burn in her eyes. "I owe that to you," she said.

"No, Raquel, you owe that to *Espíritu*. There's nothing I could have done to make you eat; you had to decide to eat for yourself. Espíritu is the One who changed your heart and gave you that desire." Sara smiled, tears in her own eyes. "And I'm so glad He did," she said. "Just your being here is birthday present enough."

Raquel choked on her tears. "You're just trying to make me start crying so you'll look better than me!" she teased.

Sara laughed. "You don't ever have to worry about *that!*" she said, embracing her friend. "Even on your worst days, you *still* look better than me! I *am* jealous of your hair, though!" she added.

"My hair?" Raquel asked, a hand going to her head. "But I thought you liked it better long."

"I do!" Sara laughed. "It's starting to grow out long again, but you hadn't even noticed!"

Raquel felt of her hair; it was down past her shoulders.

"I know it's not as long as you want it," Sara smiled, "but give it time. The King is making *all* things new! *'Therefore, if anyone belongs to the Prince, he is a new creation; the old has gone, the new has come!'*"

Chapter 35

Revenge

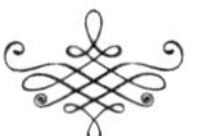

Tentación had now lost two major battles in Raquel's life, and Raquel imagined that the sombra probably wasn't too happy about it. Any day now, he would take his revenge.

Raquel would be ready. She had all her armor now; she'd seen the hilt of the sword of Espíritu in its sheath in her reflection. If the blade was anything like the hilt, the sword was magnificent: The hilt was gold-plated with two red rubies resembling Espíritu's eyes on both sides with a cursive letter "E" in the center of one side. It was driving Raquel crazy that she could see it but couldn't touch it. She knew, though, that the sword and everything else would materialize as soon as a sombra showed up. She almost couldn't wait for that to happen… just so she'd have a chance to use it!

About a week before school was out, Raquel was at her locker after last period putting her books away and keeping out the ones she would need to study for finals when someone grabbed a hold of her shoulders and spun her around.

It was Gabe. She hadn't spoken with him since prom night, and he'd seemed okay with that—content to completely ignore her. Today, however, he seemed far from content to ignore her; he was staring her down with a fierceness in his eyes.

Gripping her so tightly by the arms that it hurt, Gabe started cussing her out. Raquel suddenly forgot all about the pain in her arms; she'd never seen Gabe look or sound like this—not even on prom night. He was calling her every name in the book. As the shock wore off, though, Raquel found herself enraged; he had *no right* to be treating her like this! She started struggling against his grasp, which just made him grab a hold of her tighter. "You're gonna wish you didn't run out on me that night!" he hissed.

"What, am I the first girl smart enough to run out on you?" Raquel fired back.

He looked angry enough to strike her, but since they were in a public place he restrained himself. "You little—"

"How many other girls you been with, huh, Gabe?" she interrupted. "How many other girls have you used for your own animal-like self-indulgence? Can I help it if I'm smart enough to call it quits?"

He released her, much to Raquel's relief. He stuck a finger in her face. "You may think it's over," he snarled, "but this is *far* from being over!"

"Oh, it's over," Raquel assured him. "And I'll tell you something else, Gabe: If I hear even a *hint* of another girl liking you, I'm gonna tell her to stay as far away from you as possible!"

He sneered. "Jealous, huh?"

"This is *not* about jealousy, Gabe!" Raquel informed him. "It's about me cluing girls in to the slimy worm that you are!"

A fire leapt into his eyes. He grabbed her by the arms again. "I could make up just as many rumors about you, you little tramp," he wheezed.

"I never slept with you, Gabe, and you know it!" she whispered abrasively.

He smiled shrewdly. "But nobody else knows that, do they?" he smirked. "Plenty of people saw us leave together on prom night—an *hour* before it was over! It wouldn't be difficult at all, would it, to get people talking about the girl who can't say no!"

The implications of what he was saying pierced Raquel's heart like an arrow. There was only a week of school left, but Gabe could make it miserable for her—and guarantee that her stained reputation would follow her into high school. She felt sick at her stomach. Why did she *ever* involve herself with this guy in the first place?

"So it's up to you, sweetheart," he said, releasing one of her arms and gently stroking her face. "You keep my reputation clean, and I'll keep yours clean."

She slapped his hand away. "Don't call me sweetheart," she ordered. "You've never cared about me any more than a wolf cares about its next meal! And you can spread whatever lies you want to about me, Gabe; it's not gonna stop me from spreading the *truth* about you!"

He studied her for few seconds—searching her eyes. He released her. "You think the truth sets you free?" he laughed mockingly. "The real world doesn't work that way, sweetheart."

She smiled triumphantly up at him. "It just did."

The cocky smile dissolved from his face. "You're gonna regret this."

"Nope," she shook her head assuredly. "The only thing I regret, Gabe, is that I ever fell for you in the first place. Looks aren't everything, and you've got a heart of stone. I'll find someone who will treat me like the princess I am."

Gabe laughed loudly at this. "So you *do* think you're a princess! Oh, that's hilarious! Do you honestly think that when I treated you like a princess, I really meant it?"

"No, I don't," she said, amazed at his admission. "I don't think I'm a princess because of *you*, Gabe. I'm a princess because of I'm a child of the King, and that's how He treats me."

At the mention of the King, Raquel was astounded to see a look of fear actually flash across his eyes.

"I'm His daughter," she informed him, "so messing with me means messing with the King. Do you *really* wanna do that, Gabe?"

He snarled and uttered some profanities under his breath before turning and darting down the hall.

Raquel breathed a sigh of relief as soon as he was gone. The King had helped her to be brave while confronting Gabe, but now she found that her heart was beating rapidly and her knees were so weak she thought she would collapse. "Thank You, King," she breathed. "Thank You for helping me to stand firm against all those fiery darts."

She had a feeling there would be more.

She came home to an empty house. Raquel sat down Indian-style on the couch and opened up the Book of Light:

Yet for us there is but one King, the Father, from whom all things came and for whom we live; and there is but one Lord, the Prince, through whom all things came and through whom we live. But not everyone knows this...

This was as far as she got before a fireball sent the Book sailing out of her hands. More angry than fearful, Raquel jumped up to retrieve it and got blasted by another fireball—knocking her to the floor. She looked up to see Tentación marching toward her.

Remembering her newly-received sword of Espíritu, she drew it from its sheath and aimed it at the sombra. Tentación stopped short of reaching her. Breathing heavily, Raquel got her feet up under her and stood, facing the huge shadow. The sword of Espíritu felt so natural in her hand—as though it were designed specifically for her. She was now covered from head to foot in the King's armor—her head protected by the helmet of salvation, her feet fitted with the shoes of peace.

Not even a trace of fear filled her heart as she confronted the dark shadow. It was huge, but the King she served was bigger. She'd read in the Book of Light that very morning some verses that she'd committed to memory. She decided to share them with the sombra: *"'What, then, shall we say in response to this?'"* she quoted. *"'If the King is for us, who can be against us?'"*

The sombra took a step closer, and Raquel reciprocated the action to show the creature that she was not afraid. Tentación took two steps back.

"'He who did not spare his own Son,'" she continued quoting, *"'but gave him up for us all—how will he not also, along with him, graciously give us all things?'"*

Tentación began to circle her, looking for a weakness. Raquel kept her sword stretched out in front of her.

"'Who will bring any charge against those whom the King has chosen? It is the King who justifies. Who is he that condemns? The Prince—"

At the mention of the Prince, Tentación leapt at her—claws extended and fangs bared. Raquel slashed at the dark shadow with all her might, cutting the sombra across the forearm. Tentación stumbled back and inspected the damage. It had not been a mortal wound, and now the creature was angrier than ever.

But Raquel was not exactly happy herself. *"'The Prince who died—'"* she said, picking up where she'd left off, *"'more than that, who was raised to life—is at the right hand of the King and is also interceding for us.'* That means," she said, interpreting for the sombra, "that the Prince is alive and well and that He answers our requests, in case you didn't know."

Tentación took another flying leap at her. This time the sword of Espíritu caught on the sombra's wing, and as the sombra scrambled to get away the sword tore the wing all the way through from one side to the other leaving a gaping hole. The creature roared in pain and held up the wing with its one good arm—again assessing the damage. Tentación's flying days were over.

The creature looked at her and roared with wide-open jaws. But Raquel had more. "*'Who shall separate us from the love of the Prince?'*" she quoted. On the word "Prince," the sombra released the wing it was still holding in order to cover its ears; the wing fell useless to the floor. Tentación could only manage to cover one ear now because of his first injury. "*'Who shall separate us from the love of the Prince?'*" she quoted again, purely for the enjoyment of seeing it tormented. "*'Shall trouble or hardship or persecution or famine or danger or sword? As it is written: "For your sake we face death all day long; we are considered as sheep to be slaughtered." No, in all these things we are* more than conquerors *through him who loved us.'*"

It was clear the sombra was weakening, but it seemed determined not to give up. With its one good hand, it sent a fireball hurtling straight for her face. Before she had time to block it with the shield of faith, the visor on her helmet came swinging down so that her face was protected. But the force from the impact alone sent her flying backwards into the computer desk. She hit her head on the desk but didn't get knocked out since her head was protected by the helmet of salvation. The sword of Espíritu lay next to her where she'd dropped it after falling. Tentación wasted no time and came at her, reaching for the sword. It got there before she had time to grab it and the sombra snatched it up. The moment the sword's hilt came in contact with its hand, however, the creature immediately dropped it again and took several steps back—shaking its hand as though it had been burned. The sword must have had the same effect on sombras as the Book of Light itself.

Raquel grabbed up the sword and jumped to her feet—lifting the helmet's visor so she could see better. She needed to attack *now* while the creature was at its weakest! "*'For*

I am convinced," she shouted, *"'that neither death nor life, neither criados nor sombras…'"*

Tentación cringed but could no longer cover his ears—what with one wounded hand and another wounded arm.

"'…neither the present nor the future, nor any powers, neither height nor depth, nor anything else in all creation, will be able to separate us from the love of the King that is in the Prince, our Lord.'"

The sombra had met his match; unable to withstand any more verses—and unable to escape by flying—Tentación broke into a run straight for the dining room, its tattered wing dragging behind it and causing it to run off-balance. Raquel easily caught up with it and thrust the sword of Espíritu into its side. The giant shadow lurched and then fell—right through the dining room table and coming to rest beneath it.

Raquel found it only appropriate to quote one final section of verses to Tentación while watching him fade:

"Temptation comes from our own desires, which entice us and drag us away. These desires give birth to sinful actions. And when sin is allowed to grow, it gives birth to death."

Chapter 36

Reconciliation

Raquel still didn't know how to sing, but she was quickly falling in love with songs in the Book of Light. There was one song in particular—a whole chapter—that she found and was now reading daily:

O LORD, you have searched me and you know me. You know when I sit and when I rise; you perceive my thoughts from afar. You discern my going out and my lying down; you are familiar with all my ways. Before a word is on my tongue you know it completely, O LORD. You hem me in—behind and before; you have laid your hand upon me. Such knowledge is too wonderful for me, too lofty for me to attain. Where can I go from Espíritu? Where can I flee from your presence? If I go up to the heavens, you are there; if I make my bed in the depths, you are there. If I rise on the wings of the dawn, if I settle on the far side of the sea, even there your hand will guide me, your right hand will hold me fast. If I say, "Surely the darkness will hide me and the light become night around me," even the darkness will not be dark to you; the night will shine like the day, for darkness is as light to you. For you created my inmost being; you knit me together in my mother's womb. I praise you because I am fearfully and wonderfully made; your works are wonderful, I know that full well. My frame was not hidden from you when I was made in the secret place. When I was woven together in the depths, your eyes saw my unformed body. All the days ordained for me were written in your book before one of them came to be. How precious to me are your thoughts, O King! How vast is the sum of them! Were I to count them, they would outnumber the grains of sand. When I awake, I am still with you. If only you would slay the wicked, O King! Away from me, you bloodthirsty ones! They speak of you with evil intent; your adversaries misuse your Name. Do I not hate those who hate you, O LORD, and abhor those who rise up against you? I have nothing but hatred for them; I count them my enemies. Search me, O King, and know my heart; test me and know my anxious thoughts. See if there is any offensive way in me, and lead me in the way everlasting.

It was a long song, but she never got tired of reading it. She wished she knew the tune so she could sing it.

But she could quote it. And when Mentiroso decided to show up, she would.

With a vengeance.

She read the last two lines again:

Search me, O King, and know my heart; test me and know my anxious thoughts. See if there is any offensive way in me, and lead me in the way everlasting.

That was indeed her request this morning: *Know my anxious thoughts*. Her mom had told her that her dad planned to call later on that evening, and she wasn't sure she was ready. She loved her dad—she knew that—and she'd even forgiven him, but she was still afraid. What would she say to him?

The answer was staring her in the face—shining up at her from the Book in her lap.

Before a word is on my tongue you know it completely, O LORD. You hem me in—behind and before; you have laid your hand upon me. Such knowledge is too wonderful for me, too lofty for me to attain.

The King would be with her. He would give her the words to say. He *made* her; he would help her with one phone call.

"O LORD," she said, shutting her eyes tight, "help me not to be afraid. Do like You did for the writer of this song and '*hem me in—behind and before.*' I ask for this in the Name of the Prince."

She felt better after this—more confident—but how would she feel when the phone call came?

It was almost time for school, but she turned to one more of her favorite sections of the Book of Light before packing it away in her backpack:

For if you live according to the sinful nature, you will die; but if by Espíritu you put to death the misdeeds of the body, you will live, because those who are led by Espíritu are children of the King. For you did not receive a spirit that makes you a slave again to fear, but you received Espíritu. And by Him we cry, "Abba, Father." Espíritu Himself testifies with our spirit that we are the King's children. Now if we are His children, then we are His heirs—heirs of the King and co-heirs with the Prince, if indeed we share in His sufferings in order that we may also share in His glory. I consider that our present sufferings are not worth comparing with the glory that will be revealed in us.

"'*For you did not receive a spirit that makes you a slave again to fear, but you received Espíritu,*'" Raquel said, reading that part again. She didn't want to stop reading, but she looked at the time. Regretfully, she closed the Book and stuffed it into her backpack.

Her mom was waiting for her in the kitchen. "Take this with you," she said, handing her a bagel with cream cheese.

Raquel smiled. "Thanks, Mom," she said, taking the bagel from her mom and giving her a hug before flying out the door to meet her bus.

She enjoyed every bite of it in the five minutes she had before her bus arrived. When it pulled up, Raquel took her usual seat and waited for Sara to get on.

"What's up?" Sara asked cheerfully, taking a seat next to her friend.

Sara was amazing—perky even this early in the morning. Actually, Raquel had reason to be perky herself these days. But not today.

"What's wrong?" Sara immediately asked.

Raquel bit her lip. "I'm just a little nervous."

"About finals?"

"No," she said. "Finals will be a breeze compared with this."

"What, then?"

Raquel took a deep breath. "My dad is calling me after school today."

"That's *great*, Raquel!"

"I'm *scared*, Sara. You know the situation."

"Have you talked to the King about it?"

Raquel smiled. That was always Sara's first question. "Yes," she replied honestly. "I've asked the King to help me not to be nervous."

"Have you asked the King to bring your dad home?"

Raquel felt her stomach turn. She hesitated before responding. "Yes."

"Then maybe He's gonna do that, Raquel!" Sara said excitedly.

"That's what I'm afraid of, Sara," she said, looking her friend in the eyes. "I want him to come home, but… I'm scared."

Sara took her friend's hand. She was silent for a few moments before speaking. "You're afraid of getting hurt again, aren't you?" she said compassionately.

Raquel nodded, feeling her face get hot. She forcefully held back the tears.

"That's *normal* to be scared, Raquel," Sara reassured her. "I know what it's like to have a less-than-perfect dad."

"You do?" Raquel asked, wiping away a tear that had escaped.

"You bet I do," Sara nodded. "After my mom died, my dad never used to talk to me… like *never*. It wasn't till I was ten that he started to open up a little bit."

"What made him change?"

Sara smiled. "I think it was Espíritu," she said.

Raquel chuckled, shaking her head in disbelief at the coincidence. "I was just reading about Espíritu in the Book of Light this morning," she told her.

"What did it say?" Sara asked curiously.

"'For you did not receive a spirit that makes you a slave again to fear,'" Raquel said, quoting the verse, *"'but you received Espíritu.'"*

"I can't think of a more appropriate verse for your situation," Sara observed.

"Yeah, but what does it mean, though? I mean, I really miss Espíritu, and I wish He were right here with me, but—"

"He *is* right here with you, Raquel, remember?" Sara interrupted. "He somehow lives inside you now, so His power lives inside you, too!"

Raquel looked down at her hands. "It sure doesn't feel like it."

"I understand you're scared, Raquel. I really do. I was scared, too, when my dad started to change, even though it was for the better."

Raquel looked up.

"Change is *always* scary. I wanted my dad to talk to me, but at the same time I almost *didn't* want him to, either. What would it be like? I'd gotten used to things the way they were, you know?"

Raquel nodded in understanding.

"But things are *so* much better now, Raquel. My dad talks to me more than he used to, and it's *great!* He still wouldn't win any conversation contests..."

Raquel laughed.

"...but I'm being patient with him and taking it one day at a time—asking the King to help him every day. We have to remember that our parents have been this way for *years*. They're not gonna change overnight. It takes *time* to change, ya know?"

Raquel nodded; she knew.

"If you're worried about what to say to your dad," Sara continued, "try just keeping it simple. Say, 'I love you.'"

Raquel laughed. "You make everything sound so easy, Sara," she said.

Sara smiled and squeezed Raquel's hand. "Don't be afraid to love your dad, Raquel. He needs you now more than ever. Trust me, I know."

Raquel couldn't stop the tears this time. She gave Sara a tight hug. "I'm so thankful to the King for putting you in my life," she told her.

At the end of the day, after the parent of a friend from the treatment center dropped her off, Raquel walked into an empty house—her mom having gone out. The minute she sat down, the phone rang.

Raquel immediately felt her palms get sweaty. She wiped them on her shirt.

The phone rang again.

"*'For you did not receive a spirit that makes you a slave again to fear, but you received Espíritu,'*" she quoted aloud.

The phone rang a third time.

"Help me, King," she whispered. She picked it up.

"Raquel?"

It was her dad.

Her throat constricted; she couldn't talk.

"Raquel, is that you?"

Help me, King. "Yeah, Dad."

"Hey, Pun'kin."

Raquel felt her throat close up again. He hadn't called her that since she was a kid.

"I miss you," she heard him say.

The tears ran silently down her face. She didn't wipe them away. "I miss you, too, Dad."

There was a pause on the other end. "I'd like to come home."

Raquel felt an overwhelming, inexplicable joy and peace come over her. There were no more reservations in her heart; *she wanted him to come home, too!*

"Raquel?"

Raquel suddenly realized that she hadn't responded. "I want you to come home, Dad," she said.

There was a muffled sound on the other end. Her dad was crying.

Unable to restrain herself any longer, Raquel broke down into sobs. "I love you, Dad," she said, "...and I forgive you."

It was at least a minute before she got a response from him, but his response was worth waiting for. "I love you, too, Pun'kin," he said.

Chapter 37

Relapse

Tomorrow was the last day of school. Raquel's mom had gone out to eat supper with her dad. Raquel had been invited, too, but Raquel knew it would be an emotional reunion for both of them and she wanted to give them a chance to be alone together.

Her dad would be returning the following week! Raquel couldn't believe how excited she was at this realization. She used to be glad he was out of her life, but now she couldn't wait for him to become a part of it again. Would he and her mom argue as much as they had before? She seriously doubted it. She'd seen the look on her mom's face whenever she talked about him; she was in love with him. Looking back on most of the shouting matches, it had been her mom who had caused most of them—or at least prolonged them. But her mom had changed; Raquel had seen it. She had a feeling there would be a lot fewer shouting matches from now on.

Raquel was glad to have the house to herself. With Tentación off her back—*and* out of her head—she felt a renewed sense of freedom. As far as she knew, Gabe had *not* spread lies about her around the school. Perhaps this was because Tentación had been the one giving him the idea to do so and—with Tentación out of the picture—maybe Gabe had lost the gumption to follow through on his threat. Or maybe he was just plain scared that *she* would follow through on *hers*—telling every single girl who bat her eyes at him what a creep he was! Whatever the reason, though, Gabe seemed to be keeping his mouth shut.

Today had been her last day at the treatment center. She'd attended for about two months, and she and her mom and the people at the center had decided that she was well enough to start practicing on her own what she'd learned at the center. She'd met some wonderful new friends there and would miss them greatly. She planned to stay in touch.

She no longer counted the calories in all of the foods she ate, and she felt healthier—*and looked better*—than she had in a long time. She'd learned to see herself through the eyes of the King rather than the eyes of the world. The world saw her as ugly no matter *what* she tried; the King saw her as *beautiful* no matter what. Raquel had decided that she liked the King's view of her better.

All of the fashion magazines she had kept on her dresser were in the trash now. She still cared about fashion, but she saw no reason to hold onto old issues. When a magazine showed up in the mail, she looked through it quickly to get the latest on fashion and then threw it in the garbage. Leaving the magazines lying around the house served as too much of a temptation for her to start obsessing again over weight.

She sat on the couch in front of the TV. Her mom had told her not to wait up for her—that she wouldn't be home till late. Raquel had told her that was fine, and it was. She wanted her mom and dad to have all the time they needed to make things right.

She got bored with the reality show that was on and started channel surfing. She came across the exercise program that she used to watch. She thought of changing it right away, then hesitated. What could be so wrong with watching it—just for a few minutes? It wasn't like she was going to actually start doing the exercises. Besides, she was *done* with intensive workouts; they did what they were designed to do which was to cause her to lose weight, and that was no longer Raquel's goal: her new goal was to *gain* weight.

Gain weight. The words sent a shiver up her spine.

She pushed the thought away. Gaining weight was a *good* thing, she reminded herself. It was the path to healing that she needed to stay on.

Gain weight. The phrase entered her mind again and caused her heart to jump.

What was the deal? She thought she was *done* with this never-ending cycle of negative thinking.

Gain weight and you'll be ugly.

Frustrated, Raquel changed channels, hoping that this would make the voice stop in her head. For a couple of minutes, the voice stopped—only to come back again.

Exercise is good for the body.

She found herself surfing back to the exercise program again.

Look at their bodies. You could look like that, too, if you exercise.

Raquel caught herself staring at the woman's flat stomach and again changed the channel. But she couldn't get the image out of her mind—the woman's sleek body doing sit-ups with a tightly-toned midsection and thighs. She turned it back to the station.

You could look like that.

She wished she *did* look like that. What would it take to look like that?

Exercise.

Raquel got down on the floor and started mimicking the actions of the lady on the TV. After only a short time, she could already feel her muscles getting tighter. She liked the feeling.

What was she doing? She'd already done her exercises at the treatment center earlier, and that was all the exercising she was supposed to do today!

What harm could a little more do?

What harm *could* a little more do?

She exercised for a few more minutes and found herself asking why she had ever stopped. It felt *so good* to exercise! How could this be bad for the body? Besides, how much weight could *really* be lost from fifteen minutes of exercising, anyway? Couldn't she exercise a little more than she was accustomed to *and* continue to gain weight?

Gain weight. Her heart was racing, and not from the exercise she was doing. She was trembling at the thought of gaining weight. She thought she'd gotten *over* her fear of weight gain, so what was going on? Was she going back on her commitment to Sara to get better?

Sara. Sara had been the one to give her the constant encouragement she needed, but now school was almost out and Sara wouldn't be around anymore. Raquel felt the pounding in her heart increase as fear gripped her. She suddenly felt all alone; she *knew* she couldn't beat this disease on her own.

Disease. Wasn't that too strong a word—just for wanting to lose weight? In fact, now that she thought about it, the term almost seemed silly and juvenile. *Disease*. Ha! If she had a disease, then so did everybody else in the world who wanted to be thin! The thought was laughable.

What was so wrong with wanting to be thin? Being thin had gotten her the cutest guy in school!

Raquel's stomach turned; just the thought of Gabe made her want to puke.

They're not all like him, she heard in her head. *There are actually some cute guys out there who are nice. Don't you want to look good for them?*

Yeah, she did. And wasn't that *normal?* Wasn't it normal to want to look good so that guys would like her? If she gained weight, how hard would it be for her to find a boyfriend? She certainly didn't plan on staying single forever, that was for sure! There was *no way* she'd allow herself to be the *only girl* in high school without a guy! But would any guy even *want* to date her if she gained weight? She pictured herself getting fat… so fat that guys avoided her.

The image made her shudder.

She suddenly decided that she'd been wrong to try and gain weight—this was a *big mistake!* She was going to end up ruining her life! She *had* to start dieting again!

Hurriedly, Raquel jumped up from the floor and raced to the computer—glad now that she hadn't deleted the calorie chart she'd created. She hadn't been on the computer since starting the treatment program because the temptation would have been too great not to revert back to tallying up her daily number of calories, but now the thought of *not* counting calories terrified her. How could she have been so naïve as to think that she didn't need this? If she didn't keep track of the number of calories she ate, she'd start gaining weight! She *couldn't* let that happen!

The computer wouldn't warm up fast enough for her. When it was finally up and running, Raquel immediately pulled up the calorie-counting spreadsheet she'd created. It was like a breath of fresh air just seeing it again, and Raquel gave a contented sigh of relief. *It was still here. She could continue using it. There was no reason she* shouldn't *continue using it.*

She tried to remember what she'd eaten that day. *Think, Raquel!* For breakfast, she'd had a bagel with cream cheese. Butterflies immediately began swarming in her stomach.

How many calories did a bagel with cream cheese have? A bagel alone had 220 calories *more* than an English muffin! But she couldn't remember how many calories were in cream cheese. *She had to find out!*

Her trembling hand wouldn't move fast enough on the mouse; she clicked on the old website she used to go to in order to research the number of calories in food. Seeing the site was like seeing a long-lost friend. She smiled. Why had she ever left it?

Cream cheese. She typed it in: One tablespoon had 35 calories! How many tablespoons had she eaten on her bagel this morning? At *least* two! That was 70 calories right there, and that's not even including the *bagel!* An English muffin had 63 calories, she remembered, and a bagel had 220 calories more than that, so some quick math revealed that a bagel had 283 calories! Add that to the 70 calories of cream cheese and it came to a whopping *353 calories!* But Raquel's panic increased when she considered that that wasn't *all* she'd had for breakfast! She'd also let her mom convince her to drink a cup of 2% milk—*138 calories!* For breakfast alone, she'd eaten nearly *500 calories!* And that was just for *breakfast!*

Why had she been so stupid? Why had she let her mom talk her into converting back to bagels with cream cheese? She knew better than to do that; why had she done it? Why had she let her mom convince her that eating bagels was *okay?*

Her mom was hoping she'd get fat, wasn't she? Come to think of it, her mom had been buying a *lot* of fatty foods lately! Her mom was trying to *make her fat!* The thought enraged her. How *dare* she! How *dare* she try and control what she ate! Raquel quickly scanned the chart she'd made; *none* of the foods her mom had been buying lately were on there! Of *course* they weren't; they had too many calories! Her mom was *purposely* going behind her back and buying foods that had too many calories to try and make her *gain weight!*

But Raquel was on to her tricks now. Just *let* her mom try and force her to eat all those fatty foods she'd bought! She couldn't make her do *any*—

Her thought was interrupted when she felt something touching her. She looked down: A dark shadow in the form of a snake was slowly winding itself around her legs.

Chapter 38

Deleted

Raquel screamed and tried to run but the snake had already managed to secure her legs together. She struggled to pull them loose but the black shadow only squeezed them tighter together. Raquel cried out in pain.

The snake continued winding itself slowly up her body—now reaching her knees.

Raquel reached for her sword but as soon as she touched the handle, the snake's head darted for her hand and sunk its teeth in. Raquel let out a scream and quickly withdrew her hand. *But she was defenseless without her sword!* She reached for the sword again and once again the snake's head went for her hand. She quickly withdrew it before it could bite her again, but this time the snake stopped its coiling and instead darted up to her face.

Raquel shrieked in terror and closed her eyes tight—expecting at any moment to feel a snake bite on her face. After several seconds, she finally dared to open her eyes.

What she saw made her heart quake in terror. Inches in front of her face was a giant snake head in the shape of a king cobra—its hood spanning at least two feet! It was hissing in a tone so low that it almost sounded like it was growling. A forked tongue waved about, and two glowing red eyes were fixated on her. The eyes made her gasp; they were the opposite of Espíritu's. Espíritu's eyes burned with an intensity of love; the snake's burned with an intensity of hatred she hadn't thought possible.

Raquel sat frozen in fear. The cobra seemed to be mocking her. Slowly, it lowered its head and resumed its wrapping of her. It had now reached her waist—securing her to the computer chair.

With a sudden revelation, Raquel knew who this was: Mentiroso, the leader of the sombras!

She searched her mind frantically for the verses from the Book of Light that she'd memorized. She was terrified when she realized that her mind was blank; she couldn't remember a single one! And of course the Book itself was nowhere nearby. She instantly reached for her sword again, but she was too late; she watched as the hilt disappeared beneath the cobra's coils.

With a sudden realization that had come too late, Raquel realized that Mentiroso had been the one filling her mind with lies all that evening—from the exercise program to the fear of gaining weight to the need to start counting calories again. Why hadn't she seen it? She'd let her guard down—assuming she was in the clear since she no longer needed the treatment center. She was finding out now that Mentiroso had been waiting for this precise moment of weakness in order to strike.

But it wasn't too late! She could still escape! With his lies, Mentiroso had successfully been able to draw Raquel to the computer—convincing her to turn back to her old lifestyle of needing the calorie chart, but with one simple click of the mouse the chart could be erased!

Her hand flew to the mouse just as the snake was about to bind her arm to her side. She clicked on "Select All" and was about to hit "Delete" when Mentiroso realized what she was doing and sunk his fangs into her hand. Raquel let out a cry and shook her hand violently in an attempt to shake him off—unable to use her other arm as it was presently wrapped tight in the snake's coils. Mentiroso refused to let go. Raquel could feel the venom from his fangs starting to take effect—draining her of her courage.

Ask Me for help.

She recognized instantly the voice of the King, and she obeyed.

"King, help me!" she cried.

Mentiroso released her hand and darted up at her face. Again, Raquel flinched, but she felt her courage increase as she realized that this was as close as Mentiroso could come; her head was covered by the helmet of salvation. He stared at her with hatred in his eyes, and Raquel stared right back. "You can't scare me anymore!" she declared to it. "I'm the King's daughter—"

He opened his mouth wide to reveal hideous fangs and Raquel flinched. She thought she heard a laughing sound coming from the snake as he went back to his coiling.

More determined now than ever, Raquel's hand darted for the keyboard: *Delete*.

Enraged, Mentiroso's hiss became a scream as he began to constrict himself tightly around her body. Raquel screamed in pain as her legs were squeezed tightly together—nearly cutting off the circulation.

Ask Me for help, she heard again.

"Help me, Lord!"

The coils immediately loosened around her legs.

Raquel felt her courage growing; Mentiroso was at the mercy of the King! The old snake could do no more than the King allowed.

Verses from the Book of Light suddenly lit up her mind like a beacon. She shouted them aloud:

"Finally, be strong in the King and in his mighty power. Put on the full armor of the King so that you can take your stand against the enemy's schemes."

Mentiroso again tightened his grip on her but Raquel found that her breathing was unaffected because of the belt of truth and the breastplate of righteousness that covered her. Realizing this increased her courage and she shouted out more verses:

"For our struggle is not against flesh and blood, but against the rulers, against the authorities, against the powers of this dark world and against the spiritual forces of evil in the heavenly realms."

Mentiroso was now realizing, too, that his constricting of her was having very little effect—which only seemed to infuriate him. His hissing became louder and more intense but—again, as if in subordination to a Higher Power—he loosened his grip.

"Therefore put on the full armor of the King, so that when the day of evil comes, you may be able to stand your ground, and after you have done everything, to stand."

The snake's body fell from around her. Raquel leaped from the chair and stood with the sword of Espíritu drawn—aimed directly at the snake's head. "You have no more power over me," she informed the snake. "I am the King's daughter and He fights for me! I belong to *Him*—not to *you!* I will no longer listen to your lies, Mentiroso!"

The cobra's head was now raised so that he was at eye level with her—the eerie red eyes glowing inside the dark shape. But Raquel would not be intimidated by him; the King was stronger. Other verses from the Book of Light flooded her mind and she promptly repeated them:

"'For if you live according to the sinful nature, you will die; but if by Espíritu you put to death the misdeeds of the body, you will live, because those who are led by Espíritu are children of the King. For you did not receive a spirit that

makes you a slave again to fear, but you received Espíritu.' I will no longer be afraid of the *truth*, Mentiroso!"

The sombra darted for her hand that held the sword; she slashed at him with all her might. She missed, but so did the sombra. The cobra recoiled quickly—hissing loudly and circling her. Raquel kept her sword aimed at the leader of the sombras. She stood her ground, recalling more verses:

"...your right hand will hold me fast. If I say, 'Surely the darkness will hide me and the light become night around me,' even the darkness will not be dark to you; the night will shine like the day, for darkness is as light to you."

The cobra's head darted toward her again; Raquel struck with a vengeance—cutting a huge gash near the serpent's head.

Mentiroso reared back, screaming in pain. The intensity of the hatred in his eyes grew as he raised himself up to a new height so that his head was now far above her. His breathing became heavier. Suddenly, a bright flash of light sent Raquel sprawling to the floor. She looked up to see the cobra preparing to spit another fiery dart her way.

Raquel quickly rolled out of the way just as the fire left his mouth. She jumped to her feet again—having never let go of her sword.

"For you created my inmost being; you knit me together in my mother's womb. I praise you because I am fearfully and wonderfully made; your works are wonderful, I know that full well."

Mentiroso blasted her with another giant ball of flame. She lifted the shield of faith with which she extinguished the serpent's fiery dart.

"All the days ordained for me were written in your book before one of them came to be. How precious to me are your thoughts, O King! How vast is the sum of them! Were I to count them, they would outnumber the grains of sand. When I awake, I am still with you."

The serpent breathed in deeply again and spit another venomous fireball. Again, Raquel used her shield and couldn't believe that she hadn't felt a thing—not even the impact of the blast! *The King was on her side!*

"What, then, shall we say in response to this? If the King is for us, who can be against us?"

Mentiroso reared back in preparation for another fiery blast but Raquel stepped forward and slashed through his body with the sword of Espíritu. He let out a terrible scream and quickly recoiled—moving away from her.

With every verse she quoted, she felt the King renewing her strength.

"Who shall separate us from the love of the Prince? Shall trouble or hardship or persecution or famine or danger or sword? As it is written: 'For your sake we face death all day long; we are considered as sheep to be slaughtered.' No, in all these things we are more than conquerors through him who loved us."

Upon hearing the Name of the Prince, the snake's hissing became almost deafening but it did not strike but rather continued to slowly circle her. Raquel kept the sword of Espíritu stretched out in front of her.

"For I am convinced that neither death nor life, neither criados nor sombras, neither the present nor the future, nor any powers, neither height nor depth, nor anything else in all creation, will be able to separate us from the love of the King that is in the Prince, our Lord."

Raquel fell to the floor as one of her legs was yanked out from under her. She looked down: the snake's tail was wrapped tightly around her leg. Mentiroso had worked to maintain her focus on his head so that he could catch her off-guard with his tail. She looked up to see the leader of the sombras towering high above her—his red eyes glowing, fangs bared, about to strike.

A terrible noise came from her left; Raquel turned to look. Standing in the entryway—reared up on His hind legs and shining as bright as day—was a magnificent White Horse with fire in His eyes and great wings flapping.

"Espíritu!" Raquel cried.

Mentiroso's reaction was immediate: Raquel watched in amazement as terror entered the sombra's eyes and he immediately uncoiled his tail from around her leg and dropped from his towering height down to the floor. He proceeded to slither quickly away to a far corner of the room where he lay cowering in a heap—using Raquel as a barrier between himself and the Horse.

But Raquel had no interest in helping him out. She quickly rolled out of the way.

Espíritu charged straight toward the snake, reared up, and brought His giant hooves plummeting down on top of Mentiroso—crushing his head.

Raquel shut her eyes tight.

When she opened them, the Great Horse and the snake were gone. She lay on the floor... armor gone ... the TV still on...

...the calorie chart deleted.

Chapter 39

Bendita

Raquel stood waiting for her bus to show up. Only a few students remained at the school—most of them having already been picked up and were no doubt beginning their summer vacation celebration.

Raquel had a whole lot to celebrate. Having defeated Mentiroso the night before—with help from Espíritu—she felt a renewed sense of hope and determination to stay on the safe path. She planned to keep in close contact with Sara throughout the summer so that she wouldn't have any more relapses. She even planned to ask her mom—and soon her dad, too—to keep a close eye on her. With the help of the King, she could fully recover, but not without help from friends and family. She would do whatever it took to stay healthy.

A bright light caught her attention out of the corner of her eye. She figured it was probably the sunlight reflecting off one of the buses, so she didn't bother turning to look. But when the bright light remained constant, she turned. Espíritu stood at the far end of the bus lane—beating His gigantic wings in greeting.

"Espíritu!"

Rearing up, He let out an ear-piercing, soul-searching scream. It caused Raquel's insides to shift; how she *loved* that Horse!

Could anyone else see Him? She didn't care.

He broke into a run down the center of the bus lane. Without a second thought, Raquel ran to meet Him—running along the sidewalk. When Espíritu didn't slow down, she prepared herself for a jump; as He came galloping toward her, she grabbed a hold of His long mane and flung herself onto His back—finding the task much simpler than she had anticipated. Grabbing fistfuls of His mane, she felt nothing but jubilation as they rushed past the school with breathtaking speed—the pounding of His hooves soon disappearing as His massive wings lifted them from the ground. As they took to the sky, Raquel looked back: the school was already far behind them.

Amidst the sea of blue, a bright light like a faraway star could be seen in the distance. Her eyes had learned to adjust to bright lights, and as they flew closer and closer and the intensity of the light increased, Raquel found herself able to look upon the City of Paraíso—shining like a magnificent jewel. She and Espíritu went sailing over the City's high wall with ease and all the beauty that is Paraíso was soon recalled to her. She saw again Paraíso's mighty mountains, the forest glades, the enormous waterfall on which she'd stood, the many mansions: She couldn't *wait* to live here for good!

Espíritu landed softly on a small golden bridge—His hooves clanging against the gold beneath Him as He slowed to a stop. Raquel looked around her in wonder; the bridge crossed over a gently-flowing river—the river running through a street made of gold connected by the bridge. Out of the golden street on both sides of the river grew fruit trees with lots of different kinds of fruit growing on them. Not far away were several of the mansions she'd seen from the air—looking *much* more immense up close! They seemed to have been made of costly jewels: diamonds, rubies, emeralds, sapphires… and children of all nationalities and ages were wandering in and out of them. *What places to live!*

"Do I get to stay here, Espíritu?"

Not yet, she heard Him say. He hadn't spoken audibly, but she had heard Him nonetheless.

She sighed in disappointment.

Soon, He reassured her.

She embraced His giant neck. "I love You," she whispered.

He flapped His wings in response—a gentle breeze caressing her face. She smiled, content to simply remain here in His presence.

"Raquel?"

She was so content, she didn't bother opening her eyes. Maybe whoever it was would go away.

She heard laughter. She opened her eyes; Dante stood down below them on the bridge. "I see you've gotten to know Espíritu," he chuckled.

She laughed, slowly and reluctantly releasing Espíritu's neck and sitting up straight. "I sure have," she said with a grin, absently stroking His mane.

"Have you come here to stay?" Dante wanted to know.

Raquel smiled wistfully at Espíritu as He curved His neck to look at her. "Not yet," she said, feeling her insides churn upon beholding the love in His eyes for her. "Soon."

"Can I help you down?"

She chuckled. "Sure," she said. She reached her hand down to him and he reached his up to her, but of course there was a great distance between them because of Espíritu's size. "That's okay," Raquel said with a smile, grabbing a hold of the Horse's mane. "I think I've got this." The soft mane in her hands, she slid down the side of the Horse.

"I knew I couldn't help," Dante told her as soon as she was beside him on the bridge. "I just wanted to see if you'd let me."

Raquel chuckled, her eyes sparkling. "You could say a lot has changed for me since I was here last."

"A lot has changed *in* you."

Raquel nodded, laughing. "Yeah," she smiled, "that, too."

"Kinda tough to have Espíritu inside of you and *not* be changed," Dante pointed out.

"I owe you an apology, Dante," she said, combing her fingers through her hair, "for the way I treated you last time."

He looked at her curiously.

"You know," she said, hesitant to bring it up. "How I called you 'chubby,' and everything?"

"But I *am* chubby, Raquel," he told her. "You didn't hurt my feelings when you told me that, because I'm *okay* with how I look."

She smiled at him, then looked up at Espíritu, running her fingers through His mane. "I think I am, too, now," she replied softly.

"Did Espíritu teach you that looks aren't all that important?"

Raquel laughed, still looking at the Great Horse. "Oh, yeah," she smiled. "That's just one of the *many* things Espíritu taught me."

Dante remained silent—watching as Raquel's attention remained fixed on Espíritu. When she finally looked at him again, he chuckled softly.

"Sorry," she smiled, looking at Dante while continuing to stroke Espíritu's mane.

"You don't need to apologize to me for loving Espíritu!" he laughed. "I happen to love Him, myself! Can I tear you two apart for just a few minutes, though? There's someone I want you to meet."

"Just a few minutes?"

Dante laughed. "I promise! And don't forget," he reminded her, taking her by the hand, "His presence is right there inside you all the time anyway!"

He led her to one of the gigantic mansions. "Are we gonna get to go inside?" Raquel asked in awe.

"This is where I call 'home'!" Dante told her, "and someday this is where you'll call 'home,' too!"

Raquel was too overjoyed to speak.

The inside of the mansion was vast. They entered something akin to a very fancy hotel's lobby: there were satin and velvet couches dispersed throughout with kids sitting on them laughing and talking, a giant chandelier hanging from the ceiling, a grand piano being played by a young girl, an enormous golden staircase leading to the second floor, and all kinds of other expensive-looking furnishings that you would only find in the richest of places. Raquel stood with her mouth ajar, taking it all in.

"C'mon," Dante said, laughing at her shocked expression. "Paraíso is *the King's* City; what did you expect?"

He led her over to the girl playing on the piano. "Bendita," Dante said. "I'd like you to meet someone."

The girl had brown hair and bright blue eyes. She looked like she was maybe about six or seven. As soon as Dante spoke, she stopped playing the piano and looked up.

"Don't stop playing," Raquel told her. "It sounds beautiful!"

But the girl seemed to have forgotten all about the piano. She was staring at Raquel.

"Raquel, meet Bendita. Bendita, meet Raquel," Dante said, introducing them.

"It's nice to meet you," Raquel said politely. "You're very good at playing the piano—a *lot* better than me!"

The girl hadn't stopped staring at Raquel since they'd arrived. "Raquel?" she said softly. "Is it really you?"

"Do I know you?" Raquel asked, confused.

A smile slowly spread across her face. She looked at Dante—who stood there grinning—then back at Raquel. "It's me, Raquel. JoAnna."

Raquel felt her stomach flip. "JoAnna?" she breathed. "From the mall?"

"Yeah," she nodded with a laugh. "Guess I look a little different now, huh?"

Raquel couldn't believe her eyes. There must have been some mistake. "But JoAnna was—"

"...old, I know," Bendita laughed. "When I came to live here in Paraíso a month ago, I was given a new name and a new body."

Raquel still couldn't believe it. *"You're* the one I talked to at the mall?"

"Yes," she smiled faintly. "I tried to help you by talking to your mom, but you were just a tad bit in a hurry to leave."

"JoAnna!" Raquel exclaimed, feeling tears springing to her eyes. "Do you realize you saved my life?"

Bendita was taken aback. "But..." she said, "I didn't even get a chance to talk to your mom. You were in such a hurry—"

"I was such a *jerk... that's* what I was," Raquel informed her. "I didn't want to hear the truth, but you weren't afraid to say it anyway! You helped save my life!"

"I still don't understand," Bendita replied.

Raquel took a seat on the piano bench next to her. "You may not have told my mom," she explained, "but just knowing that you knew my secret caused me to seek help for my problem. I never would have ending up telling anyone if it hadn't been for you." Raquel felt the tears running down her face.

"Oh, sweetie," said Bendita, resting a hand over Raquel's. Raquel laughed; it was strange to hear a seven-year-old refer to her as "sweetie." "Don't thank me; thank Espíritu. *He's* the One who told me to go after you that day; I was just following orders."

Raquel looked at Bendita with grateful eyes. "I'm *so* glad you did," she told her, giving her a hug.

"You said you play the piano, too?" Bendita asked, smiling.

"Oh," Raquel laughed, wiping her face. "Yeah. A little bit."

Bendita scooted over. "Play something," she said.

Raquel looked over at Dante. He was looking at her with a satisfied smile, his elbows propped up on the piano with his chin on his fists.

"I'm not that good," Raquel laughed, looking from Dante back to Bendita.

"Just play from the heart, sweetie," said Bendita, patting her hand. "That's all we ask."

So Raquel played, and the entire room stopped to listen. She played for the King. She missed a few notes here and there, but she didn't give up and quit. When she reached the end, she didn't think her song had been all that impressive, but in Paraíso there was a different opinion. All of Paraíso agreed that it was the most beautiful they'd ever heard.

The author would love to hear from you! Email B.K. Miller at BKMillerTeacher@yahoo.com and check out her website by going to BKMillerAuthor.com to learn more about *Espíritu* and *Jaime*, books 1 and 2 of the *Paraíso's Warriors Series*.

CPSIA information can be obtained at www.ICGtesting.com
Printed in the USA
LVOW11s2247131015

458131LV00001B/1/P